DON'T YOU WISH

DON'T YOU YOU WISH

roxanne st. claire

delacorte press

This is a work of fiction. Names, characters, places, and incidents either are the product of the author's imagination or are used fictitiously. Any resemblance to actual persons, living or dead, events, or locales is entirely coincidental.

Text copyright © 2012 by Roxanne St. Claire
Jacket art copyright © 2012 by Anastasia Volkova

All rights reserved. Published in the United States by Delacorte Press, an imprint of Random House Children's Books, a division of Random House, Inc., New York.

Delacorte Press is a registered trademark and the colophon is a trademark of Random House, Inc.

Visit us on the Web! randomhouse.com/teens

Educators and librarians, for a variety of teaching tools, visit us at randomhouse.com/teachers.

Library of Congress Cataloging-in-Publication Data
St. Claire, Roxanne.
Don't you wish / Roxanne St. Claire.
p. cm.
ISBN 978-0-385-74156-9 (hardback) — ISBN 978-0-375-98577-5 (ebook) —
ISBN 978-0-375-99011-3 (glb)
[1. Popularity—Fiction. 2. Beauty, Personal—Fiction. 3. High schools—Fiction.
4. Schools—Fiction.] I. Title.
PZ7.S774315Do 2012
[Fic]—dc23
2011049124

The text of this book is set in 12-point Goudy.
Book design by Kenny Holcomb

Printed in the United States of America
10 9 8 7 6 5 4 3 2 1
First Edition

Random House Children's Books supports the
First Amendment and celebrates the right to read.

FOR MY DAUGHTER, MIA KERN, WHO ASKED
THE QUESTION THAT INSPIRED THIS STORY

CHAPTER ONE

Some days it seems like half the backpacks of South Hills High whack me in the head on their way to the back of the bus. And today, the pain is epic because I had my braces tightened this morning. Each thud shakes my tender teeth, reminding me that I am the loser who sits in the front row of the bus, head positioned exactly at the point where kids step on and turn into the aisle.

Samantha Janiskowsky. *Thunk. Ouch.*

Miranda Beck. *Thunk. Ouch.*

Kyle Rotrosen. *Thunk.*

Owwwww.

Now, this last pain is not for the aching gums. This pain is inflicted by Lizzie Kauffman, squeezing my hand in a death grip. That can mean only one thing.

Sure enough, sandy hair slowly rises from behind the metal plate between us and the bus steps. Emerging like a god from the underworld, Shane Matthews climbs onto the bus, his adorable smile directed at someone behind and beneath him.

Of course, almost the entire world population is beneath Shane.

"You got that right, babe. Feast your eyes." He wiggles his butt, which only makes Lizzie crunch my knuckles harder. It doesn't matter. All pain is numbed by the sight of him, the object of our every fantasy, the subject of our every sleepover, the man candy we can only dream of tasting in this lifetime.

Shane Matthews is about to clock me in the head, and all I can do is wait in breathless anticipation.

Next to me, Lizzie mutters, "Annie, don't look, don't look, *don't look, don't look.*" She shifts her eyes as far to the side as they can go without actually getting stuck in her head. I have no such restraint.

I look.

And get a navy blue Adidas Velocity II backpack full of history and science textbooks right in the face.

Yeah, we Googled his backpack brand. We're that pathetic. I resist the urge to touch my cheek, the closest I've ever gotten to actual contact with Shane Matthews.

Of course, he doesn't even look to see who he's hit. Because to him, I am invisible. Annie Nutter—if he even knows my name, which I sincerely doubt—is simply one of the extras to fill the halls of South Hills High, so low on the social ladder that our only job is to admire the beauty, perfection, and popularity of stars like Shane.

And admire we do.

A distinctive, throaty (and totally fake) laugh floats up from the sidewalk. Lizzie and I share a disgusted look seconds prior to the appearance of silky platinum hair, gloriously tanned skin—tanned, in Pittsburgh, Pennsylvania, mind you—and a cheerleader's smile that bares a row of blinding white Chiclet-like teeth.

Of course Courtney Nicholas is smiling. Who wouldn't, if you had her life?

"Nickel-ass," Lizzie hisses. "Of course he's flirting with *her*."

Courtney doesn't carry a backpack—she probably has Blonde Mafia handmaidens who do that for her—but her Coach handbag slugs me as she saunters by. If I didn't know better, I'd think she did that on purpose.

But I do know better; I'm not even a blip on Courtney's radar.

"Nice move, Court," a girl behind her says, snickering.

"Oh, who did I hit?" she calls over her shoulder.

"Nobody," the girl says without so much as a sideways glance at my face. "Just move it so we can sit with Shane."

Nobody. My face burns, and not from the brush with either the forty-four-dollar Adidas Velocity II or whatever designer bags are going for these days. I certainly wouldn't know, since they don't sell them at Tar-ghetto.

"Don't sweat it," Lizzie whispers, pulling me to her so I avoid the final assault of the backpack brigade. "It's

November. Half these kids'll have licenses and cars by the middle of the year, and we'll be the only dweeb juniors on the bus. We'll, like, own this puppy." She pats the ripped leather of our seat and raises her voice. "Right, Geraldine?"

The bus driver shifts in her seat to set her meaty face in a frown, but there is a light in her eyes that she saves just for us. Geraldine, whose gravelly baritone and hairy arms make us certain she was a man at some point in her not-so-recent past, has a soft spot for us nobodies. Best of all, she takes absolutely no shit from the posse of populars in the back of the bus.

We love that about her. Him. Geraldine.

"Always changes when they pass driver's ed," Geraldine growls as she closes the doors. "Just you wait."

"So you wanna come over and hang?" Lizzie asks me as the bus rolls over the speed bumps—another slam to my teeth—and pulls out of the school lot. "I don't have my flute lesson until four-thirty."

"Can't. I'm going to beg Geraldine to *let me off at Walmart.*" I raise my voice so the driver hears me. "To meet my mom for a quick shop."

Lizzie stares at me. "You're going to homecoming."

"What? How did you get that out of me meeting my mom at Walmart?"

"I figure you're getting a dress and holding out on me."

I snort. "At Walmart? Jeez, Zie, I know the real estate market is sucky and my mom hasn't sold a house in two months and my dad barely makes minimum wage at RadioShack, but even we Nutters have some standards."

"Puh-lease." She gives an apologetic wave. "As if my mom isn't always broke." She waits a beat, searching my face. "But you don't have a date for homecoming, right?"

As if. "You got nothin' to worry about, girlfriend. It's you, me, and the entire season of *Degrassi* come Saturday night." I give her a reassuring pat because she truly looks worried. "Trust me, we're just going to Walmart because my dad needs us to pick up some . . ." *Junk.* "Things."

Lizzie crosses her eyes. "Your dad needs more *things* like I need more freckles."

My heart squeezes a little, but this is Lizzie, who knows my every secret. Even how embarrassing the mess at home is getting to be.

"He's working on an amazing new invention," I say, the need to defend whacktastic Mel Nutter rising up in me.

"Really? What could possibly top the button you could press on the toilet-paper thingie so that you automatically get the exact same amount of sheets every time?"

"The Rip-Off?" I sigh with a mix of amusement and shame. Really, mostly amusement over that one. "Of course he didn't like my idea for a name."

"Even though it *was* pure genius," she adds, ever the supportive friend. "The name and the idea."

"Sadly, no one in the world wanted the Rip-Off. But this one? He's being secretive about it, so it might be good."

"Whatever happened to last summer's Flip-Flop Beach Buddy?" she asks.

"Emphasis on *flop*," I tell her, the memory still vivid: a double beach towel with corner holder-downers disguised as flip-flops to keep it in the sand. "Well, nobody wanted that, either, because it really wasn't much different from a blanket held down by, well, flip-flops. Plus . . ." I angle my head toward the window. "There's a serious beach shortage in Pittsburgh."

Lizzie nods knowingly, and I love her for not passing judgment on my dad, who is spurred on by his overactive imagination and the desire to invent a household item that will merit a blue-screen TV commercial. The Snuggie. The Ped Egg. The ShamWow. Someday, Mel Nutter will punch the RadioShack time clock for good and own the infomercial world.

As we near the Walmart intersection, I lean forward. Getting Geraldine to make an unscheduled stop depends on her mood, which seems good enough today. Otherwise, I'll have to backtrack a half mile, and it's cold out there. "Any chance you can drop me at the light, Geraldine?"

She nods, probably listening to our conversation and pitying me. "You bet, Annie." She shoots a look in the rearview at the noisy kids in the back. "Let's make it quick and safe, though."

"You got it." I look in her mirror, too, but the angle just gives me a view of my own face, which so doesn't belong in the back of the bus with the cool kids. Frizzy, flyaway hair that lovely color of a brown paper bag—which would be helpful to own right now, so I could cover the eruption of Mount Vesuvius on my cheek. I try to smile, but this morning's visit to the orthodontist makes even that feeble effort almost impossible.

"Sure you can't ditch the flute lesson?" I ask as I zip my

jacket. "Mom's taking me to Eat'n Park, and you know she'd love to have you, too."

"Sorry, I can't miss my lesson. Have a Superburger for me."

"Will do." I stand as the bus slows, and instantly complaints explode from the back.

"Why the hell are we stopping here?" The noisy demand is followed by an outburst of rude questions and comments, full of false indignation and snorts of laughter.

Geraldine ignores the kids in the back and starts to weave her big yellow beast through traffic.

"Hey!" In the mirror, I can see Shane Matthews stand up, a fist in the air like some kind of blistering-hot freedom fighter. "Nobody gets special treatment!"

"Especially nobodies," Courtney adds, easily loud enough for us to hear.

"*This* nobody does," Geraldine shoots back. "Sit down, sweet cheeks, before I come back and make you sit."

"Sweet cheeks!" Lizzie looks like she might die.

I already have. Fire licks up my own sweet cheeks as I stand for the stop. I glance at Lizzie, but she's already sinking in her seat, so my gaze goes right over her shoulder and lands . . . on Courtney.

Guess I'm on her radar now. While she whispers something to Shane, she stares hard at me. Scary hard. Nasty hard. Courtney-on-a-mean-mission hard.

The whole bunch of them burst out laughing, and Courtney starts poking Shane. "C'mon. I dare you."

He looks at her, then at me, then at her.

The traffic refuses to cooperate, holding me hostage a full lane from the sidewalk.

Shane steps into the aisle. OhmyGodohmyGodohmyGod.

"I can get out here," I say to Geraldine, like she's a cab-driver and I'm in New York or something.

Evidently she doesn't hear the raw desperation in my voice. "Are you kidding me? I'll lose my license if one of Pittsburgh's finest is watching. You just wait a second, and don't bother with those morons in the back."

But one of those morons is walking right toward me. I clutch the pole, the metal slippery in my wet palm.

Every single eye on the bus is on him. And me. And him. And me.

"Hey," he says, in that low, sexy Shane voice that Lizzie can imitate perfectly.

Except now it doesn't make me giggle. It makes me want to throw up.

"Hey." I manage the whole syllable without choking.

"You going to homecoming?"

My hand slides a little down the pole. "What?" It comes out like a half choke, half squeak. From my peripheral vision, I can see Lizzie's eyes opening to the size of headlights.

"Home-*coming*," he enunciates like English is my second language. He's close enough now that I can see his eyelashes. Dark, but tipped in gold. The eyelashes of the gods. "On Saturday night."

I somehow clear my throat, and then the heavens open up and so does the traffic. Geraldine hits the gas, and I almost fall down the first step, but cling to the bar as my backpack rolls around and hits me in the chest.

Could this get worse?

"'Cause maybe you'd want to go with me."

Yes. Oh my, *yes*. It actually *could* get worse. "Excuse me?"

I know what's happening, of course. He's asking on a dare. As a joke. Behind him, I'm aware of howls of laughter, hands over mouths as the cool kids watch the drama play out.

And then . . . I have that thought. That thought no girl in this situation should ever have. Not that any girl should ever be in this situation, but if she is, the very last thing she should have is *that* thought. That stupid, idiotic, pathetic loser thought of a hopeless nobody.

What if he's serious?

I just stare at him, digging around my Shane-numbed brain and finding . . . nothing. Forget a witty retort. I couldn't tell him my name right now.

"'Cause if you need a date . . ."

"Yeah?" Did I say that? *Why* did I say that?

"My dog's lookin' for someone to hump that night."

The entire bus explodes with laughter just as the doors open and the sidewalk beckons. All I can do is look at Lizzie as I step down, into the underworld where douche bags like Shane Matthews come from, blood rushing in my head loud enough to almost drown out the sound of Geraldine yelling at him to sit the hell down or never ride a bus in this town again.

I stand on the sidewalk as the doors swoosh behind me and the bus pulls away. I refuse to turn, terrified that if I do I'll see Courtney looking out the window, her giant white teeth bared in laughter. In fact, I don't move for a good fifteen seconds while those words roll over me like Geraldine's bus wheels. The words about the dog?

No. The other words.

'Cause maybe you'd want to go with me.

Because for that one insane flash of a magical moment, I could pretend he really did ask me.

I know, that's even more pathetic than Googling his backpack.

CHAPTER TWO

My buzzing phone pulls me out of the depths of self-pity. It's Mom, telling me she's already done shopping, so she'll wait for me in the book section. No doubt she was ogling some high-end houses in *Southern Living* or some other magazine that makes her whine about wanting a nicer house. She says she only reads those magazines for work, but, honestly, they're like crack to her.

Sure enough, I find her nose-deep in the Mother of All House Porn, *Architectural Digest*, her frosted hair covering her face. She doesn't look up, but I hear her sniff.

"Mom?"

She shakes her head a little, turning away. Is she crying?

"What's the matter?"

Finally, she looks at me, her face streaked with rivers of

black mascara, her eyes red, her lower lip trembling. What the heck? She so isn't a cryer.

"What's wrong?"

Her hands are shaking as she holds the magazine out to me, saying nothing, as if the pictures and words do that for her. But all I see is some museumlike place with fountains and statues and water views from every floor-to-ceiling window. The headline reads "Living a Flawless Life."

"This could have been mine," she says in a strangled voice.

Hers? Her what? "Your listing?" I ask.

"My house."

I give it another glance, still clueless. "What are you talking about?"

"Him." She flips a page and points to a guy in scrubs, hands on hips, big phony grin. "Jim Monroe."

"Who is he?"

"Dr. Jim Monroe," she repeats, sliding her hand to another picture, where the same guy stands in front of a building with two giant gold intertwined *F*'s behind him. "The cosmetic surgeon who started Forever Flawless?"

"Oookay." I think I've seen this guy on TV, hawking a chain of plastic-surgery centers popping up all over the country like they're McDonald's, but that doesn't explain the tears. "Why are you crying?"

"I could have married him, Annie," she says, another harsh whisper, as though saying the words out loud is somehow wrong. "I dated him in college. He went to med school at Pitt."

"Really?" Totally did not know Mom had a doctor boyfriend pre-Dad. I take another look at the magazine, and

Jim. Not bad-looking, in a young Ben Stiller kind of way, maybe midforties. And, whoa, dripping in dollars. "Yowza, this guy's loaded."

She snorts softly. "Estimated net worth of over a billion."

Holy crap. "With a *B*?"

"Billion," she repeats, swiping some mascara and smearing it across her cheek. "Look at that house, Annie. Just . . . *look*."

"It's nice." Which is like saying the ocean is wet. Mom hands the magazine to me so she can dig a tissue out of her bag, and I skim the article, picking up key words. Words like . . . "twenty-three-thousand square feet" . . . "Star Island in Miami Beach" . . . "pizza oven in the kitchen." "He's got his own pizza oven?"

"Look at the last paragraph," she says, her voice cracking. "Read it."

Our tour ended in the master bedroom, where Dr. Monroe showed off the cavern of a "Hers" walk-in closet. Only there is no "her" in Jim Monroe's life. "I'm still waiting for my princess," he says with a wistful smile. "And, no, she doesn't have to be flawless, just fabulous."

I throw up a little in my mouth.

"I came so close." Mom blows her nose, and I cringe, praying that no one hears. "So close to having that."

She stuffs the tissue back into her purse and takes the magazine from me, staring at it again.

"How close?" I ask, a little fascinated by this new side of a woman I never thought about with anyone but my dad. And am not sure I want to.

"When he finished med school, he went to do his

13

residency in Florida. He asked me to go with him, but I still had my senior year left."

"And he wouldn't wait for you to graduate and marry you then?"

She hesitates, a little color returning to her face. "Well, to be honest, he never really . . . proposed—he just talked about us being together. But he would have," she adds quickly. "I'm sure he would have. But he wanted to live together first."

"Why didn't you?"

"Oh, probably because of Nana. She said men don't pay for the cow if they get the milk for free."

Yep, that sounds like my grandmother. "But this dude can pay for a whole farm." Interesting that he never bought one, staying single long past the age when it's cool. "Did you see him after he moved?"

She stares at the page. "After college I met Daddy, and I was going to go see Jim, but . . ." Her voice trails off. "Things happened, you know."

I *know*. My birthday is seven months after their wedding anniversary.

She blows out an exasperated breath and gives me a shaky smile. "Jim Monroe never really offered more than . . . cohabitation. Then I met your father and discovered what it was like when a man really cared about me. Frankly, until this minute, I forgot all about Jim. He was a go-getter, that's for sure."

Closing the magazine, she reaches to put it on the rack behind her, then shudders a little before tossing it into the cart on top of some groceries, a pair of pliers, and a thick roll of electrical cable.

"You're buying that magazine?" I ask.

"So I can get a taste of how the other half lives."

Right. The other half that we'll never be. We'll never have much money, let alone a house that could go in a magazine. At least, not unless one of my dad's so-far-out-there-it-inhabits-its-own-time-zone inventions takes off.

"Looks like the other half lives with pizza ovens," I say, ready to make light because Mom looks a little wrecked over this.

"Money isn't everything." She swipes at her face with her hands, making a holy mess out of her mascara. I don't have the heart to tell her, though. "Anyway, this is what's meant to be. I have you and Theo. And Daddy."

"Instead of a twenty-bazillion-square-foot house."

Without responding, she shoves the cart to the checkout line and starts unloading with a little more force than necessary.

I can't help flipping the magazine open to the article again. I've never seen anything like this place. A mongo curved staircase, room after room of total luxury, a master bedroom that kind of hurts to look at, it's so gorgeous.

"I can't imagine what it would be like to be that rich," I muse.

"Money doesn't make you happy," Mom insists, whipping carrots and lettuce out of the cart. "Money doesn't make you laugh when you're lonely, or make you full of contentment on Christmas morning."

Sorry, but on Christmas morning, money can make you *really* happy.

I hold out a picture of a giant pool built on the edge of a patio, the water spilling over into an ocean beyond it. "Looks like money does buy something called an infinity pool overlooking the Bay of Biscayne."

She shrugs, opening her wallet. "He wasn't capable of loving anyone but himself," she murmurs. Then she takes the magazine from my hand and plops it on the conveyor, the last item to be rung up. "I can't believe I'm spending six dollars on that."

"Did you love him?" The question sort of pops out without full brain engagement. Maybe it isn't my place, but I really want to know.

"I . . . I . . ." She slides the credit card slowly through the machine, holding her breath a little as she always does until it clears. "I did."

When she scribbles her name and flips the last plastic bag off the round bag holder, I can't resist pushing a little more. "Did you love him more than Dad?"

I stay close to her while she rolls the cart to the auto-open door. I'm dying to know the answer, but kind of scared to hear it, too. I don't want her to love anyone more than Dad.

"I loved him the way a woman loves a man she wants to change, but knows she never will."

Which makes zero sense and strikes me as a non-answer. "What did you want to change about him?"

"I wanted him to be faithful, for one thing, which I never really could be sure he was. And I wanted him . . ." She thinks for a minute as we wait for a car to pass. "I wanted

16

him to love me for who I was, and I never felt quite good enough for him. You'll understand someday."

Someday? I understood about ten minutes ago on a school bus.

We stop talking about it on the hike to the van, which is parked in another zip code. About halfway there, she freezes in her tracks with an SUV behind us.

"I really love Daddy," she announces. "I mean, you and Theo are all I live for. What would I be with Jim Monroe? Rich and lonely, that's what."

"Maybe you'd still have us." I guide her to the left to let the SUV by.

"I wouldn't have *you*," she insists, giving the cart a push toward the minivan. "Maybe I'd have some other kid. But not you. Not Theo."

She reaches for the dented hatchback—a mistake of backing into Theo's basketball hoop that would cost $2,600 to fix, so we lived with it—and yanks the door upward.

"You don't know that," I say.

"You wouldn't exist, Annie."

How does she know? "I look way more like you than Dad," I tell her. "People always say I'm your clone. So I might look just the same, only I'd be rich and living in Miami Beach." I look up at the typically gray Pittsburgh skies. "That'd be nice."

She flips a plastic bag into the back. "You are who you are because of Daddy and me. Get in, and I'll put the cart away."

I do, watching her walk to the cart return, the frown deepening that line between her eyebrows that she's always trying to hide with her bangs.

When she climbs into the driver's seat, she lets out a little sigh. "I'm not hungry. Let's just skip Eat'n Park and go home."

"'Kay." I wasn't in a Superburger mood anymore, anyway.

As she sticks the key into the ignition, she makes a little grunt. "Oh, sh—sugar. I forgot Dad's duct tape."

"He has enough at home," I say. "It's just . . . under something else."

Her eyes shutter closed for a second. "Don't I know it."

"You can show him that magazine and tell him you got distracted."

Looking over her shoulder, she backs out of the spot. "He doesn't need to see that. It would just make him feel inadequate."

"Or give him an idea for a new invention. The infinity bathtub." I laugh, but Mom doesn't. And she would totally have laughed at that, like, half an hour ago.

I lean my head against the window, still sick from the bus incident and a little sad about the rich doctor who might have been my father.

Courtney wouldn't laugh at me if I had a house so big it was in a magazine. Not when I got a Z or a Beemer for my birthday, and had . . . a date to homecoming. I sure wouldn't be wearing crappy clothes and—

Mom's hand lands on my arm, yanking me out of my thoughts. "I love who you are, honey," she says. "I wouldn't give you up for all the money in the world. It would just be nice not to have to worry about money constantly."

"Nice" is an understatement. With that much money, I wouldn't be a *nobody*. My "dad" could give me a boob job, better cheekbones, and a smaller nose. I'd be at the top of the A-list, not target practice for backpacks.

"So don't even think about it again," she says. "Because you are who you are meant to be. Annie Nutter, daughter of Mel and Emily Nutter."

"But you don't know, Mom. What if I were the daughter of Jim and Emily Monroe? What if you'd had a daughter with a different husband? Who knows if I would still be me?"

"That's a silly question."

Is it? Would I play the violin? Would I have my same lousy hair but pretty blue eyes? Would I still love Jolly Ranchers and SpongeBob, or would I be too rich and cool for candy and old-school cartoons? Would Lizzie be my BFF? Would Theo still gross me out? Would I still be the poster child for the website My Life Is Average? Or *worse*?

I think not.

"If you even existed," Mom says. "You'd be somebody else entirely if you had different parents."

"But wouldn't I have the same soul?"

Mom looks at me, her eyes clear now, but still mascara-smudged. "I have no idea. Nobody can answer that question."

But I think about it all the way home.

CHAPTER THREE

If *Architectural Digest* did a pictorial on our home, it wouldn't be called "Living a Flawless Life." More like "Navigating the Nutter Clutter." The minute I make my way through the maze of discarded printers, car parts, and rusted tools in the garage and manage to get into the kitchen, Theo comes bounding up from the basement, hollering for our attention, with Watson the Howling Basset on backup.

"This is it!" Theo announces, drama-king style. "Dad has done it this time!" He opens his mouth and burps. Every word my ten-year-old moron brother speaks is punctuated with an exclamation point and a belch.

"What are you doing home so early?" I ask, dumping Walmart bags onto the counter.

"Dad picked me up from school to help him. Wait till you see this!" He grabs my arm. "Where's Mom?"

"Getting the rest of the stuff."

"You gotta come downstairs!" he insists, pulling at my arm.

"Okay, okay." I slip out of his slimy touch just as Mom comes in.

"Mom! Dad's got the best idea ever! This one is killer! We're gonna be rich!" Theo shouts.

Mom and I share a quick look, but Theo misses it, of course, as he digs through the Walmart bags and yanks out the electrical cable. "Did you get the duct tape? 'Cause that'll really finish the whole thing."

Mom's shoulders sink as she reaches into one of the bags, and I know exactly what she's looking for. Not duct tape.

"We forgot it," she says.

"No biggie. Dad rigged it up with something else."

Of course he did. Dad's middle name is Rigged It Up.

"Tell Dad I . . ." Mom inches the magazine out of a bag and avoids my gaze. "I'll come and see whatever it is later," she finishes weakly. "You go down, Annie."

I follow Theo down the basement stairs to find Dad standing next to a full-length mirror, the kind you might hang on the inside of a closet door. His curly brown hair is messed, like he's been running his hands through it a zillion times, and his glasses are crooked from being pushed up his nose. But behind those nerdy horn-rims, his eyes are bright with a look I've seen so many times.

Hope. Enthusiasm. Sheer lunacy.

"C'mere, Annie," Dad says, waving me past a carton overflowing with old telephone books. "Stand in front of this mirror and get on that scale."

"Hey, is that my laptop?" I almost choke at the sight of my secondhand el crappo Averatec on the floor. It's the only computer I have! It's completely taken apart, with a circuit board on the floor connected to other tiny electronic gadgetry I suspect was all taken from the discard bin at RadioShack.

"I had to borrow the motherboard," Dad says. "I'll put it back together again."

"Yeah, that's what you said about my flip-flops," I mutter. "What's that other stuff?"

"A solid-state relay, some rectifiers, and a couple of PIN diodes."

"And is that Mom's digital scale?" I shoot a look at Dad. "Do you actually *want* to die?"

"Just get on the scale, Annie. You'll see."

All I can see is my precious—if cheap and as slow as a diseased turtle—laptop disassembled next to the digital scale that we got Mom for Christmas last year. Still, I step on the scale, because when Dad is in this mood, you have to humor him.

"Look in the mirror."

On the left side of my reflection, a series of red numbers and letters appears: *70 in. 143 lbs. 20.5 bmi.*

"See?" Dad says. "Height, weight, and body mass index."

"Not mine," I say, doing some quick math. "Unless I gained twenty pounds and grew five inches."

"Well, that's a little glitch," he admits, coming around

the front of the mirror. "I can only get it to register one set of information now, but I have a friend at Process Engineering, and he's going to help me iron that out. But wait, Annie. Here's the amazing part. This mirror and scale combination alone would make a very cool product, don't you think?"

"Yeah, if you want a full-body view while weighing, that's a neat idea, Dad." Not sure it would sell, but then, what invention of his does?

"Now comes the good part," he says, kneeling down to the electronics on the floor. "Nobody can touch this contraption but me because it's so delicate that an ant could ruin it by walking over the top. But . . ." He takes out something that looks like an iPhone knockoff, obviously used and refurbed by RadioShack, and starts to flick the screen.

"Watch the mirror, Annie."

At first, the change is barely noticeable. My waist narrows. My hips flare. My boobs . . . whoa.

"Holy cow, Dad. That is so not my body."

"Look at your face."

My hair has grown, my eyes have widened, my skin has cleared. Dear God, I got cheekbones.

"Dad!" And the image moves . . . as I do. "This is unbelievable! How are you doing that?"

"I programmed about a hundred faces in here, and I'm just picking the best of the best. I used that iPhone app Famous Faces, where you can put your picture in and replace all your features with celebrities'. Now look at you. Like it?"

Like it? "It's perfect!"

"Then voila!" The phone makes the click of a picture,

and he holds up the screen to show me. "Saved on the phone in a new app."

I look from the phone to the mirror to my dad. And back to the mirror, because, wow, I am hot.

"Those numbers will change on the side when we get this thing wired right," he adds quickly. "So you know what weight you're shooting for to have that particular body. Doesn't it just rock?"

Oh, God, Dad. Please don't say that. Ever. "It's pretty cool," I say, getting off the scale.

"Pretty cool?" Theo chokes instead of burping, for once. "Dude, this is, like, the freakiest."

The freakiest? Theo is worse than Dad, if that's even possible. "But why would people buy it?" I ask.

"Visualization, Annie!" Dad's eyes are wild. "It is the key to success. Just ask any sports psychologist! Use your mind to picture what you want to be, and you'll be it. Now you can visualize in full color, and then put it on your iPhone so you can carry your image with you as a constant reminder of how you want to look. Just think what motivation that could be to a dieter!"

"But I can't get my eyes to look like that."

"Maybe with the right makeup."

"Or plastic surgery," I say dryly, fighting the urge to sigh. Dad's inventions are brilliant and ridiculous, and so is he. "So, uh, who do you think would buy this, Dad?" I ask.

"Only the six billion people who've downloaded that Famous Faces app." He takes the phone and waves it. "This country is obsessed with looks and weight loss. This is the most incredible combination of the two in history!"

Easy to see where Theo gets his drama-king gene. "That's saying a lot, Dad."

"Well." He shrugs modestly. "It needs work, obviously. I have to somehow create a permanent motherboard and computer that attaches to the mirror, but once I do, and I patent the smartphone app, then I have sole ownership of what will be known as the hottest new invention of this millennium. I could get this into every health club in America."

"Or into every plastic surgeon's office." Mom's voice comes from the top of the stairs.

"So true, Em. Come and look at this!"

"Really, Mom," I call. "You need to see what I'd look like if I were perfect."

"You *are* perfect," she says softly.

I almost snort with laughter, but something strange about her tone makes me stop.

"Of course, this is just a prototype," Dad says quickly. "We need to get a really high-end computer and a special—"

"And where are you going to get the money for a really high-end computer?" Mom's voice is cold as ice as she slowly makes her way down the stairs.

Dad looks a little taken aback. "You remember the idea that woke me up in the middle of the night a couple of weeks ago, Em? I really think I nailed it. First you see what you weigh. You love that, right?"

"Especially if you're five-ten and weigh a hundred and forty-three," I add, trying to make light.

"Those numbers are just a placeholder." Dad dips his head to see Mom's face as she reaches the last few steps. "Mom knows why I used one-four-three."

Theo and I know their little inside message. One, four, and three are the number of letters in the words "I love you." Dad always signs notes to Mom like that.

She navigates the last few steps deliberately, like she's thinking about every single movement, not just trying to avoid the stacks of old newspapers. *You never know when you'll want to find an article*, Dad would say.

And then I notice what she's holding.

Architectural Digest.

"Anyway," Dad adds, filling in the awkward silence. "I told you I'll figure that out later. You know I hate details. I'm a big-picture kind of thinker."

Mom stands very still, looking at the mirror. Neither Dad nor Theo seem to notice that anything is wrong, but I do. I see that drawn look across her mouth, usually a sign she's about to lose her temper. I see her eyes glisten, like she's been crying again. And the magazine in her hand shakes. Once when she was shaking, I asked her why, and she said she had PMS.

Maybe that's why she was crying over that stupid article in Walmart. Maybe that's why she's looking at Dad like he's The Biggest Loser, and I don't mean the kind who'd love to own a mirror that helps you visualize a perfect body.

"Well, perhaps you need to be a smaller-picture kind of thinker, Mel."

He gives her a quizzical look. "What's up, honey?"

"Why are you doing this?" Her voice has a funny hitch in it.

Dad blows out a breath. "I know what we talked about

last night, Em, and I promise, I swear, I'm throwing everything out this weekend. Tomorrow. As soon as I—"

"*This,* Mel. This . . ." She sweeps her empty hand toward the mirror. "This complete and utter waste of time."

"Mom!" Theo jumps up. "Don't you want to see what you'd look like with Angelina Jolie's lips?" God, he is so clueless.

"Yeah, Em. Try it. I'm telling you, this is the big one." Dad sounds pretty clueless, too. But on he goes. "And this isn't just for fun! It has commercial potential. Everyone in this country is hung up on self-improvement and celebrities. Not to mention iPhone apps! It's the perfect combo of our biggest fixations. I call it—"

Mom pitches that magazine so hard, it sails across the room like some kind of wild colored airplane, all six dollars' worth of gloss and glitz, and *wham!* It slams into the nest of electronics, sliding the motherboard, cracking the diodes and rectifiers and whatever else there is. The contraption yanks the mirror so hard the whole thing tumbles forward, shattering with a noisy crash.

"*Picture-Perfect,*" Dad finishes with a whisper.

No one moves. We all just stare at the jagged jigsaw puzzle of mirror shards and computer parts and really bad ideas.

Then Mom runs back upstairs, shoving a whining Watson into the kitchen and banging the basement door behind her.

Theo throws his arms out, his mouth wide in speechless surprise. Dad stares at the stairs, his expression as broken as his invention. Then he steps over the glass and the carton

27

and all the newspapers and follows Mom, quietly closing the door, leaving us alone with what was once the prototype of Picture-Perfect.

Theo lets out a loud belch, and I just kneel down and carefully start to pick up the pieces.

CHAPTER FOUR

The whole night royally sucks. I can't get on Facebook—which I am dying to do, because there has to be something on there about the bus incident. In fact, when Lizzie doesn't call after her flute lesson, I'm pretty sure that means I am Facebook-ruined for life.

And we don't even eat dinner together, which is really bizarro for the Nutter house, since Mom and Dad insist on it most nights if everybody's home.

To top it all off, a storm moves in, pounding our roof with nonstop rain, which means I have to get the bucket from the mudroom and put it in the hall where the ceiling leaks. Lightning and thunder add to the doom and gloom of a really dismal day.

Mom and Dad disappear for hours in their room, the soft

sounds of their conversation drifting out if I walk by the door. Or stand there and listen. Not that I would *ever* do that.

Dad comes out and says Mom is resting, claiming she's just a little upset about "things," which usually translates into "money" or "Dad's latest trip to the lunatic fringe." Those are the only two things they fight about.

I bet Jim Monroe doesn't fight with his wife about— Wait. He doesn't *have* a wife. I wonder if Mom is thinking about leaving Dad and going to hunt down her rich ex-boyfriend. Maybe she thinks she could fill that "hers" closet with clothes and shoes. She is fabulous, if not flawless.

My heart thuds down to my feet. Do I want to be rich *that* bad? That I'd wish a *divorce* on my parents? I study Dad for a minute, trying to compare him to Jim Monroe. There is no comparison. Jim is better-looking, loaded, and probably hasn't kept the rusted parts from every barbecue grill he's ever owned.

"Starving!" Theo whines from his room. "Where's food?"

"I'll make pancakes," Dad says quickly.

"Pancakes?" My brother and I are in complete unison for once.

"Breakfast for dinner," Dad says. "I'll make eggs, too. And bacon. The real way, not in the microwave."

Theo is too dumb and hungry to even notice how strange that dinner menu is, and I decide to let it go. Chocolate chip pancakes and the works it is, but Dad doesn't eat, so Theo and I take our food into the den and eat in front of the TV until some pretty serious lightning kills the cable, and Theo leaves me alone.

I give my bacon to Watson and sit in the lonely den for

a few minutes anyway, the smell of our breakfasty-dinner lingering in the air, the rumble of thunder and the steady drop of water in the hallway bucket the only sounds I hear.

It is kind of impossible not to compare our family room to the house that Forever Flawless built.

We have the green leather sofa—pleather, Dad calls it, since it really is more in the plastic family than top-grade super-leather. The edges are torn, and Dad has covered them with clear tape.

The carpet, once beige, has a pretty noticeable charcoal-colored path where we all walk in and out of the room. Next to Dad's chair is an unopened box of lightbulbs (buy three hundred, get one free!) that hasn't found a home in . . . four months. Under the coffee table, a set of old silverware Mom wants to throw away but that Dad says he might be able to use for some invention.

The landfill isn't just the basement anymore, I think glumly. Pretty soon I won't be able to bring my friends into the den, either. I head into the kitchen, which feels dingy and cluttered and as cheerless as our torn pleather and worn carpet.

No wonder Mom cried over Jim Monroe's palace.

I turn out the kitchen light and walk to my room, wondering if I can work any magic with the broken laptop. I pass Theo's room, where he is on his computer—an ancient IBM that has a monitor the size of a small building—with Watson snoring on the bed.

"Night, Theo."

He looks up. "Is Mom sick?" he asks.

"I don't think so."

He opens his mouth, and I hold out my hand. "For God's sake, don't burp."

He burps.

"Real cool and classy, you idiot."

"Who wants to be cool and classy?"

I do! And pretty and popular, and God, I don't want to live in this dingy house on Rolling Rock Road with Dad the hoarder and Theo the burper anymore!

But I just walk away. In my room, I close and lock the door, drawn to the *Architectural Digest* magazine I've left on my bed. Once more, I skim through the *Flawless House*, as I now think of it; then, disgusted and envious, I throw the magazine under my bed and turn my attention to the broken laptop on my desk.

"Better give you last rites, old Averatec." I set it on my pillow, optimistically plugging it into the wall, and the little green light comes on but the screen is blank. No surprise, because it has no circuitry, thank you very much, Dad.

On the nightstand next to me, I see Dad's off-brand smartphone that I brought up from the basement. What if I connect the phone to the laptop with my phone charger cable? Possible to run the old Averatec off the iPhone?

Only the daughter of a RadioShack salesman could have that idea. The cables fit—also because only a daughter of a RadioShack salesman would have a cast-off universal phone charger that some customer left in a box at the store. I plug it into my computer, hit the On button, and miraculously the screen flashes to life.

"Oh, my God, it works!"

I wait for the Averatec logo to pop up, but when it

doesn't, my heart sinks. This is a fool's errand. If I want to get on Facebook that bad just to read the nasty post–Shane bus episode comments, I could borrow Theo's computer. Then he'll read about it, and—

My face fills up the screen.

Whoa. Not my face. *That* face. That face Dad created and saved on the iPhone! I reach to tap the Escape key, but my finger hovers, not quite ready to part with that image.

Because . . . what would Shane Matthews say to *that* girl?

When he asked her to go to homecoming, he'd mean it. And he'd be sweating out a rejection. Man, what would it be like?

I can't even imagine. Where would a girl like that live? My mind skitters to the magazine I've just thrown under my bed. She'd live in that house, with that billionaire for a dad, and—

A white flash of lightning blinds me for a second, instantly followed by the loudest smack of thunder I've ever heard. All the power goes out.

Damn. Just when I got the computer to work.

The only thing still lit is the little flat-screen phone in my hand. I glance at it to see if it has a flashlight app, but freeze at the sight of me on the screen. Again, not the real me. Not plain Annie Nutter with paper-bag-brown hair and braces and zits.

Everything is pitch-black but that tiny screen and that beautiful, beautiful girl.

Why can't I be that girl? Why can't I live her life, in her world, with that face and that house—

Another strobe flash of lightning steals my breath, so

close that I feel the voltage ping through me, lifting every hair on my body, like the bolt has hit my window.

The impact knocks me forward, right into the computer. My chest hits the screen, slamming the computer backward as sparks of electricity ricochet through my body.

I try to cry, to move, or think, but . . . I'm paralyzed, suspended, hot and cold and sweaty and dry, all at the same time. All I can do is shift my eyes to the phone in my hand.

I can still see her. I can still . . . see . . . her.

Something buzzes under my pillow. I try to lift my head, but every muscle in my neck feels heavy, and there's a fog deep in my brain. But the pillow vibrates again, a soft hum from underneath.

What is that? The computer? Did I bring it back to life?

I slip my hand under and touch something smooth and slick. Dad's cheapo phone? Light pinches my eyelids, still stuck together.

So I've slept, long enough for it to be daylight.

And those damn vibrations start again, this time with a soft beep.

I manage to pry my eyes open and feel under the pillow until I grab the rounded edge of a . . . *What?* I pull out an iPhone.

A real one. No off-brand here.

This one is so new and shiny, it looks like it has never been touched. Was it my birthday and I forgot?

I blink again, vaguely aware that behind the iPhone is something bright and blinding green. The pillow.

My pillowcase is pale blue. But I can't quite comprehend

the change of sheets because my brain is processing the screen of the iPhone.

Alarm 7:01 a.m.

I turn it over, frowning at the engraving on the back. I run my finger over the words.

Ayla Monroe.

Who is Ayla Monroe, and why do I have her phone?

CHAPTER FIVE

The phone vibrates again and freaks the crap out of me. I swipe my hand over the screen, and it stops. I stare at it, then at the pillow with the chartreuse case.

I mean, *pillows*, plural. There is more than one, which is weird and wrong. I have one pillow on a twin bed. But now there are four, five, six pillows on a . . . huge bed.

Chills tiptoe up my spine, lifting the hairs on the back of my neck. Very, very slowly I shift my gaze from the ginormous bed to the rest of the room and am assaulted by vibrant colors and a whole wall of arched windows draped in yards and layers of fabric.

What the *eff*?

This place is humongous! Even with big pieces of

furniture and clothes strewn over every square inch, I feel small and lost.

I hear my throat gulp, a mix of fear and disbelief, or maybe I'm doing a sound check to be sure I'm awake. Because this cannot be real.

Where am I?

I turn. The walls are neon lime-green and turquoise, with splashes of bright pink and the occasional dark brown accent. Even a sofa by the windows is satiny chartreuse with one curved armrest, like an old-school Hollywood starlet loungey thing.

Oh, my God. Look at that flat-screen TV! Like a freaking movie theater. I'm vaguely aware that I'm climbing out of the bed, my gaze flicking from one unbelievable sight to another. One whole wall is a bookcase with a huge desk, a hot mess of papers, and pictures and junk. In the middle is a laptop—as new and insanely expensive as the iPhone I'm still holding—with a stylized A floating around as a screen saver.

Next to it, a rose in a crystal vase, with a card leaning against it.

Is this some kind of joke? A reality TV show? Am I being punked?

It has to be a dream. Either that or I'm dead and this is . . . Oh, if that's true, then the big guy totally overlooked all those times I punched Theo and sent me straight up to the Good Place.

As I take a step, something silky brushes my legs and I glance down, expecting to see my old striped sleep pants and SpongeBob tee. Instead, silver silk flows over my legs, a long . . . nightgown? I hate nightgowns. Still, this one is so soft and sheer, it's like wearing flower petals and air.

I lift the material to reveal my toes. Well, someone's toes. Toes painted a bruising violet and decorated with teensy-tiny rhinestones in the shape of a teardrop.

I wiggle; they move. They *are* my teardrop toes.

I pinch the flesh on my arm, hard, and feel the pain. Does that mean I'm awake and this isn't a dream? It has to.

Or . . . No other explanation even suggests itself to me.

I take a few steps. My bare feet hit cool hard wood, dark and gleaming, and then sink into the edges of a plush throw rug in the middle of the room.

There are shoes everywhere—heels and wedgies and brightly colored sneakers. As I navigate my way over them, I notice the inside of one sandal, decorated with interlocking C's and the word *Chanel*.

Over by the Hollywood Barcalounger, a door is partially open, all dark inside. The closet? Curious, I make my way over and give a nudge.

Without me touching a single switch, soft rose-colored lighting lifts from the floor up, like an electric sunrise, illuminating . . . Oh, my *God*.

For a second, I can't breathe.

This is somebody's *closet*.

No, no. Calling this a closet is like calling the Empire State Building an anthill. It's the size of my whole room and then some. One entire wall and around a corner is for shoes and bags, and someone has filled every inch. On the other side, jeans and tops and dresses and *stuff* are hung sloppily on green and blue satin hangers. In the middle, the open drawers of a huge four-sided dresser spew more clothes.

It's like Forever 21 has dropped out of the sky.

I back out and close the door, and the lights dim like in a stage production. That effect is just too much.

There's one more door in the room, and I'm starting to feel like Alice in Wonderland. Pretty certain it's a bathroom, I turn the knob to find I'm right.

Inside, acres of creamy marble, a tub the size of most people's pools, a glassed-in shower with—holy crap—six showerheads? And one giant one at the top? It's like a car wash in there.

Fluffy white towels are dropped all over the floor, little mountain ranges you'd have to climb to get to the vanity.

And the *vanity*. Like being in Sephora after an earth-quake. Every inch is covered with products and brushes and earrings and more *stuff*. Milky white ball lights surround the mirror, giving it that Hollywood feel again.

The *mirror*.

Do I even dare look? I mean, I have to, right? But surely that'll be the thing that ends the dream, and I don't want it to end. Everything will melt away, and I'll look like someone else or some old witch and the magic spell will be broken. Even if I'm not a witch, seeing Annie Nutter in this setting would just be a big fat letdown.

I study the purple toes. The teardrop. The clump of towel by my feet. Slowly I lift my gaze, holding my breath, bracing for . . .

"Oh!" The exclamation comes out the second my eyes focus, my hand slapping the gasp back into my mouth. I think it's my hand. It *has* to be my hand, because it's moving in a mirror that I'm in front of, so that's me, isn't it?

I take a step closer. Yes, that is most certainly me. Only . . . improved.

And not the combined facial features of celebrities, either. This face is mine, only so much better.

I lean a little closer, expecting it all to end any second. Theo will come burp me awake—his favorite form of morning torture—or the clock radio will blare or the phone will ring or something will end the dream that just got really, really good.

But none of that happens. I get even closer, squinting in disbelief; then my eyes widen in happy shock.

Look at my hair! No, not *my* hair. Not the thin, drab, lifeless, flyaway hair that Mom always apologizes for having given me. This hair is just . . . shampoo commercial–worthy.

I touch it, unable to resist running my fingers through the chocolate locks with caramel-colored highlights expertly woven in. Stick-straight, too, like someone spent the whole night flat-ironing it, which they'd have to, because it's so damn thick.

And my eyes? They're still big, wide-set, but the blue-gray I'm used to seeing is green now, almost emerald. Contacts? I blink, but nothing changes.

My fingers graze my skin, which is buttery smooth. My cheekbones are more prominent; my nose is a tad smaller but still mine. And look at that chin! Is that a little cleft in the middle? Omigawd, is that not the cutest thing *ever*?

I take a step back, smiling. The braces are off!

I'm freaking beautiful!

The realization makes me giggle a little. I put my hands on my hips to give those incredible locks a shake over my shoulders, but the move pulls my gaze south, to the V-neck of the silky nightgown I'm wearing.

To . . . my cleavage.

I grab my chest. Now, these, thank you very much, are boobs. A handful at least. Maybe a C-cup! Su-*weet*!

Sliding my palms down, I slip over a narrow waist and I turn, tightening the nightgown so I can see the shape of my backside.

Well, goodbye, No-Fanny Annie. Wait till I tell Lizzie her nickname is no good in this dream.

I laugh a little, my hand to my mouth for the auto-cover of braces, only to remember that the braces aren't there. I realize I'm shaking, from shock or pleasure or terror. Placing both hands on the counter, which feels solid and real, I lean all the way into the mirror and look right into those gorgeous greens.

"Annie Nutter, this is a dream."

I nod back in total agreement. I've always had Dad's hyperdrive imagination and some wild and crazy dreams to go with it. Nothing quite like this, but still.

"This is the best dream you've ever had," I tell the reflection. "So just go with it. Before you know it, you'll wake up on Rolling Rock Road, boobless, buttless, Chanel shoe–less."

I inch back a few steps, unable to wipe the smile from my face. "Now, dream," I say to my imagination. "What should I do next?"

Get dressed.

Oh, like that'll be a supreme hardship. I start to climb

over another towel but stop, picking it up out of habit and shaking it open to hang on the towel rack.

As I smooth the velvety cloth, I notice a turquoise-colored A embroidered on the corner. A for *Annie?*

Still smiling at the wonder that is my dreamy imagination, I head to the closet for some fantasy threads.

The underwear drawers are a mess of silk and lace, an array of the sweetest little strips of colorful satin I've ever seen. Even the bra I choose—which I certainly need with these most excellent bazooms—is lemon-yellow with a flower made of teeny little pearls that take my breath away.

I pick designer jeans labeled *7 for All Mankind* and step in, somehow not at all surprised that they fit like, well, a dream. Rolled in the top drawer, I find five—no, six Juicy Couture T-shirts, all with the tags still attached. I choose a deep purple to match my funky toes and bite off the price tag, but not before checking it.

He*llo?* What idiot would pay $198 for a T-shirt? Wait'll I tell Lizzie about this.

I could spend an hour picking shoes but settle on some cool Michael Kors platform espadrilles and leave the closet, still marveling at that magic light when I close the door. Back in the bathroom, I try a little dream makeup, not surprised that the MAC and Bobbi Brown go on better than HiP from L'Oréal.

When I look at the finished product, I smile again. I might never want to—

"Miss Ayla!" A loud knock on the bedroom door jolts me out of my thoughts. But, thankfully, not the dream. If Theo wakes me now, his death will be slow and painful. "Are you awake, Miss Ayla?"

The voice is female, lightly accented, a little desperate.

"It is a school day, Miss Ayla. You must get up right this very minute." She jiggles the handle furiously. *"Please."*

I walk to the door and unlock it, opening it to find myself face to face with a dark-haired woman in a crisp navy dress with an apron over it. Under one arm, she carries an empty wicker basket.

"Oh, my God!" She steps back, her hand to her mouth, her eyes wide.

"What? What is it?"

"I don't believe what I see."

Well, join the club, lady. That seems to be the way things go around here.

But I just invite her in, dying to know more.

CHAPTER SIX

As soon as she walks in, chaos breaks out. The iPhone starts beeping. Loud, heavy footsteps clomp outside the door, and suddenly there's a big teenage boy in my doorway wearing earbuds and a look of sleep-deprived disgust on his face. From somewhere in the house, a woman calls, "Ayla! Trent! Breakfast!"

The basket lady reaches up and yanks the headphone out of the boy's ear and screams, "Can you believe she is awake and dressed!"

She's so loud, like he's deaf or still has the bud in, that he steps back from the impact of her voice. Then he slides a look up and down me, shrugging.

"Good thing. 'Cause I'm leaving in twenty minutes. If you don't like it, walk your ass to school."

"There's no bus?"

He chokes a little, like he almost wants to laugh, then looks at the woman. "You're right, Loras. Some alien came and took Ayla. Somebody with a sense of humor and the ability to tell time and get out of bed has arrived in her place."

For one insane moment, I cling to this alien theory. That's one explanation, anyway.

He sticks the earbud back in and disappears as the woman hustles by me into the room.

"Is so nice to see you get up by yourself, Miss Ayla!" She stoops over to pick up some clothes and toss them into her basket.

Do I usually need help getting up?

"Here, I'll get that," I say. Even though *I* didn't drop yet another Juicy T-shirt, it's still kind of embarrassing to have my . . . Wait a second. Is this my dream mother, this Loras?

She freezes in the act of cleaning, staring at the T-shirt I just picked up, her eyes widening. "Are you sick, Miss Ayla?" She reaches toward my forehead. "Fever?"

"No," I say, gently moving her hand. "I'm fine. I'm . . ." *Just new around here.* "Hungry."

"Go and eat, then. I get your room, Miss Ayla."

Ayla again. Like the A on the towel. And the name on the phone . . . Ayla Monroe. Props to the dream for a truly sick name, by the way.

"Thank you," I say, probably smiling like a fool. But who wouldn't be happy when you look like a model and live like a queen? "Sorry for the mess," I add as she bends over again.

Once again, she gives me an incredulous look. Whereas my real mom would probably have dumped the basket, pointed to the piles of crap, and said, "Grounded for life."

But this Dream Mom—

"Your mother is downstairs in the kitchen," she says.

So this is the help. Well, duh. Dream would never skimp on something like support staff, would she?

"Oh, good. I'll go see her." Because I'm dying to meet the mom of my dreams.

I start toward the door, and Loras stops me with a hand. "Miss Ayla?" She's holding out the iPhone. "I've never seen you go anywhere without this." She says "this" like "thees," with a Spanish accent.

I take the phone. "Thank you . . . Loras."

She beams at me, and I smile back. Awkward! On the way out, I glance at the phone.

`Message from Jade Sterling`. I touch the phone and read: `don't 4get me! Trent said I could ride with u. am not going with bitch mom. cu.`

Meaningless. But somehow, I know where to go, moving slowly as I drink it all in. The size, the scope, the luxury, the bomb-diggity staircase that curves forever. I stand at the top and just stare down to the jaw-dropping entryway, a wall of glass looking out over water and blue skies.

Wait, I've seen this staircase before. That view. That very statue in a fountain at the bottom of the stairs. In a movie? In a . . .

Magazine.

Every nerve ending in my body tingles as I stand stone

still, gripping the smooth wood banister. I am living the flaw-less life! This is Dr. Jim Monroe's house.

Of course. *That's* why I'm dreaming this! That's why it's so vivid and real, so alive that I can smell the money oozing out of every corner.

Ayla . . . *Monroe.*

Oh, REM sleep is a wild and wonderful thing, isn't it?

For some reason, this realization comforts me. It's like, if I know why I'm dreaming something, then it isn't a night-mare, not so scary and uncertain. Not that anything about this is scary.

Still, good to know that this is just a product of a maga-zine article and an emotionally electrified day. Wait'll I tell Mom about this dream! I swear, I'm gonna tell her every single detail I remember.

With a little bounce in my step, I head down the stairs, not really that surprised that I know where I'm going. Dreams are like that, senseless and crazy.

And fun. This will definitely go down as the best dream ever.

Toward the back of the house, I turn left and head through a short passageway with counters and cabinets on either side. I think I've heard Mom, when in realtor mode, refer to this as a butler's pantry, leading to a kitchen. There, another woman, wearing the same uniform as Loras, is cooking.

She's light-haired, broad-shouldered, and huge. Like, linebacker huge. And that big teen guy, who I'm going to guess is Trent, is at the table scarfing cereal.

And another woman has her back to me, looking out

over a patio, and, oh, there's the infinity pool! Beyond it, a forever view of water, boats, palm trees, sun, and a sky that's Windex-bottle blue.

I clear my throat. "Mom?"

The woman doesn't turn, and I realize she's talking on the phone. Instead, she holds up one finger, as if to say, *Just a second*, and keeps talking softly.

I walk closer, and the lady at the stove glances my way.

"I wouldn't believe it if I didn't see it with my own eyes." Her words are also slightly accented, but definitely not Spanish. She scowls at me, not nearly as sweet as the woman cleaning my room.

"Believe what? That I'm up and dressed?" Apparently this is some kind of major coup for Ayla.

"And dressed so . . . simply," she adds.

I glance down at what has to be a six-hundred-dollar outfit. If this is simple, I can't wait to wear complex.

She waves me toward the table. "I have your yogurt chilling, Miss Ayla."

Do they all have to call me Miss? When she angles my way, I see that she has a gold name badge pinned to her uniform that says *Mathilda*. Are there so many staff members that they need IDs?

"Thank you, Mathilda."

That earns me another fierce look. Am I not supposed to use her name?

"Is it in the refrigerator?" I glance at the side-by-side Sub-Zeros. "Refrigerators," I amend.

"What are you doing?" she asks, blocking my way like a human wall.

"Um . . . getting the yogurt?"

She gives me the same look Loras did when I picked up the T-shirt. "Sit down, Miss Ayla. I promise you it's not strawberry. You don't have to test me."

"I'm not . . ." I close my mouth and nod, then head toward a table that could seat at least ten.

As I get closer, Mom-on-Phone turns away even more, still hiding her face, murmuring. The boy, who I'm going to take a wild guess is my dream brother, pops the earbud and glowers at me. His green eyes match the ones I just admired in my mirror. His hair is lighter, his face the male version of great-looking.

"What the hell's up with you?" he asks, all accusation and disgust.

"Nothing." *Just don't screw up my dream, bonehead brother. I'm not ready for it to end.*

"Why are you acting like a freak?"

I scowl at him. "How am I acting like a freak?"

"What do you want? I'm not letting you drive today, so you can take that learner's permit and shove it where the sun don't shine. It's not my fault you and your posse are too dumb to pass driver's ed. You want to drive that car Dad gave you? Find someone else with a legit license to sit next to you."

I have a car? Of course! It's dreamland! "Nah, but I need a ride to school. With Jade," I add, kind of smug for catching on to this gig so fast.

He lets out a grunt like I've punched him. "That little skank never shuts up."

I want to defend my friend, but just as I open my mouth,

a place mat flutters down in front of me, and Mathilda sets a glass bowl of yogurt on it, a mint sprig at a jaunty angle. Spoon, napkin, and a tall glass of OJ.

I half expect her to bow.

"Thank you," I reply, looking up at her.

She stares at me as if I've spoken in another language. But the woman on the phone has ended her call and turned around, and she approaches the table, stealing all my attention.

"Are you still determined to do this?" she asks.

I blink at her. Mom? Holy smokes, she looks different. All shiny and smooth and tight. Her face is kind of amazing and weird at the same time. Her eyes are bright, brows high. There's not a wrinkle in sight, and her hair is silky, thick, and definitely not bottle blond. She paid big money for that highlights job.

"I'm going to take that as a yes," she replies for me, parking a hip on the corner of the table.

She's in a body-hugging knit dress, with several heavy necklaces hanging around her neck. Whoa, this mom's been hitting the gym and skipping the ice cream after dinner.

"You look great, Mom." The words are out before I know it.

She tilts her head to the side, her eyes narrowing in distrust. "You don't have to do that."

"Do what?"

"Put on this act."

"It's not an act." It's a *dream*. Didn't everyone else get the memo?

"Why are you wearing that?" she asks.

I automatically check for a bra strap showing, which would be what usually upsets Mom about a T-shirt. "Uh, because I like it?"

"You told me you hated Juicy."

At two hundred dollars a pop? "Well, I took the tag off," I say. "Did you want to return it?"

Trent snorts and looks up at her, some kind of silent communication passing between them. "I know, dawg. She's all effed up today."

I don't know what to be more surprised at—how everyone seems to think I'm different, or the fact that this kid can say "effed up" and call his mom "dawg" and get away with it.

"Ayla, I saw the card when the rose arrived." She frowns. Sort of. More of a Botox frown attempt.

The card . . . the rose. Dang, I should have read it. I opt for a shrug.

"I'm not going to tell you what to do," Mom says, her voice—her whole being, actually—so oddly taut. "It's just that—"

"Use a condom, nitwit," Trent says, picking up his cereal bowl to chug the milk, suddenly reminding me very much of Theo, except Theo is ten and wouldn't mention a condom in the kitchen if his life depended on it.

"Exactly," Mom says. "Be smart. I like Ryder. I just want you to realize your own value."

I have no earthly idea how to respond.

"I have some raincoats you kids can use," Trent says, holding his bowl out in midair. The cook magically appears to relieve him of it. He gives me a smart-ass smirk as he lifts his shirt and shows off an impressive six-pack. "Obviously, I have plenty of need for them."

"Obviously." Just like obviously, you're a tool.

Mom smoothes her dress, eyes cast down. "Has anyone seen Dad?"

For a moment I sense an uncomfortable silence, noticing that Trent is suddenly preoccupied with his place mat. Mathilda twists the faucet with a vicious jerk.

Mom's gaze lands on me. "Did you see him yet today?"

Didn't she see him when she woke up? "No."

"Did he . . ." Her voice trails off. "I'll check his room."

He has his own room? As she starts to walk away, Mathilda sidesteps and puts out a hand to stop her, shaking her head.

Mom closes her eyes for just a second, and even though she's been tucked and 'toxed, I see the corners of her mouth draw down, just like they did on the basement stairs back in . . . real life. "Thanks, Tillie."

Tillie? That monster is as much a *Tillie* as . . . I am an *Ayla*.

As Mom's walking out, she presses her phone and puts it to her ear.

"Hey, I changed my mind. I'll be there at one, so order my Manhattan at twelve fifty-nine." She laughs as she disappears down the hall, but it's a hollow sound. "Yeah, you were right. He never came home."

Only then do I realize she never mentioned school. Or said *Have a nice day* or *Don't you think that's too much eyeliner?* or anything.

Just "Realize your own value" and "Use condoms." Jeez.

Across from me, Trent is standing up. "Hey, if we're picking up the whole country of Skankovia, we gotta fly. Let's go."

"To school?"

"No, the mall, shit-for-brains. Meet me in the garage."

I'm still hungry, but it doesn't look like Tillie's going to cough up a bagel and cream cheese, and I don't dare attempt to touch her fridge again.

I scoop up the bowl, which is heavy—real crystal—and take it to the sink. When I reach for the faucet to rinse, a large hand lands on my arm.

"What is with you today? Why are you doing this?" Blue eyes slice me, the first set to meet mine today and look truly dubious.

"You know this is all a dream, don't you?" I ask.

Her gaze never wavers. "It's a rare day when you recognize that, Miss Ayla. Give me the bowl."

I let her take the crystal out of my hands. "I was going to clean it."

Her eyebrows rise like mountaintops. "You've never cleaned a dish in your life."

Okay, the rules in this house are different. And definitely in my favor. But Ma-Tillie the Hun is dangerously close to making me wake up and have this dream end, so I book to my room before she can drag me back to reality.

There I find a bag—Fendi, which feels freakishly like plastic, who knew?—and a pair of Donna Karan sunglasses. I check out the rose and read the card.

A flower 4 u, since u r giving me urs.
Ryder

Ayla's getting deflowered by a guy who writes love notes in text speak? Dream, this is juicy. *Just go for the ride, Annie. I mean, Ayla.*

I slide on the sunglasses, covering my dazzling green eyes. Because this dream is so bright, I gotta wear shades.

CHAPTER seven

The dream does not disappoint.

From the moment we leave the garage—which is like a hotel parking lot stocked with so many cars I lose count—and Trent the Tool guns a spiffy blue BMW over a bridge to leave someplace called Star Island, the day is unreal.

Sunshine, blue skies, palm trees, tropical breezes, and aquamarine water remind me that Billionaire Jim lives in Miami, and today, so do I. We go to another exclusive neighborhood with gabillion-dollar houses, called Cocoplum. There, Jade Sterling, who is no skank, ambles to the car slowly enough for me to drink in every detail. She is a little bit of everything—Asian, Hispanic, black, white, with some island flair thrown in for added spice. Her skin is like toffee, her hair ebony and perfectly straight, her clothes right off the New York runway.

She joins me in the backseat because Trent refuses to let either of us in the front, and greets me with a curled lip.

"What are you wearing?" The question is a mix of repulsion and uncertainty.

I root around my memory for the label. "Seven for all . . . the men."

She almost laughs. "Cute, A-list. But Juicy? Like, to *school*? It's so pedestrian." Jade's in a stunning black miniskirt with a cream-colored off-the-shoulder sweater and big chunky jewelry. "I thought we decided all Marc Jacobs on Tuesdays," she whines.

"Dang. I forgot." I give her a big grin. "Let's do it tomorrow."

"Tomorrow is Dior. And, Jesus, Ayla. Jeans? Seriously?"

"I like to wear jeans to school," I tell her.

She rolls her eyes. "Then so will every single kid in Crap Academy by the end of the week."

"Really?" Too bad I can't stick around to see that.

"Oh, don't get all modest on me now. You are Ayla Monroe, baby." She taps Trent's seat. "Can we put the lid up, Try-Hard? This wind is totally wrecking an hour of straight iron."

Trent responds by gunning the engine, killing Jade's hair and earning a middle finger from her in response.

I laugh, and she spears me with a dirty look that's more playful than nasty. "And of course A-list's hair is perfect no matter what."

"It is?"

"Bish, puh-lease. You have everything and then some."
The playfulness fades to dead serious.

Okay, then. I have everything and *then some*. This is my first real clue that if this Ayla chick thinks she has a sweet life inside the mansion, it gets better outside.

And better it gets.

Trent ditches us the minute we park, surrounded almost immediately by a group of very cute senior guys. Jade tries to flirt with a couple of them, but they barely notice her. A few say hello to me, probably because I'm Trent's sister.

Or maybe not. The first little bits of attention kick up my heart rate as we cross the parking lot to a two-story Spanish-style building, past the sign that says JOHN J. CROPPE ACADEMY. Not because I'm nervous, or even a little apprehensive.

I'm not going to lie—I'm totally psyched.

And can I just say that if this all-five-senses-in-overdrive is a *dream*, then the other things I've been experiencing at night for the past sixteen years have been complete amateur efforts.

I'm barely up the stairs, driven by that feeling of vague familiarity, when the smell of books and Axe mixes with the sound of kids shouting, F-bombs dropping, and the slam of locker doors.

I feel eyes on me, a lot of them. And it seems that the kids kind of step back as I enter the main hall, a low rumble of conversation, my name spoken in a whisper.

Is this what it's like to be überpopular?

"There you are." A male voice, a big, warm body behind

me, a possessive hand on my shoulder, the cloying scent of something much higher-end than Axe. "God, you look hot in jeans."

I slow my step, then stop, still not turning.

"Didn't you like the rose, babe?" Warm breath tickles my ear. "Or are you still pissed off about the whole beer thing?"

Am I? Something is sending the skitters down my spine. Irritation or . . . attraction? Time to find out. Slowly I turn, and am face to face with . . . a chest. Sizeable, too. I lift my gaze to the throat, where an Adam's apple moves up and down in a swallow. Then my gaze travels over a square jaw with just a hint of whisker, to steel blue eyes and dirty blond hair that falls over a forehead and kisses a brow.

"You're not pissed," he says, a perfect smile mesmerizing me. "I can tell when you look at me that way."

There isn't any other way to look at a guy this hot. I manage to inch back and cop a total attitude of disinterest. "Hey, Ryder."

He slides his hand around my neck, tunneling under my hair and instantly zapping every cell in my body. Instinctively I duck away from the touch. It's too hot. Too familiar. So maybe I am pissed at him.

"C'mon, Ayla. How many times do I have to say I'm sorry?"

"Many, Rye-Bread." Jade grabs my arm and tugs at me. "At lunch. We gotta go."

I almost laugh out loud, because Rye-Bread is exactly what Lizzie would nickname him. Not that Lizzie and I would actually ever breathe the same air as this guy.

But Jade drags me away, a few kids separating me from Ryder. I'm not at all sure how I feel about this.

"He's gorgeous," I say softly, the words out before I can really stop them.

"Yeah, Ryder Bransford has always been your weakness," Jade tells me. "But, dude, you want him to grovel, right? You told me you weren't going all the way until he begs for mercy like a beaten dog."

"I said that?" I blink at her. "I love dogs. In fact, why don't I have one?"

She snorts a laugh. "You're whack this morning, Ayla. Let's go. Bliss is waiting for us. She went to the Falls yesterday and totally scored at Bloomie's."

"Scored what?"

"Jewelry, I think. She's in our bathroom."

"We have our own bathroom?"

Jade lets out a hoot of laughter. "Oh, my God. I love you today." Around the corner, Jade smacks open a heavy mahogany door marked ELEVENTH-GRADE LADIES and stares down a group of five or six girls inside. "Out, *stat*." She flicks her fingers like they are no more than annoying mosquitoes.

I feel my jaw drop at the order, but they look from her to me and start to gather their things.

Am I a mean bitch or what?

"Cute top, Ayla," one says, the words barely audible.

"Thanks," I reply brightly, earning a look of shock and awe from her and a few others.

"I like Juicy Couture," another says.

Jade chokes softly. "Pedestrian. Told you."

The second girl's face explodes crimson as she reaches down for a flute case. My heart squeezes in sympathy.

"Are you in band?" I ask her.

She looks up, clearly not trusting this exchange. She expects me to zing her, I realize.

"Uh-huh," she says, swallowing and switching the case to the other hand.

"Flute?"

"Yeah."

I give her a friendly pat on the arm. "The heart of the orchestra, I always say."

Her mouth drops open a little, but the others have left, and Jade snaps her fingers in the girl's face. "Cease and desist, Flute Fly. My friend here ate way too much sugar for breakfast."

The girl says nothing but moves to the door, studying me, still trying to decide, I think, if that exchange was for real or not.

As she opens the door, I can't help asking, "Hey, what's your name?"

"Candi." She's hesitant, like that beaten dog Jade mentioned. "Candi Woodward."

"I'm Ayla Monroe."

She laughs uneasily. "I know."

"Out, Candi Cane," Jade orders. "And do your new best friend, Ayla, here a favor and stand guard. Send any more like you away until we come out. Got it?"

She nods. *Jeez, grow a spine, Candi.*

The last stall door pops open, and a blond head pokes out. "What is all the locomotion out there?"

"Ayla dropped some 'nice' pills this morning," Jade says, giving me a withering look. "Are you running for class president or something?"

"Something," I say, cursing myself for being such a loser. Popular girls don't act like that. I have to at least pretend I belong in the bathroom with them, or I'll be out with Candi and the rest of the music geeks playing palace guard before this dream is over.

"Get in here," the girl in the stall orders. "And look what I got you girls."

"Bliss Tremaine for the win!" Jade says, scampering toward the stall.

I follow, peeking in to see a cloth draped over the closed toilet seat, and gold on top of it. A couple pairs of earrings, a bracelet, and a long, heavy chain.

"Nice!" Jade says. "I call the hoops." Then she inches aside to make room for me. "Unless you want them, Ayla."

I glance at the jewelry and at the petite girl with long blond hair and big eyes a blue I've never seen on anything but a doll or a colored contact lens ad. Bliss crosses her arms and adds a smug smile.

"I know. My expertee knows no boundage."

Expertee? Boundage? What language does this girl speak? She ignores my look of dismay and gives me a nudge. "Take what you want, Ayla."

"It's free?"

They both laugh so sharply and loudly, it startles me.

"You are hi-*lar*-ious, girl," Jade says with an elbow to my arm.

"How'd you . . ." I manage to gulp the cocktail of fear and excitement that rises in my throat. "Get it?"

Bliss shrugs. "Fire alarm went off in Bloomie's last night. I walked out with two grand in gold." She brushes her knuckles and blows on them, reminding me of Trent at breakfast. "Beats the eighteen hundred you did in Bal Harbour last week. So, dude, consider this a challenge to top."

I stole eighteen hundred dollars' worth of stuff from a store? Why?

"You guys," I say, shaking my head. "I . . . I . . ." *Am rich.* Seriously, sickeningly loaded. Why would I steal?

But something stops me. The look in their eyes. The air of expectation. The thrill of getting my name whispered in awe by the nobodies, and having a groveling boyfriend who looks like a rock star.

This is living the flawless life, right?

Anyway, it's not real. It doesn't matter. This doesn't count.

"I like the bracelet," I finally say.

"Yours." Bliss grabs the bangle and hands it to me.

Jade takes earrings while Bliss digs into a bag so designer I don't even know where to look for the label.

"You have Brighton in first period English lit," she says. "So you can be late." She pulls out a jewel-encrusted case and pops it open, revealing three perfectly rolled joints. "I need to chillax before chem."

I feel my knees weakening. I've seen pot, smelled it, but never smoked it. And I sure as heck don't know anyone who has the nerve to light up in the bathroom.

"Oh, for Chrissake, Ayla," Bliss says, her Caribbean Sea eyes narrowing as she fingers a joint. "I know you said you weren't getting high at school, but that doesn't mean *we* can't."

Next to me, Jade stiffens. "C'mon, Bliss. Ayla is entitled to not get loaded."

"And act douchetastic with the invisibles," Bliss adds with a smirk.

The *invisibles*. That's what they call . . . us.

"It's okay," Jade says, waving a hand like she can make the discomfort in the little stall go away. "She can throw a bone to the kids once in a while."

"Not if she wants to stay A-list, she can't," Bliss fires back, like they aren't totally talking about me in the third person.

I snag the joint from Bliss's fingers, unwilling to walk the path to unpopular. "Puh-lease. I write up the damn A-list every morning." Rolling the white stick, I launch an eyebrow north. "And you better be nice, Bliss-full-of-yourself, or you won't be on that list tomorrow."

"Bliss-full-of-yourself!" Jade giggles and points at Bliss. "Owned! And with a nickname worthy of my approval."

"Owned" is right. My head feels light, like I'm drunk on my own coolness. Did I just shoot down a popular girl and threaten to delist her? God, I love this dream life.

Bliss forces a laugh as phony as her blue contacts. "And I knew 'Straight Ayla' wouldn't last when you gave her *that* name last week, Jadie. Here, let me light you."

I put the joint to my mouth, not worried about choking

like a noob. Because evidently, I can do anything in this life, including smoke pot in the eleventh-grade bathroom and dis the coolest girls who've ever even talked to me.

"Hey!" A voice comes from the door before we light. "Verderosa's coming!"

Instantly Bliss whips around and flips the cloth cover over the jewelry on the toilet, folding it like a pro and dumping the whole thing into her bag. Jade pushes me out the stall door, muscling past me to twist on the faucet and pretend to be washing her hands.

The door pops open, and a teacher type marches in, her eyes sharp. "What's going on in here?"

My heart, trained for years to fear authority, squeezes. My fingers do the same over the joint.

"Pee and poo, Mrs. Verderosa." Bliss beams with a smile of pure innocence. "What do you think?"

"Get to your classes," she says, pointing to the door.

Jade just tsks and strolls by the woman without making eye contact, and Bliss does the same. Mrs. Verderosa is staring at me. The joint crumbles in my damp palms, and my heart is back in high, high gear.

"What do you have, Ayla?" Her gaze slips to my hands.

Oh, dream. Why did you go here? I close my eyes, certain that when I open them I'll be back in bed, awakened by my galloping pulse.

No such luck. "Nothing, Mrs. V."

She tilts her head with suspicion and holds out her hand, palm up. "Give it to me."

One hand is holding drugs. The other, stolen jewelry. Slowly I raise the bracelet, praying it's the lesser of two evils.

She barely glances at the jewel-encrusted bangle. "Nice."

"Thanks."

"A gift from your father?" There's some serious nasty in the question.

"From . . . a friend."

She puffs air out of her nose, like she has no doubt what this "gift" is. Contraband.

"That's about a week's salary for me," she says. "So if I were you, I wouldn't lose it."

Then she turns and walks away.

Seriously? I breathe again, swamped by relief. Slipping the bracelet on and stashing the joint in my bag, I saunter across the bathroom, sparing a look in the mirror. Nothing's changed. I'm beautiful, I'm cool, and apparently I'm invincible.

I wink at my flawless reflection and head to the hall. There, Bliss grabs my arm. "What the hell was that flutey girl's name?"

"Candi Woodward," I answer, barely thinking about it, even though a truly popular girl wouldn't have bothered to remember the name.

"She's dead to me," Bliss says.

"Why? She's the one who warned us."

"*After* she told Verderosa we were in there, getting brownie points from teacher, props from us. Does she think we're stupid? Snitches get stitches."

"Whatever, Bliss." I dismiss her with the same ease I did in the bathroom and walk past her, instinctively knowing that maintaining the upper hand with Bliss is key to my success.

"Hey," she calls, snagging my bag to stop me.

I flatten her with a contemptuous look.

"Gimme my joint back," she says, but the bite is gone in her voice.

"See you at lunch," I reply, heady with the charge of power.

She backs off. "Sure."

Holy crap, this is amazing. I can snuff out bitches and outsmart teachers. Could this possibly get better?

I head down the hall to find out.

CHAPTER EIGHT

When I open the door to English lit, the teacher's back is
to me as he writes *symbolism* in red marker across the white-
board. Every eye in the class turns to the door, and there's
a rumble of comments ranging from "You're toast" to "Of
course *you're* late" to "She's wearing *Juicy?*" from two brats
in the back.

The teacher, Douglas Brighton, according to the name-
plate on his desk, lets out a put-upon sigh.

"I have rules in this classroom," he says without turning.

I search for an open seat, but the only one is in the dead
center of the class, requiring me to struggle through a maze
of tightly cramped desks and chairs to get to it. But some girl
instantly shoves her seat forward, and another guy inches his
desk to the right so I can sail through.

Make way for royalty.

Damn. Back at South Hills High I would have had to beg, plead, and humiliate myself for some space. No, back at SHH, I would never be late for a class. Especially not because I was in the bathroom talking trash, doing drugs, and taking stolen jewelry.

"I know this is first period," the teacher continues, his marker still squeaking on the board. "And I know you all need your precious sleep, and I know that most of you stayed up until two on Facebook. However, every one of you knows how I feel about first period tardiness. My class is not an excuse to sleep late."

I'm *almost* to the open seat. One more kid, this one wearing some kind of brimmed fedora hat, has to move his chair.

He just stares straight ahead, chin on hand. Jerk.

"So this will be your only warning," Mr. Brighton says. "Next time—" He snaps the marker top and turns, beady eyes narrowed through John Lennon round-rimmed glasses. Instantly his face softens. "Ayla." He shakes his head, a genuine smile dawning. "You've never been a morning person, have you?"

I go with it. "I rock after lunch, though, Mr. Brighton."

Everyone laughs like I just said the wittiest thing.

"Mr. Zelinsky, please let her through," he orders Hat Boy, who gives his desk enough of a pull for me to shimmy between it and the seat in front of him. My backside grazes his desk, and one of the boys in the back mumbles, "Nice view, huh, Charlie?"

I expect color to rise to my cheeks, but my face remains

cool as I level the speaker with an icy gaze. How fun is this? I don't blush in this dream!

The recipient of my dirty look, however, doesn't have such good luck, as he brightens while the kid next to him— oh, it's my boyfriend, Ryder—leans over and grabs the heckler's T-shirt.

"Shut up and move so she can sit back here," Ryder snarls, then turns and completely annihilates me with a sexy smile.

I glance at the pack of cool kids in the back—you don't have to know them by name, they're the same in every school, real or imagined. Two pretty girls are doing some hair twirling and boob adjustments, and there are a couple of jocks, and Ryder. That's where I belong, I just know it.

"Please, Ayla. Take a seat." Mr. Brighton might be running out of love for me, so I slide into the closest desk with a quick shrug toward Ryder, who suddenly looks confused. Like he's not sure if I'm blowing him off or not.

Which is just laughable, considering he is el major hottero, as Lizzie would say. She'd obsess over his every move, cataloging his colors (yellow on Monday, red on Tuesday), analyzing his every syllable on Facebook. And probably never get the time of day from him. And now he's worried that I've dissed him.

Ohmi*god*, this is so much fun. I can barely keep from laughing out loud, looking around and taking it all in. But instinct tells me I shouldn't.

Still, after I get situated and the chattering stops, I can't resist one more silent message to Ryder, a raised brow that just says *Maybe you're not worth fighting for*. It has its intended effect—he narrows his steely eyes and gives a stone-cold-sexy look of determination.

I ignore the little shiver that runs through me and turn to face the teacher, who's straight out of "English teacher" central casting, with a ponytail and a blue denim button-down.

"What are the chances you've completed the reading assignment I gave you three weeks ago?"

A collective groan confirms that the chances are zero, making Croppe Academy no different than any other school.

"Look at the person next to you, right now."

Everyone does, and my gaze lands on the rim of the hat.

"Now take that person's hand."

More groaning, and some laughter, a few outcries of "gay" and "retarded." I reach my hand, but that boy is tucked low into his seat, long legs extended. His face is in shadow, some dark hair curling out around his neck. Guys who wear anything but baseball caps are complete wannabes; that law has to be universal no matter what world I'm inhabiting.

Still he clenches his jaw, refusing to look at me. I try to imagine myself in his shoes, which, sadly, isn't hard. How would I feel if I had to reach over and hold hands with Courtney Nicholas's boyfriend du jour? I'd want to crawl into a hole.

I'd be sympathetic to his situation, except he lost me with the hat and attitude.

"Whoever you are holding hands with is your partner." Mr. Brighton walks down the aisle between the boy and me. "Mr. Zelinsky, do you have a problem?"

The kid just closes his eyes, then reluctantly takes my

hand. His palm is warm and surprisingly dry. If the situation were reversed, my sweat glands would be set on Drench.

"I'm working under the assumption that at least fifty percent of you have read the book. So we're having a pop quiz on it right now, and you get the benefit of a partner's help."

The resounding "Get out!" and "No way!" makes everyone drop their partner's hand, including Zelinsky and me.

"I understand if you have a good reason to be behind on the reading." Mr. Brighton tilts his head toward me. "Ayla, for example, was busy with her father during the dedication of the new gymnasium and indoor swimming pool he had built."

He *did*? Way to go, Dr. J. No wonder the teachers tiptoe around me.

As Mr. Brighton returns to the front of the classroom, I lean a little closer to Zelinsky. "What book?" I ask him.

He slides a look at me, and for the first time I can really see him. Deep, dark eyes, clear skin, a recent first-time shave over a squarish jaw.

"You don't even know what book he assigned?" he asks in a shocked whisper. "Man, you're dumber than I thought."

I give him a hard look, the same one that worked on Bliss.

"*Lord of the Flies*," he says.

"Seriously?" I ask. He rolls his eyes, and I resist the urge to grab his shirt in my enthusiasm. "William Golding's *Lord of the Flies*?"

"No, Justin Bieber's version. Did you read that?"

I want to give the bird to Hat Boy, but I'm too happy that my Day of Good Fortune is holding steady.

71

"I need three symbols in *Lord of the Flies*," Mr. Brighton announces. "And their *meaning*, people. You have fifteen minutes to talk to your partner, craft some answers, and write them out. Scores count as a quiz grade. Fifteen minutes."

He punctuates that with a dramatic twist of a white kitchen timer.

"Did you read it?" I ask Zelinsky.

"I had something else to do."

Hat shopping? I'm about to tell him it's his lucky day, when my Fendi bag vibrates, and I pull out my iPhone.

Ryder: Don't forget about me.

"Okay, everybody. Push your desks together and work!"

Zelinsky moves his desk with little enthusiasm, then pulls out a piece of paper. "So we're burned," he says.

Of course no one would expect Ayla to have read the book. I put my elbow on his desk and sneak a peek under the brim of the hat. "I read it last year," I tell him.

His eyes widen, well beyond surprise and deep into incredulity. "You *read*?"

"Amazing, isn't it?"

Then he shakes his head, wheels visibly turning as his features show doubt. "Why'd you read it last year?"

Because every sophomore in South Hills High AP English had to. "Extra credit."

"Yeah, right," he snorts. "The only extra credit you do is with an American Express card."

I hear my mom's voice in my head: *Extra credit is not optional.* I just clear my throat. "Excuse me, have we actually met?" I ask.

"I'm Charlie."

"Hi. I'm—"

"I know who you are." He searches my face a little. "You seriously read the book?"

"Yep. And *not* SparkNotes, either." Digging for a pen in my bag, I steal another look at Ryder, who is staring at Charlie's head like it's target practice. He's jealous?

I give him a three-finger wave and smile, then hand my pen to Charlie, mentally calling up the three essays I wrote on Golding's symbolism, the lowest grade an A-, thank you very much.

The noise level rises around us, but I whisper to Charlie, "Face paint. The conch. Butterflies. Write those down."

He leans back, blown away. "Really?"

"Well, you could argue that rituals are symbol—"

"No, I mean, you're not playing me? Like, you *know* this stuff?"

"It's a fluke," I assure him. "Like everything else today."

He starts to write, dividing his attention between the paper and me. "I might have pegged you wrong."

"Thought I was just a dumb, rich, popular girl?"

His color deepens. "You have that reputation."

I nudge him to write. "C'mon. This is timed. Face paint is a big symbol in the book. They use it for fun at first. Then it becomes camouflage. . . ."

As Charlie madly writes what I'm saying, I feel some weird pressure on me. Eyes. Attention.

Get used to it, Annie. You are no longer invisible.

Still, I look up from the paper, and the room is somewhat

hushed, and all twenty sets of eyes are staring at me, a whole classroom full of disbelief, and displeasure.

Oh, now I get it. I'm upsetting the feng shui of this school or something. This is not how Ayla Monroe is expected to act. This is how Annie Nutter acts. Do I want to blow what's been a perfectly wonderful dream day by showing off my lit skills?

"Okay. What else besides face paint?" Charlie asks, clueless to the strange dynamics in the room.

I push my hair off my face, warm from the unexpected attention of the class. "Um . . . whatever. Just write whatever."

"The conch?" he prods. "Didn't you say something about the conch? And bumblebees?"

"Butterflies," I say softly, aware that I'm vibrating again. I touch the phone screen.

Ryder: r u high?

He would think that. Gorgeous, cool girls don't sidle up to geeks and ace pop quizzes.

Charlie taps the paper. "What about them? The butterflies?"

I hit the screen to compose a note to Ryder. Ha ha, I write. Lame, but I'm in a pinch here.

"Ayla?" Charlie insists. "Butterflies?"

The phone vibrates; Ryder is clearly an industrial-strength texter.

Ryder: how much longer?

Me: for what?

Ryder: very funny. i'm dyin here.

For sex? My stomach flips around a few times, and I stare at the screen.

I've never really made out with a boy. I mean, I've kissed a few, and even got tongue in eighth grade when Justin "Cheeto Boy" Reddick laid one on me after lunch, and I don't think I've eaten a cheese puff since that day.

And at last year's Spring Fling dance, fellow orchestra geek Alan Schumake did kiss me for a good, solid three-point-five minutes in the band locker room. (Lizzie was timing, as we had long ago decided five full minutes that included tongue and at least a side brush of boob constituted bona fide making out, so it didn't officially count.)

And now that hunk is telling me he's dying for . . . the real deal?

"Butterflies are what?" Charlie insists, tapping the phone so I'll pay attention to him.

"They're cute," I say with a quick smile. "And maybe good luck, or is that ladybugs?"

He puffs out a breath of disgust. "I knew you were playing me. Shit. We're toast on this test."

"Quiz," I shoot back. "It can't be worth as much toward the grade."

The room is pretty quiet; everyone is listening to this conversation. So this is what it's like to be the polar opposite of invisible. I'm the center of attention, and for some reason, I feel like I have a reputation to maintain.

Ayla's reputation, not Annie Nutter's. I can't mess with this . . . this . . . alternate reality I'm in.

"Two minutes!" Brighton announces.

"Why didn't you read the book, anyway?" I ask Charlie. "You seem like a smart kid." Except for the unfortunate hat choice.

"I'm interested in other things. Why else do you think I'd be in DK lit and not AP?"

"DK?" That's a new one.

"Dumb kids."

The phone buzzes with a text from Ryder again.

Ryder: gimme what you got!!

Seriously? I don't know what shocks me most, Ryder's style or the fact that Ayla is a dumb kid. "In my school, we just call it regular lit," I say to Charlie.

He frowns. "This is your school."

"Only briefly." And something tells me if I screw with this dream state, I'll be back in South Hills High before that timer dings.

"What should I write?" he asks, impatience growing.

"Whatever," I say, sliding over my texts with total disinterest. "Say anything."

"One minute."

For some reason, my stomach is churning and I feel my palms dampen. Like, it's killing me inside to deliberately fail a quiz. Who would want to be like that, anyway? Who would throw a test just to maintain an image?

Um, me. A-list Ayla.

But I am screwing this kid in the process, because I know the answer to the butterfly symbolism, and I know about the conch, too.

He blows out another breath, and I lean over. "Nature has no regard for man. Like when the butterflies are—"

He scowls at me. "What?"

"Just write it," I urge in a whisper. "No regard for man."

He does, considering the words. "I actually get that. What about the conch?"

Jeez, I gotta do this. Still, I fake like I'm reading a text on my phone.

"The conch, Ayla?"

I glance at him, caught by the glint in his dark eyes. "If it mattered so much to you, why didn't you read the book?"

"'Cause I'm a science geek. Do this, and when you're stuck in chem later this year, I'll return the favor."

Except I'll be in Pittsburgh and he'll be a dream I had once.

"Wrap it up, class!"

"It's a symbol of order, leadership, and power." I click to the text that just came in.

Ryder: i need answers!

Me: not now

I hit send before reality hits me. He's not sexting, he's trying to cheat. Jeez, I'm dense. I turn to look at Ryder, but the teacher is already collecting papers, and my boyfriend looks madder than hell.

Annie wouldn't cheat, but Ayla? From what I know of this girl already, yeah. Of course she'd give her answers away. Most kids do, especially the cool ones.

Mr. Brighton passes Ryder and his partner—ironically, the kid who heckled my butt—giving them a look of disgust when he picks up a blank paper. When he reaches us, he takes Charlie's paper and reads it, nodding.

"Well done, Mr. Zelinsky."

"I had help," Charlie says.

Mr. Brighton raises his eyebrows in a silent *Yeah, right,* but Charlie tips his hat back a bit and angles his head toward me. "I really did have—"

"It's okay." I stop him with a hand to the arm. "Team effort."

Brighton nods and moves on, the silence behind him suddenly uncomfortable. Then the bell rings and I snag my bag.

"Hey," Charlie says as I scoot away. "Thanks."

I manage a totally disinterested look. "Forget about it."

"I had you all wrong," he adds, with a smile that's surprisingly sweet.

"No, you didn't," I assure him. Then I escape into the hall before Ryder can catch up with me.

I try to blend into the student traffic, but it doesn't take long before I realize that *blending in* is no longer part of my daily life.

CHAPTER NINE

The minute I leave fourth period, I'm flanked by Jade and Bliss. A few others trail like a wake behind me, but my right and left are instantly bookended by besties.

"Ryder is pissed beyond description," Bliss announces. "He's epileptic."

"He's epileptic?" I couldn't tell that.

"I mean he's just crazy furious with you."

I frown at her. "Do you mean apoplectic?"

"Whatever," Bliss shoots back. "He's not happy."

I shrug, but inside I'm kind of disappointed, and a little mad at myself for blowing it with the hot boyfriend before I've even gotten to know him. I've been kind of hoping to wake up having had at least a moderate dream make-out.

Considering how real this whole thing is, I might be able to convince Lizzie to count it.

A funny twist squeezes at my gut, the same one that's been annoying me all day.

Considering how real this whole thing is.

When is it going to *not* be so real?

"Oh, don't look so upset, Ayla," Jade says, shouldering me toward a bank of lockers. "Bliss is exaggerating."

"I am not." Bliss leans against the locker right before I open it, crossing her arms and flipping back some blond hair, revealing sizeable diamonds in her ears. Stolen, no doubt. "We cut third together and he told me."

I smell a whiff of pot on her, although her eyes are bright. In my school, popular girls don't get high during the day, just stoner kids do. But this isn't my school. This isn't even my life.

Which doesn't stop me from wanting to know everything Ryder said.

"What did he tell you?" I ask, nudging her to the side so I can get to my locker.

"Ryder and I talk about a lot of things, Ayla." There's an unmistakable challenge in her voice. "You know we've always had a special friendship."

I give her an incredulous look, trying to decipher exactly what that means. "How special?"

Bliss gives a dramatic and vague shrug. "All I know," she says, "is that he's sick of waiting for you to give it up."

"Give what . . ." I stop before I sound like a complete moron. My V-card, of course.

"A flusterated boyfriend is not a happy boyfriend," she singsongs.

"Flusterated?"

"Speak Bliss," Jade whispers to me.

"And an unhappy boyfriend is an ex-boyfriend," Bliss finishes haughtily.

"And then what?" I shoot back, taking the bait. "He's your *next* boyfriend?"

"Stop it, Bliss," Jade chides her. "Why are you always trying to get between them?"

I slam the locker door hard enough to startle her. "You know what happens when you skate on thin ice, Bliss?"

She frowns, the metaphor obviously lost on someone who annihilates the English language every time she opens her mouth.

"You fall and you freeze to death." I ice her with a look that matches the threat, a zing of endorphins shooting through me.

Bliss pales for a second, then turns, defeated but refusing to show it. Feeling smug, I let them bookend me all the way to the cafeteria, the three of us parting the invisibles right down the middle like Moses and the Red Sea.

Wow. Nice. Is this what I'm missing while I sit around with orchestra kids and discuss the miserable song selections for Winter Musicfest?

I follow their lead for salads, but only because the line for pizza is too long. Maybe because I have a feeling it's super-uncool to chow down on the good stuff, even though the french fries smell out of this world. Bliss and Jade don't look like they've ever eaten a french fry in their lives.

There's no evidence of seniors in this lunch period, so we obviously get the best tables on a veranda just outside the cafeteria, with a view of palm-tree-dotted lawns. In one fast scope, I find all the usual gatherings, from potheads to math geeks and everything in between.

Our table seats ten, and there are six girls around it, including us. The others are pretty quiet, clearly deferential to the three of us.

The hierarchy of Crap Academy, as the school is universally known, is becoming crystal clear. And the social strata are not that different from my real school. There are invisibles (nobodies), wannabes (subpar), almost-could-be's (lower class), just-about-there's (middle class) . . . and then the top of the heap. The popular kids, as they are known in every world, real or . . . whatever this is.

Right now, it doesn't matter what this is, because I am a popular kid, so far at the top of that heap that I could get a nosebleed.

I'm digging through the salad, looking for a crouton or something of substance, when two strong hands smack down on my shoulders and squeeze.

"What the hell was that all about, Ayla?"

I don't have to look; I know it's Ryder. But I turn anyway, still not used to how insanely cute he is. But he doesn't look too cute right now. He looks . . . *apoplectic.*

"Told you," Bliss whispers as she circles glossy lips over a wide straw and looks up at Ryder. For a second, it's not clear who she's talking to, him or me.

"Move over," Ryder says to her, giving her arm a dismissive tap.

She slides, not happy about it.

Ryder climbs onto the stone bench, his thigh pressing against mine, his mouth to my ear. "Now you owe me."

Chills explode over my skin, cascading down to my toes, which curl in my Michael Kors platforms. I close my eyes to hide the response, and put plenty of indifference in my voice. "I don't owe you anything, Ryder. You should have read the book."

"Very funny, Ayla." He flicks his tongue over my ear-lobe.

Oh. My. *God.*

"I'll forget the quiz on Saturday night," he says, his hand possessive—and really high up—on my thigh. "You know why they call it home*coming.*"

I whip around to him. "Saturday is homecoming?"

He laughs. "Among other things, as you know. And everything's arranged."

"We're going together."

His smile is dead sexy. "Whatever you want to call it, babe. My parents will be in the Keys as of Saturday morning, with my brother. My *casa* is your *casa.*" His fingers slip another inch up my jeans. "My bed is your bed."

"Seriously?"

He leans back and narrows his eyes. "We agreed, Ayla. Homecoming is the night."

So, it looks like I have a date for homecoming after all. A date . . . to do the deed. *Take that, Shane Matthews.*

"You are not going to change your mind." There is just enough of a subtle threat in his voice that I look up and spear him with a look.

"I might change my mind . . ." I give him a slow, sly smile. "About my dress."

"No, you don't," Jade interjects. "I'm in white Stella McCartney, Bliss is in black Versace, and you're wearing the yellow Vera Wang. We've been planning this since last year."

Ryder moves even closer. "I don't care what you wear. I just want to take it off."

"O . . . kay." Shoot, my voice cracks. To cover, I pick at the salad, finally locating a lone crouton, but I'm aware that the entire cafeteria is watching like we are their own personal soap opera. Well, we kind of are.

That's the price of popularity. And sitting here at the "it" table with the hottest guy I've ever talked to, telling me he wants to take off my homecoming dress (Vera Wang!), well, shoot, I guess I'm paying whatever moments like this cost, because I have never had one before.

I turn to him, our lips barely an inch apart. "Anything can happen between now and Saturday, Ryder." Like I could wake up and these people could disintegrate into thin air.

They will, won't they? By Saturday? By tomorrow when I wake up? Of course they will.

That hand goes so high, he's just about in my crotch. Has any boy ever touched me on the thigh? Maybe by accident, when I shared a music stand with Conner Bondi.

But this is a dream. Even though there's nothing about that hand that says it's imaginary. The nagging starts deep inside me again.

"Why does this seem so real?" I whisper.

He smiles. "Because it is, babe. And it's gonna be even more real on Saturday night." He squeezes my leg. "Got it?"

Heat coils through me, easily as much from embarrassment as an unfamiliar response.

"What the hell do you want, Candi Cane?" Jade's voice throws ice water onto my little party.

I turn from Ryder to see a girl walking by me, holding a tray, and I instantly recognize Candi from the bathroom. She's staring at me, a question in her gaze.

Bliss slams down a water bottle and stares at her. "Your days are numbered up," she says, butchering the expression enough to get a little chuckle from the table. But she takes it as encouragement, pointing a finger at Candi. "You busted us."

Candi's face turns a lovely shade of purple. "I did not."

I feel everyone's focus at the table shift to me, as though, in my position of power, it's my job to support Bliss and fire another warning. Of course, I know what I should do—what any Queen Bee in this chair would do. I should remind the little nobody just who's in charge here.

"Candi," I say, trying to make my voice sound lofty as I dig through my brain for just the right thing to say. The right way to show my status and hers, because that's what's expected.

"What?" she asks, her eyes full of hope. I can practically read her mind, and not because this weird dream state I'm in has given me that capability.

Don't insult me, she's thinking. *Don't make me look like the fool we both know I am.*

All I can think about is Shane Matthews and the shame on the bus. I can't be like that, can I? "Thanks for the heads-up in the bathroom today," I finally say. "That was cool."

"Hey, sure. No prob." She just smiles a little and bounds away, but Bliss drops both hands onto the table with a drama-queen exhale.

"'No prob'?" Bliss mocks. "Who *says* that?"

"This from the queen of wordkill," I say, expecting a laugh from the table. But they're all kind of looking at me with the same expression: disappointment and doubt.

"What?" I shoot back. "I'm just not feeling the meanness today, okay?" I slide a look to Ryder. "I'm too happy."

He gives me a really hot smile and another leg squeeze, but Bliss is having none of it, smacking her plastic fork onto her tray. "Well, thank you, Ryder, for turning our little Ayla into the Patron Saint of the Invisibles."

I look out toward the tables and trees, just to avoid her face, which is really starting to get on my nerves. My gaze lands on the boy in the hat, sitting alone at a table with a broken umbrella, the sun blazing on him and his fedora.

"Hey." Ryder says with a different kind of pressure on my leg. "What is it with you and that loser Zelinsky?"

I brush his hand away. I don't know where I got these cool put-down moves, but I'm using them for all they're worth.

"Like I'd even talk to him."

"You talked to him plenty in lit."

Standing now, Bliss raises her eyebrows. "She's been on crack all day."

"Shut up," I order her.

"You are different today," Jade pops in, pulling a straw from her mouth and pointing it at me. "You're, like, acting all weird."

"Hell, yeah," Bliss chimes in, straightening like she has a purpose in life and is itching for more support. "Kissing up to invisibles, wearing two-year-old shoes, and pulling answers out of your ass in lit class."

These Michael Kors are two years old? "Shut up," I repeat. I'm going to have to do better than that to stop the train that is Bliss.

Ryder scoots back. "How did you know that stuff about that book anyway?"

"Maybe I *read*, Ryder."

He snorts. "Clothing labels."

I get ready to argue, then stop. What's wrong with me? There are a lot of benefits to this world, this life, this lofty position. And I've done enough to wreck the delicate balance for one day. Across the grass, I see Candi, sitting at a table full of musicians, the band and orchestra geeks. Do I want to go back there?

No, I do not.

I glide my hand up on Ryder's arm. It's not painful feeling those muscles, trust me. "I'm just, you know . . ." I bite my lip so it's wet and full. "Excited about Saturday."

He smiles—a sinful thing, really—and shoots a look at Bliss. "Get off my girlfriend's case, bitch." He stands, taking his tray, kissing my cheek on the way.

When he leaves, I glance over his shoulder at Charlie Zelinsky, who looks a little disappointed in me.

Too bad, Charlie. I've done my good deeds for the day. As long as I'm in this bizarre world, I'm staying at the top of the food chain. Whatever it takes.

Someone smacks a card or something in front of me, and I inch back to see what it is. A Florida driver's license? With my picture on it.

"Consider it a peace offering," Bliss says, looking smug. "Check the birth date."

I squint at the tiny numbers. "That's wrong."

"She's just so cute when she's like this!" Jade exclaims.

But Bliss looks dubious. "Look, I held my end of the bargain. We each have one of those. Your mom has some fundraiser tonight, right?"

I have no earthly idea. "Right."

"And your dad is never home."

That, I'm pretty sure, is true. "Never."

"With this thing, you are licensed to drive . . . and drink. Jade and I will be there at nine, and we hit Mynt in South Beach by ten."

I blink at her, barely past "drive" . . . and "drink." "It's a school night."

They look at each other, openmouthed. "I'm telling you, she's precious."

Bliss narrows her eyes. "I think she's some kind of imposer pretending to be Ayla." She might butcher the language, but she's smarter than anyone else around here.

"Shut up," I say, taking the license. "Tonight's going to be insane."

Why not? There *is* no tomorrow on this planet.

CHAPTER TEN

By the time the three of us are dressed to "go to a school function," as I felt compelled to tell Tillie when she brought what looked like a thousand-dollar order of room service up to my bedroom, we've each been through six different outfits, a dozen pairs of shoes, and enough makeup to paint the red carpet.

My room looks like the backstage dressing area for the final runway show of *America's Next Top Model*, and despite the fact that I haven't had a sip of the vodka that Bliss brought in a water bottle, I'm high on life.

And five-inch Louboutin shoes. You know, with the red bottoms? In Pittsburgh, we'd look like hookers. In Miami Beach, I have a feeling we'll fit right in. On our way out, as I'm stuffing my fake ID and cash into a Kate Spade bag,

I have a wave of . . . emotion. This is going to end when I wake up, and all I want to do is seize the moment of what might be the most wild and fun thing I've ever done or ever will do.

Soon we're clattering and giggling our way downstairs, where I expect to see . . . someone. Anyone.

A parent, a sibling, even one of the ubiquitous staff. But there's not a soul in sight.

Bliss is giddy, shredding every other word she uses in an effort to seem smarter. And she looks gorgeous in black leather hot pants and a red halter. Jade is just totally chill, all in her signature color of cream with only one splash of burgundy in her accessories. I went with a black miniskirt and soft pink top, cut low over my well-endowed boobs and cropped short at my waist.

In my whole life, I've never felt pretty, but tonight I am magic itself. The garage is stocked, with keys hanging on a wall like valet service at a high-end hotel, and my hand hovers between keys for a grown-up-looking (but very sleek) silver Mercedes and a much safer Lexus SUV, when Bliss grabs another set.

"Come on, Ayla. Take the freaking Aston."

Somehow, I doubt that's the car my dad bought me for my birthday.

Bliss clicks the remote entry and the lights of a cobalt blue sports car flash, and even I, who know next to nothing about cars, realize she just picked the most expensive car in the garage. Maybe the world.

"I don't know. . . ." I eye the machine and think of the

dented ten-year-old Toyota Sienna I've been learning to drive. "Will we all fit in that?"

"Jade's tiny. We'll slide her in the back." Bliss is already headed toward the car. "You want me to drive?"

After vodka? "I can handle it," I say, snagging the keys from her and dropping into the driver's seat, which smells of leather and spice and . . . no cologne Mel Nutter would ever wear.

Oh, my God. I've never even met my dad, and I'm stealing his best car.

Oh, well. I may wake up by the time Dr. Jimbo gets home.

"You can drive a stick, right?" Bliss asks.

"Sure." We shoot forward like a rocket in response, and all three of us burst out laughing. "Maybe. I drove one once in driver's ed."

I'm not very good at it, but somehow we manage to get off Star Island, down the big causeway, and over to Miami Beach, laughing our asses off the entire way.

"Cruise the strip!" Bliss hollers, and we turn onto Ocean Drive and go four miles an hour with everyone else, getting hooted at by all the guys, and of course, Bliss hoots right back.

Like everything else in this freakish dream, Miami Beach is vibrating with color, wildly alive. The hotels are bathed in pastel lights, and the sidewalks are crowded with barely dressed beauties and seriously intense men.

"You girls are hot!" calls a guy in a red Corvette.

"You got that right!" I holler back, my pulse beating like the constant thrum of bass from cars all around. This is insane!

We finally get to Mynt, and I hand the keys over to a darling valet who winks at me and promises to protect the Aston on his mother's life.

"You better," Bliss says. "'Cause Daddy'll kill her if it gets dented."

"Wait, do I care?" I ask Bliss. "I never even see the guy." And who cares if I'm in trouble? I'm in a rule-breaking, risk-taking, earthshaking kind of mood and am so not worried about the quibillion-dollar car or the always absent dad.

Arm in arm, the three of us head to the front of the line and instantly get ushered through glass doors bathed in neon green light.

Inside, it's almost black except for flashes of green, pink, and white. Everything is shaking with bass, noise, people, glitter, and bone-skinny models looking incredibly bored and beautiful. Bliss drags us to the bar, and we don't even get carded.

A minute later, she hands me a mojito with a big sprig of mint—I guess everything stays in theme here. I've never had one, so I sip slowly, my eyes widening at the delicious taste.

"I'm driving," I say to Bliss.

She rolls her eyes. "The night is young, girlfriend, and so are we!"

"You'll dance it off," Jade says. "Oooh, look over there. Mother lode of hotness."

There are a few really nice-looking guys—who have to be in their twenties—giving us the eye, and for a minute, I almost do one of those classic *Who me?* turnarounds.

One with really perfect hair gives me a chin nod, then angles his head toward the dance floor.

I just look back, but Jade elbows me. "Are you crazy? He's asking you to dance. Or are you playing hard to get?"

In my life I haven't played hard, easy, or in-between to get. In fact, nothing in sixteen years has been quite like this. Tomorrow I'll be Annie again, but in this crazy dream, I'm beautiful, rich, cool, and about to dance with a guy who looks a little like Taylor Lautner, so I'm totally going for it.

With a cool nod back at him, I set my drink on the table Bliss has claimed, and meet him on the dance floor.

Just getting there is an experience. Sweaty bodies, leather dresses, heady colognes, and a few spilled drinks block my way. But Taylor's determined, and so am I.

We meet in the middle and start moving to a song I've never heard and won't remember. It has a beat, and because the gods of this fantasy world love me so much, I dance like Jennifer Lopez.

As I turn, he takes my hands and pulls me into him. "You're gorgeous," he says, a little drunk, but the words still get me.

"I know!" I add a silly giggle to soften the cockiness of it, but come on. I *am* gorgeous. And I never have been before in my whole life.

He grabs me again, a little friendlier. Okay, like hand-on-ass friendly. "Wanna do some blow?"

For a second, I don't have a clue what he just asked. I inch back and out of his palm to let the words settle in. Thank God Lizzie got me hooked on the crack that is bad Canadian teen soap operas, because only on *Degrassi* have I ever heard cocaine called blow.

"Not tonight," I say coolly. But as soon as the dance ends, I manage to slip away, and he gets the message.

There are more guys at the table with Bliss and Jade, but I don't really talk to them. Instead I have some water and drink in the glitter on the dance floor and the wild green and pink lights and the very scantily clad girls who dance on the balconies like they're part of the show.

The Black Eyed Peas start screaming about what a good, good night it is, and Jade grabs me.

"Woo-hoo, Ayla! This was our song in, like, eighth grade."

"Way to let everyone know how old we are," I say into her ear, but I let her pull me onto the dance floor, and I have a flash of dancing to this same song with Lizzie . . . in my basement.

This is so much better that I let out a little "Woot!" and raise my hands and scream the words while the whole world flashes mint and raspberry.

"This is amazing!" I scream to Jade.

She's laughing and pointing and singing, and then suddenly her entire expression changes to sheer horror.

I spin around, terrified about what it could be. It has to be Bliss doing something—

"Jesus Christ on a hot dog bun, your dad's here, Ayla."

The minute she says it, I meet the angriest, harshest stare I've ever seen, and instantly recognize the man from the magazine. He's smaller in real life, narrow-shouldered and mad as hell.

"Am I in trouble?" I ask her as she gets next to me in a really nice show of solidarity.

"Are you sober?" she asks.

I barely drank the mojito. "Enough."

"Then hope for the best."

He marches toward me. "When you get home, I want to see you."

Wow, that's not too bad. He must be cool. "Okay, Dad." The word feels weird on my lips, but I say it anyway. "Midnight too late?"

Just then a woman saunters up to him, a stunning James Bond girlfriend type wearing a tiny black dress and a lot of jewelry. "I'm thirsty, sweetheart," she says, her eyes on me. "Get me a drink."

"Midnight is fine." He starts to walk away. "In my office. And I need your brother there." He slows his step and leans close to me. "And let's just agree we haven't seen each other."

Holy . . . *hell*. I'm in collusion with my own father? My mouth opens but nothing comes out. That's it? No *What are you doing in a nightclub, young lady?* No *What are you doing driving my expensive car with nothing more than a learner's permit?*

This is . . . *unexpected.*

Bliss stumbles over, kind of drunk and giggly, but Jade looks like the wind's gone out of her sails, too. It's a quarter after eleven, and I just want to go home and get ready for a midnight rendezvous with a man I kind of can't believe is my dad.

If that meeting even happens. Because surely this dream will end at midnight, like all good fairy tales.

* * *

95

But it doesn't.

At midnight, wearing a T-shirt and Agent Provocateur sleep pants (so not SpongeBob), I head downstairs, guided by some mental GPS that hasn't been wrong yet today.

My dad's office is at the far end of a long wing on the first floor, and I feel a little like the Cowardly Lion headed in to see the Wizard. My bare feet pad along the cool marble until I reach two polished wood doors, closed tight, lighted columns like bodyguards protecting the entrance.

For a moment I flash to the basement on Rolling Rock Road . . . Wow, did my mom have a range of taste in men. These two couldn't be more different.

With a swallow that hurts my bone-dry throat, I knock lightly, even though I've been invited—er, ordered, to the place.

"Come in."

Pushing the door open, I blink at the dim room, lit only by the soft lights around a super-modern glass bar that looks an awful lot like the one at Mynt, only the colored lights are blue, not green. There's a desk on one side, and a squared-off sitting area with two long and extremely uncomfortable-looking sofas.

He's in the same clothes he had on at the club, a white business shirt, tie loosened, sleeves rolled up. He has the same dark brown hair I do, and some of that Botoxed perfection my mom sports.

He doesn't look at me, so I check out the room some more. Not only is this dad not a hoarder, his office is practically empty. What kind of work does he do here, anyway?

"Hey," I say to break the awkward silence.

He knocks back a drink, then finally looks at me. "Trent's on his way down, too," he announces.

"Okay." I take a step closer. "So, what's up?" Besides the fact that I used a fake ID, drove without a real license, and hung out in a SoBe club on a school night?

He turns, so I get a good look at his handsome, hawkish features, and his eyes, also green like mine. "I thought I'd call an impromptu family meeting."

"Oh, well, Mom's not home yet—"

"I know," he interjects. "That's why we're meeting." He gestures toward the stiff-looking bench. "Sit."

I feel a little like a dog, but perch on the edge, feeling awkward inside and out. "So, what's on the agenda?" I say, a tease in my voice to break the ice.

"You'll see. If Trent ever gets in here." He strides over to the desk and pulls out the chair. He's really going to sit there? I guess he wasn't kidding about a meeting. "That's another bad trait he picked up from your mother—serial tardiness. That won't help his cause in life."

It's midnight, for crying out loud. How serially tardy can he be? And does Trent have a cause in life? Besides being a jerk? I decide to keep my comments to myself until I can figure out which way the wind blows in the room.

I hear footsteps in the hall, apparently not moving fast enough to suit Jimbo, who rolls his eyes and shakes his head a little. "Any day now, Trenton!" he calls.

Finally, my big brother cruises in, shirtless, shoeless, and, of course, wired with earbuds. He pops them out and frowns at both of us. "What up?"

"Sit down, Trent. I have an offer that could change one of your lives."

Trent looks as perplexed as I feel, but drops onto the sofa and slaps his bare feet up onto the barren coffee table.

"Must you?" Jim asks him, looking pointedly at his toes.

"I must. What the hell's going on, Dad?"

"I'm about to transform your existence. Is that important enough?"

I sit up a little straighter, but Trent, ever the tool, just shrugs. "I already know about the split, Dad. I'm going with Mom."

They're splitting up? So the blonde in the club was more than arm candy? I eye Jim for his reaction, but he gives none.

"We haven't made that announcement," he says quietly. "If your mother is talking divorce, it's because she's seeking it, not me."

"What's going on?" I ask, feeling clueless and oddly frightened. Am I the only one who thinks divorce is a scary, scary thing?

Trent spears me with a look. "Earth to Ayla. Mom and Dad hate each other. Oh, wait, you're not in that sentence, so it doesn't matter to you."

Jim saves me from digging for a suitable comeback by pushing his chair out dramatically. "We don't hate each other," he says, standing slowly, sliding his hands into his trouser pockets. "It's just that . . . we have different ideas about how a marriage should work."

"Yeah, dude, it works like this," Trent quips, hatred and disrespect rolling off every one of his words. "You come home and sleep here at night, and don't tap your patients in your spare time."

My jaw drops at this, but Jim stabs a finger toward Trent. "*You* are out of line, mister."

"And so are you." Trent stands. "I don't have time for this shit. I'm outta here."

"Sit down," Jim barks. "Or you're cut off from every dime I have."

Trent glares at him, then me, slowly returning to his seat.

I can't help giving him a snotty grin. "Nice to see you have a price," I say.

"You should talk, MasterCard whore."

"Stop it," Jim says, coming around the desk. "I have an offer to make to both of you, then you can take your bickering out of my sight. Just hear me out."

We both look at him, waiting.

"One of you is going to take over the reins of my business."

Whoa. Where did that come from? I look at Trent and notice his jaw tighten.

"I'm ready to make that official by signing a contract to that effect."

"Wait a second," I say, holding my hand up. "I'm sixteen. Do I seriously have to even think about this yet? And don't we, like, have to go to med school?"

Jimbo blows out a "Pffft" and waves his hand. "You hire doctors, you don't do the slave labor."

Trent shoves back on the sofa. "This is totally effed up, Dad. You already promised me I'd be CEO of Forever Flawless when I get out of college. Ayla's not capable of managing her bathroom vanity, let alone a multimillion-dollar business."

"And you are?" I shoot back. Not that he's wrong about that, but still.

"I have twice your IQ, three times your common sense, and quadruple the ability to think about people other than myself. This is a moot point, Dad."

"Not anymore. I'm turning this into a little contest."

"What?" Trent and I ask in shocked unison.

"I want something, and one of you can get it. If you do, I'll formalize your future."

"What do you want from us?" Trent asks. "Just come right out and make your demands and don't make it some kind of stupid contest. Everything's a freaking contest with you."

"I need information." Jim directs this to me, as if he just can't take another minute of his son's contempt. Can't say I blame him. "I believe your mother is hiding something from me."

I can't help but choke. This from a guy whose sign-off at Mynt was *Let's just agree we didn't see each other here?*

"I want to know what she's hiding," he says.

Trent puffs in disgust. "You want dirt that isn't there," he says, his voice tight.

"I want a fair fight," Jim fires back. "And I don't want to lose everything I've ever worked for because she's got a wily attorney."

A chill slithers up my spine. The whole conversation is kind of grossing me out. Would he actually ask his own kids to dig up dirt on their mother just so he doesn't get taken to the cleaners in a divorce? An hour after I saw him cheating on her?

"I need your help in order to keep the business financially sound and my empire—which will someday belong to one of you—intact. The one who is willing to go the greatest distance will have proven to be the one who is most worthy of the CEO title in the future."

He avoids our gaze by looking at his nails, which are clipped and buffed. For one sharp instant, I remember my "real" dad's hands—inventor's hands, he used to call the calloused palms and cracked fingers. Maybe he has crappy hands, but he isn't a snake.

Trent is nearly imploding, working to hold in his reaction.

"Dad," he says, his voice tight, "you know I'm gonna side with Mom on anything."

"I know you're very close to her, Trent. And that was real sweet when you were six years old. But you're a man now, and—"

"I'm not going to spy on my own mother."

Jim lifts an eyebrow as if he doesn't believe him. Then he looks at me. "Ayla and I have a closer relationship, don't we?"

Oh, so that's why I'm not in trouble for stealing the Aston.

"Because you're both made of the same crap." Trent stands. "I'm not going to help you, Dad."

"Then, you'd better figure out what you're going to do with your life, because the gravy train is about to end."

Trent mumbles something that sounds suspiciously like "Screw you"—or worse—and walks to the door. Just as he's about to leave, he throws one more look at me. "You guys deserve each other."

Wait a second. Did I die and get reincarnated in a daytime soap?

"Well, Ayla?" Jim asks when we're alone. "Are you in or not?"

"I'm not sure," I admit.

He laughs softly. "You want to negotiate, huh? Okay, I noticed the Aston was parked in a different spot when I came home. How'd it drive for you? Maybe we can upgrade your last birthday present."

Holy cow, talk about sweetening the deal.

"I still don't know. Is there no hope for you and Mom?"

"I'm willing to make compromises; she is not."

Do the compromises include the thirsty blondes he's . . . *tapping*?

"Why don't I give you a little something in advance?" He goes back to the desk chair and sits down, pulling out the drawer. "I've never really understood Trent's blind loyalty to his mother."

Blind loyalty? "Well, she is his mother," I say.

He pulls out a black card . . . a credit card. As he holds it between his finger and thumb, the light catches the American Express logo in hologram.

"In your name." He flips it, Vegas dealer–style. "Unlimited."

"That's . . . nice."

"Money comes and money goes," he says, his eyes glinting. He holds it out to me. "I can terminate this at any time.

I need some answers, Ayla. She's no saint. I have to give my lawyer something, and fast, or we're going to be out a lot of cash."

We're . . . like we're in this together.

"And I know I can count on you," he adds with a smile that looks an awful lot like the one I've been seeing in the mirror today. Ayla has a lot of genes from the Monroe side, that's for sure. But I'm not sure I like all of them.

"I don't know, Dad," I say, even though calling him that feels so wrong deep inside.

"What don't you know?"

Why I'm here. Where this is. And what it all means. "I just don't know . . . if I'm in this for the long haul," I say vaguely. "I might leave . . . soon." Like tomorrow, when I wake up back on Rolling Rock Road.

He laughs softly. "You're not going anywhere, Ayla. Just do what you're best at."

"What's that?" I really want to know, but I'm a little scared what the answer is going to be.

"Play both ends against the middle, that's what. How could I blame you?" His lip quirks. "You've inherited so many of my most impressive traits."

He snaps the card onto the desk, next to a single pen. That's all that he has on his huge block of gleaming wood. Just imagine how much of my dad's junk this surface could hold.

But this man, this dream dad, is so not like my dad.

He slides the card toward me. "Go ahead. Take it. Use it. And do your job. Sneak around a little. Ask some questions. See if you can get her to trust you."

Blood money, that's what he's offering. Well, blood credit. But maybe with this card, I can convince my new best friends not to steal. With that pathetic rationalization in my head, I reach for the card. As I do, Jim's phone beeps with a digital melody, and he grabs it before the third note and presses it to his ear.

"Well, hello there," he says softly, pushing away from the desk and getting up to walk to the bar, his voice so different and . . . warm.

What's she thirsty for now? Or is this someone else?

I stand there, but he gives me a dismissive wave and shoulders the phone, laughing softly.

"I thought you'd like that," he says, his tone entirely different. "It was the least I could do after . . ." He glances back to see me riveted to my spot; then he points to the door. "Get out," he mouths.

I turn and walk out of the room, knowing instinctively to close the door behind me. As I reach the end of the hall, I turn to find Mom standing right there. Her expression is pained as she looks down at the card in my hand.

"What's that for?"

I just stare at it, then her. "Um, Dad gave me this for . . . supplies. For a school project." The words taste sour in my mouth. Have I ever flat-out lied to my mom before?

But this isn't my mom. This is some other woman who . . .

Who is she? She is Emily, deep inside, the same person I just shopped with at Walmart—

That's when all this started. That day in the store, that magazine, that iPhone app and the Picture-Perfect mirror.

Maybe Jimbo is right. Maybe she does know *something*. Like what I'm doing here.

I stuff the card into my back pocket. "Mom, can I talk to you?"

She looks at me, her eyes impossible to read, like there's a veil over them. Not the bright, open eyes of my mother, my *real* mother.

"I'm tired, Ayla."

"It won't take long." I angle my head toward the hall. "Let's go into the kitchen and . . ." With Mom, it was always tea. I'd drink hot chocolate at night, and she'd drink tea. "Have some tea."

She frowns, a creaseless effort. "I don't drink tea, Ayla. And I'm too tired to talk." She passes me, heading up the stairs.

"But, Mom, I really want to talk to you."

She shakes her head and continues on her way.

"You're just going to ignore me?" I call out to her. I mean, she is my mom. On any planet.

She turns around. "I already talked to your brother, Ayla. Don't waste your time trying to suck up to me. Nothing's going to change."

I stare at her back as she makes her way up the curved staircase, moving like an old, tired, aching woman, even though she looks much younger now.

I hear her sigh as she turns and disappears at the top.

Wow. The Monroe family is a hot mess.

Maybe this is a weird twist of my dream, a message telling me I better watch for warning signs back at the Nutter house.

Divorced parents . . . it's like my very worst nightmare. Like the world cracking underneath me.

I head to my turquoise and green room, close the door and lock it. Falling on the bed, I dig out the American Express and flip it around just the way Jim Monroe did.

Then I stop and read the name.

Ayla Anne Monroe.

My middle name is Anne. Taking some bizarre comfort in that, I turn over, curl my arms around one of the pillows, and close my eyes.

When I wake up from this, I'll be back on Rolling Rock Road. I'll be Annie Nutter again, awake, alive, and without my own Sky's-the-Limit AmEx, conniving dad, and miserable mom.

It's been fun, but I'm kind of looking forward to being home.

CHaPTer eLeven

"Meeees Ayla!" *Thump. Thump. Thump.*

What is that sound?

"You will be late for school! Get up, Miss Ayla!"

No. This is not possible. I slide under the comforter, blocking out all light, but not all sound.

Thump. Thumpthumpthump.

Jeez, she could lead the drum line in band.

"Get up now, Miss Ayla!" The doorknob jiggles furiously. "Mr. Trent is almost ready to leave."

Oh, my God. *Nothing* has changed. Not the room, not my clothes, not the maid screaming at the door. I am still Ayla Monroe. And I have got to figure out why. Or *how.* Or . . . how long it's going to last. I have to figure out something, or I'm going to lose my mind.

"I'm sick," I call out in a groggy morning voice.

Stumbling out of bed, I find my footing—my still-purple-with-crystalline-teardrop footing—and get to the door.

"What is the matter, Miss Ayla?" There's no sympathy in the question. Just a lot of disbelief because Ayla probably lies on a regular basis and no doubt is a lot better at it than *this* Ayla is.

"Stomach," I say, adding a dramatic moan. "My . . . my . . . monthly visitor." I cringe as I channel one of my mom's most pathetic expressions, and hope it works.

"Miss Ay—"

"You are *not* skipping school."

Mom! I fiddle with the lock and whip the door open to face my mother, who somehow manages to look pretty darn put together this early. Full makeup, hair styled, top-of-the-line clothes.

"I need to talk to you, Mom," I plead, looking past Loras, who's waiting to dive into the room, basket at the ready. "I have to ask you something. Privately."

For a minute Mom softens, and I see a flicker of the woman I know in her eyes as she looks at me. That caring look, the one she has when she strokes my hair even though she knows I hate to have my hair touched.

"Are you okay?" she asks, the first real glimmer of concern I've seen since I arrived here.

"Actually, no. I'm not."

She studies me for a moment, her expression unsure. "I have to say . . . you don't seem like yourself."

"You have no idea." I grab her wrist to pull her in, my decision made. I'm going to tell her everything. She's my *mom*. She has to believe me. I've never lied to her in my life.

Not in my other life, at least. And, of course, I can't speak for Ayla, who seems to have a less than stellar track record for things like that.

"Come in here and talk to me."

"Into your room? Since when?"

"Since . . . since this new me. I'm a new me," I insist. Because I *am*. And I'm going to tell her. "I need to tell you something. I need to *ask* you something." Like who the heck am I and how did I get here?

She still doesn't move. "What's wrong, Ayla?"

"Nothing's wrong, technically." Because I kind of like this life. But it's not mine. "It's . . . complicated. Please."

"Go, Emily." Jim Monroe's voice startles me from around the corner, followed one second later by his stern expression. "Your daughter is reaching out for you, and you're standing there like the ice queen we all know you are."

Her eyes narrow at him. "Don't tell me you slept in your own bed for a change."

He ignores the comment and waves toward me. "Go talk to her. She needs you. It's obvious. She's calling out for help, and you are her mother. Talk to her."

I feel viselike pressure on my temples, a feeling I've never had before but somehow I know is familiar. Like both of these people have a hand on my head and they're squeezing until my skull cracks.

Mom shifts a frosty look my way. "I can't. I'm late for a meeting."

A meeting? With her lawyer? Behind her, over her

shoulder, I catch Jim's glance, and I don't mean to, but somehow I feel like we're communicating silently. And by the way Mom closes her eyes, I can tell she thinks so, too.

But Jim notches a brow and nods at me. He likes this approach; he thinks I'm holding up my end of the bargain. I'm not, but there's no way to explain that to either of them.

"Get dressed and go to school, Ayla," Mom says, stepping away. "Your theatrics won't work with me. Save them for your dad."

"Mom, seriously, please." I am so not going to school until I get some answers. "I can't go to school."

"You're not sick," she says.

"I . . . didn't do my homework."

She almost smiles. "You'll figure it out."

"No, I had this paper. For English lit, and, Mom, I cannot go to school without writing it. I just need to miss first period. Then, maybe . . ."

Jim clears his throat. Subtle he's not. "Let her do her homework, Emily, and then you can drive her in an hour late. Would that work, Ayla?"

"Um, yeah. That'd be a start."

"It's settled, then." Jim pivots and heads back down the hall.

For a minute, Mom fights for composure she doesn't really have, then she strides toward the steps without a word. Loras just stands there, unsure what to do next.

I start to close my door, but don't want to slam it in her face. "I have homework to do, Loras. Can you come back later? Please?"

She raises her eyebrows.

"Tillie is right," she says in a hushed whisper. "You are a witch."

"I think she meant bitch."

Loras shakes her head. "She meant witch. Go do your work, Miss Ayla. I'll come back later."

Oh, great, so now the help thinks I'm a witch. Well, whatever. I have to find out what I am before I can set anyone else straight. So the minute I'm alone, I lock the door and head to the computer.

I'm not exactly sure what I'm looking for, though. Can you Google "woke up and I'm a different person"?

Like I'm on autopilot, I log on to Facebook and type my email as my user name and *theoisabrat* for my password.

No such account exists.

Goose bumps cascade up my spine. Why wouldn't Annie Nutter have a Facebook page? I mean, even if . . . I'm *here*? Wherever I am.

My fingers hover over the keyboard, and I realize there's a lump growing in my throat.

If Annie Nutter doesn't have a Facebook page, does she even exist?

Very slowly I type *Ay* and an email address pops into the box, giving me hope that I can get onto Ayla's page easily and navigate from there. But the hope is dashed when the password box stays blank. Dang. How will I ever know her password?

I try *trentisatool*, but it doesn't work. Because Ayla isn't Annie and she doesn't think like I do. How does she think? I

111

close my eyes and channel my inner Ayla. She loves clothes, makeup, shoes, and . . . Ryder.

I type *Rydersgirl.*

Access denied.

Ryderswoman. Ryderschick. Rydersbabe. Nothing. The goose bumps have turned to a fine sheen of sweat, and I know I'm going to have to give up this attempt soon. I close my eyes, take a deep breath, and just let my fingers move the way they always do when logging in to Facebook. Without thinking.

TheAlist.

I'm in.

I skip the news feed and profile and slide up to the search box, type *Lizzie Kauffman* into the box and then click on my best friend's name and the group picture I instantly recognize from last summer.

I'm in that picture, I know it! I can't read her page, of course—we're not friends—but I click on her profile picture to enlarge it. There were five of us, inseparable that day at Lake Erie. Sarah, Mia, Jessica, Lizzie, and . . .

I'm not in that picture, though. I squint at the girl standing where I remember I was, a dishwater blonde with angular features that are kind of familiar, but I can't quite place her.

Why isn't that me?

"I remember that picture," I whine under my breath. "Why am I not in it?" We were by the canoes, wet and screaming and happy and . . . Who is that girl?

Oh, my God. Oh, my God. Oh, my *God.* "That's Nickel-ass." What is Courtney Nicholas doing in my place?

I remember I had one hand on Lizzie's shoulder, and the

other was giving a thumbs-up to Lizzie's mom, who'd taken the bunch of us to the lake that day. Courtney isn't giving anyone the thumbs-up, but it's definitely her. On a really bad hair day.

The lump in my throat is bigger, closing things up and forcing tears to my eyes.

"Where am I?" The question is a croak now, and I feel the first tear meander down my cheek, when I blink and realize that the answer is obvious.

I'm here. In this house. In this family. In this world I don't know but somehow seem to understand. Before I leave Facebook, I hit the friend request and send it to Lizzie.

Maybe . . .

But she never accepts people she doesn't know.

I Google a few things—including Courtney Nicholas, but she doesn't have a Facebook page—and even try digging up my dad's RadioShack location, but his name isn't listed as an employee. I try Mom's real estate website. No such URL. Even Theo Nutter doesn't show up on Facebook.

It's like we never existed.

I return to Ayla's page, and there I am. Dozens of pictures. Backstage at a concert, on a yacht, toasting champagne glasses with Jade and Bliss, a link to a video called "My Slammin' Sweet Sixteen Party at Edge in SoBe."

Ayla had her sweet sixteen at a nightclub in South Beach? I had mine at the Moose Lodge in Lawrenceville because my dad had a customer who belonged and we got it for a discount.

So why am I complaining? This glorious, glamorous life is so much better.

I click on the video and watch as my face comes into focus. There's loud music—a live band. Holy God, it's Never Shout Never. Christofer Drew played at my party?

The camera is jumpy, but I can see I'm in a sparkly pink minidress, and I look like I'm about to walk the red carpet at the People's Choice Awards. Mesmerized, I turn the sound up.

"So what day is it, Ayla?" It's Jimbo's voice, so he must be working the video cam.

I look right at him and give him a snotty look like he is all things stupid and annoying. "August twelfth, Daddy."

So Ayla and Annie have the same birthday.

"Do you love your party?"

On the screen, Ayla just laughs, throaty and sexy, and, really, who laughs like that? "Yeah, except I really wanted to fly everyone to St. Bart's instead of going down the street to SoBe," she says.

Holy crap, what a bitch.

She turns from the camera as someone approaches. It's Ryder, looking damn good. He reaches for her, and she accepts his hug, but pulls back to give him a less than affectionate look.

"Where the hell's my drink?"

I hate that girl.

The band starts the next song, and there's a lot of screaming. Christofer Drew—ohmigod Lizzie would die!—gets up to the microphone.

"Where's the birthday girl? I need some help on this one," Chris says.

I watch in silence as Ayla takes the stage, lets Never

Shout Never sing happy freaking birthday to her, and every-one toasts with champagne.

So, okay, that didn't happen at the Moose Lodge.

What is wrong with me? Why can't I just appreciate being here, wherever the hell I am? Life's great, and who cares if I'm a bitch? I don't have to *act* like Ayla Monroe to *live* like Ayla Monroe.

But a little tendril of confusion wraps around my heart. Why am I changed on the outside but not on the inside?

What if I were the daughter of Jim and Emily Monroe? Who knows if I would still be me? Wouldn't I have the same soul?

As the Walmart conversation with my mom replays in my head, I clutch my chest, where I always imagine my soul resides. Is that what happened, somehow?

Little sparks flash behind my eyes, and all of the answers to the questions of the last few days are right there. I am Ayla Monroe . . . but somehow, some way, I've got Annie Nutter's soul. Now I just have to figure out a way to make these two coexist.

Holding that thought, I shower, dress—I go with Jade's suggestion for all Dior—and apply a little makeup to my pretty face.

No, this totally doesn't suck.

I open the door and head downstairs to find Mom. Maybe I won't tell her just yet. Or maybe I'll ask some questions, find out a little about her history, like when she married Jimbo and why.

Tillie is in the kitchen. "Good morning, Miss Ayla." She hands me a crystal bowl of yogurt, and as I reach for it, I smile.

"I'm not a witch," I whisper. "And thank you."

"Then, why do you say 'thank you' after sixteen years of being the world's biggest brat?"

"Because I've changed."

That earns me some more intense scrutiny, as though she can figure out what happened by looking into my eyes. "True," she says. "Something is different."

"It certainly is." I spoon the yogurt and slide it into my mouth, watching Tillie clean with competence and speed. Maybe she can shed some light on this world.

"So, how long have you worked for us?"

She frowns at me. "It's not strawberry, Miss Ayla. I don't need a lecture on what you eat and don't eat. I have been with this family long enough to know what's what."

Yeah? Too bad I haven't. "Where's Mom?" I ask.

"She left for an appointment."

Disappointment pulls at me. "She was going to take me to school."

"There's a limo on the way, Miss Ayla. You'll get to school."

A *limo*? Yes I will get there, and in style, it seems.

I swallow any questions along with my yogurt. Stop fighting the tide, Ayla. It's time to embrace every limo-filled moment of this new life.

CHAPTER TWELVE

When the stretch pulls up to the entrance of Crap Academy, there are a few kids dotting the lawns and circular drive. But my eye is drawn to the fountain in the middle, where Charlie Zelinsky is sitting on the stone wall, oboe case at his feet, phone in his hand, geektastic fedora low over his face. He looks up as the car slows and the driver gets out to open my door.

I'm not quite ready to leave the luxury that is my very first limo ride. But I'm comforted knowing it won't be my last. Evidently Jimbo keeps this monster stretch on 24/7 call, with Marcel, a gray-haired grandfatherly type, as the driver. I slide out, and Charlie watches, tipping back his hat, then sliding some off-brand aviators down his nose to pin me with a long stare.

He probably hates me. All the invisibles hate the popular kids; that's the law of nature. They hate us, and they want to be us.

Us. *That didn't take long to embrace*, I think with a wry smile.

Confident in my school status for the first time in my life, I square my shoulders, nod my thanks to Marcel as he holds the door for me, and head toward the steps, planning to cruise right by the nobody who caused me such grief in English lit.

But Charlie surprises me, holding up his hand with an easy smile. Despite my desire to glide by like school royalty without so much as a sideways glance, I hesitate. It's the smile, I think. There's something about his smile that's genuine. And, jeez, kinda cute.

I mean, he might be a geek, but in my old life he'd be the object of my late-night if-only-I-had-a-boyfriend sessions with Lizzie. Of course, my standards were much lower then.

"Brighton read our stuff on symbolism to the class," he says.

Great. Now there's no doubt that one of us had to know what we were talking about on that assignment. Something tells me that Charlie didn't hog all the credit, further eroding my position as a Queen Bee who doesn't care about grades.

"Cool." My brain wants me to move on, but my legs are like lead. No, worse than lead. They're on their way over to him. "So, I take it we got an A."

Why did I say that? Ayla wouldn't care what her grade is.

His smile widens, revealing really straight teeth and one

dimple. One lone dimple that kind of grabs my heart, it's so cute.

No, Ayla. Not cute. *Invisible*.

"Which might balance out the fact that you're going to fail chem," he teases.

"I am not," I shoot back. "And how the heck would you know, anyway? I didn't see you in my chem class."

"And you won't. I'm taking advanced physics."

Nerd alert! "Of course you are," I say, inexplicably drawn to him. "That's why you offered chem tutoring."

He shrugs and raises his head enough that I can really see his face under the brim. "Only if you need it."

"Why do you wear that stupid hat?"

"Why do you wear those stupid shoes?"

I look down at the booties, admiring the buckles. "Sorry, but there's nothing stupid about these shoes."

"There's nothing stupid about this hat."

"Just the person who bought it."

His smile disappears. "That's where you're wrong."

Oh, sensitive, is he? "Sorry," I say, softening the tension with a smile. The fact is, I'm still held like a magnet two feet away from him.

Of course, if a boy had talked to me this long and this casually in my old life, I wouldn't have dreamed of walking away. So, chalk this social faux pas up as a noobie mistake, because I'm not used to the fact that every boy in Crap wants to talk to me.

Still, I don't move, and neither does he.

"Why aren't you in class?" I ask, mostly to break the beat of awkward silence.

"Why aren't you?"

"Do you always answer a question with a question?" I inch closer. Why? I don't know, but I do.

"If I can," he admits. "I take college classes at night, so I don't have a full six-period day. I'm free during third and fifth. But you are officially cutting, which I know is your MO."

"Is it? How *do* I get away with that?" I try to make it sound like a sarcastic joke, but I'm hoping he knows the answer.

He snorts a soft laugh. "Ayla Monroe, daughter of one of the school's biggest benefactors, darling of the faculty lounge, owner of the Can Do No Wrong title . . . are you asking me a serious question?"

"Are you always so sarcastic?"

When he doesn't answer, I give his arm a little nudge. I'm that close to him now. And staying. "Question with a question."

He laughs, and so do I, and for one crazy second, we have eye contact. Long eye contact. The kind of eye contact that sends a little baby butterfly flitting around my stomach.

"Ayla!"

I spin at the sound of my name, freezing like a criminal caught in the act when I see Jade and Bliss bounding down the stairs. As much as anyone can bound in four-inch heels.

Bliss blasts Charlie with a dirty look.

"What are you doing?" she demands, like he broke the law or something. Well, I guess he did. Invisibles don't talk to the most popular girl in the school. Doesn't he know the immutable laws of physics?

"Aren't you supposed to be in class?" he shoots back at her, flicking his gaze at me. For a flash, we share an inside joke, answering a question with a question.

The flash is long enough for Bliss to see it. "Nice lid, cowboy," she says, walking up to the fountain, Jade right in step with her.

"It's not a cowboy hat," I tell her, bracing for her to say something really mangled *and* mean to Charlie. I don't know why, but I just don't think I can stand it after he's been nothing but nice to me.

"You like that hat?" Bliss asks me, a challenge in her tone. "'Cause I think it looks kind of . . . highness."

"Highness?" Charlie whispers to me.

"I think she means 'heinous.'"

He stifles a laugh, and that makes Bliss's eyes flash in anger as she marches closer.

"You have a lot of nerve laughing at me," she says to him.

"I'm not—"

She snags the hat right off his head, and he tries to grab it, but she's too fast. In a second, she's got it on, copping a pose while Jade hoots.

"How do I look?" Bliss asks, hand on her hip, diva-style.

"Cut it out," I say, an old, familiar heat rising up from my chest. I've seen this a million times, only I've never had the nerve to talk back to a kid doing this.

"Give it," Jade demands, reaching out.

Bliss flips the hat to Jade. Charlie is up, but they're way too fast, scampering around the fountain with heels clickity-clacking, and he obviously doesn't want to look like a fool running after them.

"Over here," I say, enough play in my voice that I hope they'll fall for it. Because the minute I have that hat, I'm giving it back to its rightful owner.

But the hat flips between Jade and Bliss again, high in the air.

I steal a look at Charlie, seeing his whole face and hair for the first time. Funny, he doesn't look too much like a science geek who takes college classes in eleventh grade. Not as cute as Ryder, obviously, but kind of a young, in-need-of-a-makeover Ashton Kutcher. Only skinnier and not as tall. And not as sexy.

So, not Ashton Kutcher.

"Hey!" he says as the hat narrowly misses a fountain spray and the two of them giggle like banshees.

There's got to be a better way to handle this. I round the fountain and get in Bliss's face, gearing up to deliver a deadly warning and underscore it with The Look.

She hesitates under my gaze, but the hat's sailing her way. I reach up to catch it, but I miss, instead sending it right into the fountain.

Charlie swears under his breath, and the hat bobbles in the water behind me.

"Nice one, Ayla," Bliss says, offering a high five.

Jade scampers around the fountain, tossing long black hair over her shoulder like she has just finished a hard afternoon's work. "You gotta quit socializing with the invisibles, Ayla," she says, her voice low in warning.

"Why?"

They both stare at me, but Bliss's expression shifts and softens.

"You're right, Ayla. Talk to all the losers you want, whenever you want. It's fine." She gives me a nudge. "We were going to hit Miracle Mile. You comin'?"

I turn to see Charlie shaking off the hat, which is drenched. He won't even look at me, and my heart sinks a little. He thinks I knocked the hat into the water on purpose.

"Or would you rather stay with your new friend?"

Bliss's question is swaddled in sweetness, but I know better than to trust her. Of course, if I'm caught so much as talking to an invisible, I could lose my perch on the pile of popularity, and guess who is ready to hoist herself up and fill in the vacancy?

"Let's go," I say quietly, without even looking at Charlie.

The fleeting connection is gone anyway, and that's the way it's supposed to be. I head off with my friends without looking back. They might not be the greatest girls in the world, but they breathe the rare air, and I still want my lungs full of that, too.

The boutique- and restaurant-lined street in the heart of the Gables is packed with tourists and shoppers, and as we navigate the crowds and sip caramel macchiatos, my friends grill me.

"Why do you suddenly find it necessary to befriend the homeless?" Bliss demands.

"Don't you mean the hopeless?"

"No, I do not."

Jade steps in between us, where she is metaphorically most of the time. But this time, I think she's siding with Bliss.

123

"Honestly, Ayla," she says, "you could really ruin our rep by talking to people like that jerkwad Zelinsky."

Do popular kids really think like this? I mean, I've been watching them from afar since whenever "popular" happens—so, what, fifth grade? I know the lessers certainly know their lives can change on a dime with even a nod from the popular kids, but is it vice versa, too?

"He's just a nice science geek," I say, still determined to defend him, but my voice has grown weak. Along with my conviction. Cutting class and drinking coffee with the most popular girls is by far better than flirting with nerds. "He's going to help me in chem because I helped him in lit."

They both stare as if my hair has changed color.

"Yeah, about that freak accident in lit," Bliss says, accusation in her voice. "It's been all over the school. I assume you SparkNoted that book, right?"

"Duh. Like I really read *Lord of the Flies*." I sip my coffee, averting my eyes. "So I'm going to let him make sure I don't fail chem."

Jade shakes her head. "Nobody talks to him, Ayla. If you talk to him, one of two things is going to happen." She holds out perfectly French-manicured fingers to count. "One, he becomes popular by week's end."

Bliss exhales as though the world just ended. "That is so not going to happen. But we might lose our position."

"Then we probably don't really have it, do we?" I say.

"What is wrong with you, Ayla? You're acting like some kind of lunatic. Like, who *are* you?" Bliss asks.

Good question.

"Chill, Bliss," Jade says quickly.

"I'm not going to chill," she snaps. "I'm reminding little Miss Get Hot and Bothered over a Needs Scholarship Kid that she can't drag us into the lower ranks because she's becoming some kind of . . . of . . . philanthropologist."

"He's on a needs scholarship?"

They look at each other in disbelief.

"Dude." Bliss puts her hand on my arm, her tone softer, like she's speaking to a child. A stupid child. "Did you forget? He lives in a cardboard box."

"What?" Something inside my heart slips. Does she mean he really *is* homeless?

"Not anymore," Jade says. "But his mother *was*, like, a hobo or something, for crying out loud. Then she was on the news, and he was all over the papers and *Good Morning America* as some boy genius living under a bridge."

"Next thing you know," Bliss continues, "we got Box Boy at Crap because the powers that be thought paying his ride was a 'good PR move.'" She uses air quotes and a sarcastic tone. "So we're stuck with him, even though half the school's parents tried to fight it. Who wants a homeless kid here?"

"No one," Jade says. "And we sure as shit don't talk to him."

"He doesn't still live in a box, though," I say with hope. Because for some reason, this idea just rips me inside.

"Might as well," Bliss says. "It's an apartment in Hi-a-le-ah." She whispers and drags out the offending town's name, syllable by syllable, as though she can't really bring herself to let the word be spoken from her lips. "And his mother cleans *offices*, Ayla."

"He doesn't belong at our school, and he sure as hell doesn't belong talking to you." Jade points at me.

"He's still . . ." A *person*. But something stops me from saying that. "Not even that bad-looking," I finish weakly.

"Oh. My. God." Bliss stares at me with incredulity. "You really are psychopathetic."

I fight a laugh at this latest malapropism. "Just psychopathic, but I'm not. I just talked to the guy. I don't understand the big deal."

"The big deal," Jade says, deep into her peacemaker role, "is that we"—she makes a circle with her finger that indicates the three of us—"only talk to certain people. Some of the cheerleaders, not all. Some of the jocks, and the occasional noob or invisible, yeah. That's all fine and kind and stuff. But this guy." Again, she shakes her head as if I just don't get it. "Nobody even wants him at school, and talking to him? Just . . . no, Ayla. No."

Inside, a war rages. It's physical, a tearing in my chest, right down the middle. Part of me—the new, rich, popular, cool, pretty part—just wants to agree and move on.

"I guess," I concede.

But Bliss doesn't notice, because she has stopped walking again, this time in front of a glitzy-looking boutique called Mia Cara. She's mesmerized by a jeweled belt in the window.

"Now, that," she says with a sigh, "could eradiate all your sorrows."

"I don't have any sorrows that need to be eradiated *or*

eradicated," I say with a smile, giving her a friendly squeeze. "But I do have my brand-spanking-new American Express Centurion card, so let's melt that sucker."

Bliss freezes me with a look. "You're not going to take all the fun out of it, are you?"

Damn. Somehow I knew she was letting me off the hook too easily. "I don't know, Bliss," I say coolly. "Depends on your idea of fun. I love to shop."

She leans very close to my ear. "Well, I love to shop*lift* and, *mia cara*, it's your turn."

I've never stolen anything in my life.

"Jade and I will do the D and A."

"D and A?"

"Distract and annoy," Jade says as though I should know. "You get the belt. And maybe that cute little gray leather clutch next to it. Win!" She looks hard at my Fendi bag. "Open it and clear space. Remember, we're the decoys. I'll buy earrings or, if we have to, try something on."

"What's wrong?" Bliss demands, probably smelling the sweat that's starting to make my armpits sticky.

"Nothing." *Everything.* "I'm fine." *I'm sick.* "Why . . ." *Are we doing this?* "Are we waiting out here?"

"So you can get your shit together," Bliss says darkly. "If that's even possible anymore."

She gives me a hard nudge toward Mia Cara. "Get me the freaking belt or it's going to be all over Crap Academy that the Queen Bee has lost more than her honey." She looks ridiculously smug with her pun. "You lose everything. In-cluding us."

"Then, maybe you weren't worth anything."

"Ayla," Jade whines. "Guys, stop this. Let's go in there and make it fun. It's always fun. You call it your favorite high, A-list."

Dear God, I do?

I stare at the belt, the purse, and my still unfamiliar reflection in the window. So who's going into that store . . . Ayla or Annie?

chapter thirteen

They're experts. That much is obvious as we walk in and one of two salesclerks is instantly on us asking if she can help. Jade and Bliss take her full attention, getting her to help them find some tops. While the other lady rings up the only other customer, Bliss shoots me a look, surreptitiously pointing to the hanging belt display.

The one she wants is out of view of the cashier. Their salesgirl has gone to the back to find a size zero for Jade, and I casually round the display and finger the jeweled belt.

The price tag is a mere $189. A day's allowance for this crew. Is it really some kind of incredible high to flip that thing off the hook and drop it into my bag?

No.

Unless the high is walking out the door without having a store security alarm blare and three armed guards throw you down, cuff you, and remind you that you'll never get a driver's license or get into college or spend another day outside of a prison cell.

I slide my wet palm over my skirt and hear the footsteps of the other clerk coming from the back.

"I have a double zero. Do you want to try that?"

Jeez Louise, who wears a double zero?

I do, now. This is my life. Cool girls. Hip stores. To-die-for clothes. And . . . shoplifting.

How bad do I want to fit in?

If I don't do this, am I on my way down the high school food chain again?

My hand reaches for the hook. I look around, not seeing any eyes on me, no security camera, no other customers. Jade and Bliss have the clerk's full attention, the other salesperson is busy bagging some clothes.

I close my fingers over the belt, slide it off the hook, glance down to the opening of my handbag to aim, and . . . make my final decision.

I step away from the display, re-shoulder the bag, and walk over to my friends, who pull me into their conversation about jeans and tops.

"You ready to go?" I ask, an edge in my voice.

Bliss's eyes widen enough for me to know I've broken some golden rule of shoplifting.

"Let me grab these earrings," Jade says quickly, waving them at me as she heads to the cash register. "I can't live without them."

My heart is still clomping triple time as she pays and we head toward the door.

Bliss is quiet, Jade is texting, and as I step one foot out the door, a man appears on my right.

"Miss, open your bag."

"Excuse me?" I ask, vaguely aware that every cell in my body has turned to liquid.

"Are you kidding me?" Bliss asks, dumbfounded.

"Open your bag here or at the Coral Gables police department." He pulls out a leather wallet and shows me a badge. "Miracle Mile security."

"Knock yourself out," I say with full Ayla flair, popping open the Fendi bag. "I don't think you'll find what you're looking for."

He flips my wallet and makeup bag to the side, knocks around some mints and a hairbrush, frowning.

"No contraband. Sorry," I say as snottily as possible.

He digs deeper; then his hand slows. "You're sure?"

Oh, shit. The joint I'd taken from Bliss is still in there. I didn't shoplift, but I'm about to be busted for drugs.

He gives up the search and levels me with a gaze. He's young and kind of cute, and I see his eyes travel over my face. My pretty, pretty face, which can get away with anything.

"Get back to school, ladies."

Oh, yeah, there are some serious benefits to beauty, and I just reaped some big ones. I lock arms with Jade and stroll on past the ladies watching from inside Mia Cara.

"Dude," Jade whispers. "How the hell did you pull that off?"

"I smelled trouble."

"You are, like, the luckiest person in the universe," she adds, giving my arm a squeeze. "I thought we were toast."

Bliss nestles to my other side, her look not quite as admiring as Jade's. "Didn't take the belt, huh? You really have changed, Ayla."

"Back off, Bliss," Jade insists. "She saved our ass."

Bliss sniffs dismissively. "Not what I'd call it."

"What would you call it?" I fire back, unable to resist. "*Masturbate* when you mean *masterful*?"

She's not amused. In fact, she's just pissed enough for me to remember: The only thing stopping Bliss from being me is . . . *me*. And the more I become Annie instead of Ayla, the sooner she can slide onto Ayla's vacant throne.

When I get home, I find Mom upstairs in a huge exercise room, sweating to the sounds of Katy Perry. Well, not exactly sweating. Her back is to me, and she's bent over a leather bench, a free weight in one hand, but it doesn't appear to be moving.

"Hey," I say, staying at the door, our relationship so weird and strained, I don't even know if she wants to talk to me.

She looks up to the mirror and meets my gaze, then exhales, dropping the weight with a thud. "Oh, it's you." Disappointment darkens her voice.

Mom doesn't like me very much, I'm beginning to guess. "Who were you expecting?"

"A new trainer." She touches a remote and lowers

the volume of the music. "I wanted him to think I was warming up."

"Well, go ahead," I say, stepping into the room. Three walls are mirrored, and there's high-end gym equipment everywhere over a shiny oak floor. "Don't let me stop you."

She lifts a shoulder and places her hands on narrow hips encased in black spandex. "I haven't exactly started. But God, I need to. Which is why I'm trying a new trainer."

"You're in great shape, Mom," I say as I get closer to her.

She tilts her head a little, like she doesn't trust what she heard. "Thanks."

I'm not lying; she's an easy fifteen pounds lighter than the Mom I left behind, and more muscular. With the fixed face and thick hair, Emily Monroe is hands down more attractive than Emily Nutter.

Which reminds me exactly why I wanted to talk to her. "When did you and—" I can't call him Jim, but I can't think of him as Dad. ". . . my father get married?"

The distrust darkens her blue eyes. "Why?"

There's no easy answer for that. "I'm just curious. Did you marry him when he left Pittsburgh, or—"

"*Why, Ayla?*" She drops onto the workout bench.

"I need to know for a . . . school proj—"

"Why are you doing this?" Her voice is sharp, so she takes a calming breath before continuing. "Look, I know we have our differences. I know . . ." It takes her another second to collect herself. "I know we don't agree on anything and you will side with your dad on everything that matters because you two are so much alike—"

"We are?" I get a funny feeling in my gut. I am not like that man, not at all. Unless, deep down, in the *soul* . . .

I don't know why, but I feel the answer to what and how and why I'm here lies in these questions. I have to ask them.

"You are," she tells me softly.

"I just want to know some stuff, Mom." I close the space between us and perch on the edge of her bench. "About . . ." Her life, her history, my being here. "You."

"Jesus, Ayla, do you think I'm an idiot? He wants anything he can use against me, and he's paying you to get it." She snorts softly. "That man thinks money solves everything."

I sigh, adjusting my technique. I have to remember I'm Ayla, not Annie, and that's who Mom thinks she's dealing with. And, worse, she thinks I have some agenda to help Jim. I'd like to tell her I don't, but I have a feeling she won't believe me.

"That's not why I want to know," I say. She just looks at me, all skeptical and tight. "I need to . . ."

"You want to decide which one of us you're going to live with?"

I blink, horrified. "Do I have to make that choice?"

"Don't be naive, Ayla. The court makes the decision based on what you say you want."

"So you really are getting divorced."

She looks like she's going to laugh. Or maybe cry. Instead she turns to the mirror and speaks to her own reflection. "After the last one . . . Lisa . . ." She shakes her head, lips tight. "I don't even care that there's a new one. After a while,

134

they all run together. The patients, the nurses, the franchise owners, the . . . women of his *flawless* world."

There's so much sadness in her voice, I could cry.

"You deserve better than that," I say.

She meets my gaze in the mirror, and I realize what's so different about this Mom. Not the glossy skin or better body. Not the high-end haircut or the sizeable studs in her ears. It's her smile.

There isn't one.

"I'm glad you finally realize that, Ayla. Is it because you're in love yourself?"

I frown, not even sure who I might be in love with. "Ryder?" I ask, the impossibility of that obvious in my voice.

"You don't love him?"

I don't know him, but from what I saw . . . we are a long way from love. "You know, there's a difference between thinking a guy is hot and being in love with him," I tell her.

"Oh." Her whole being seems to relax a little. "I had no idea you were getting so mature."

"There's a lot you don't know about me, Mom." Like *who I am*. "But I really am interested in, you know, the history of you and Dad." I suddenly see the right angle. "So I don't make the same mistakes."

She gives me another long exhale, but no answer, clearly struggling with what to say next.

"You met in college, right? He was in med school?" I need to know if this Emily's history is the same as *my* Emily's history. Because, somewhere, somehow, they had to diverge. "Then he . . . came to Florida? Right? Did you follow him?"

"Not until I finished school and had some time. Then I came down here to . . . tell him something. He can be very . . . persuasive. Even . . ."

"Even what?"

She shakes her head, shutting down. "It doesn't matter, Ayla. Everything has changed since then. Especially me." Sliding hands over her hips, she turns side to side. "I'm not that girl anymore."

Yeah? Welcome to my world.

"You look great, Mom," I say absently, skimming my mind for how to get her to tell me more.

"I could," she agrees. "If I could get rid of this belly." She laughs softly. "Guess I should have thought of that before I married a man who recommends that ironing boards get lipo. Looks like I married the wrong man."

I sit up straighter at the tone of pure regret in her voice. Did she marry the wrong man? "Was there ever anybody else before Dad?" I ask.

Her eyes close a little. "No one who could have convinced me not to marry Jim Monroe."

"But someone," I prod. Someone like Mel Nutter. Did she ever meet him? Did she choose Jim Monroe over him?

Her attention is back on the mirror, and she's turning to the side, sucking in her stomach. "Do *you* think I should have lipo?"

The sudden change of subject throws me. "Are you kidding? Look at you."

"I am, but I don't think I see what you see."

"Obviously not, if you'd suggest something as stupid as lipo."

She sucks in harder, making her gut concave. "I wish I could just see what it would look like. Just to have an idea of what is possible."

"Maybe someone will invent that," I say, unable to keep the irony out of my voice. "A magic mirror that shows you with a dream body. And you could pick your favorite celebrity body parts just to create the perfect person."

"Holy hell, that's a brilliant idea!" Jim Monroe's voice surprises both of us. I startle. Mom freezes. "I'd put one in every Forever Flawless location in the country."

"What are you doing here?" she asks.

"I live here," he replies coolly. "Ayla, I need to talk to your mother."

"Okay." I glance at her; she's pale and stiff. The little glimmer of closeness we almost had disappeared the moment Jim entered the room. "Do you want me to leave?" I ask her, wanting her to know I'm not on his side completely and I can't be bought with a black AmEx card.

But she looks at me like I've spoken Greek. "Since when does what I want matter to you?"

"Never mind," I say, knowing it's not the time to convince her of anything. "I'll talk to you later."

As I pass Jim, he puts a hand on my shoulder, stopping me. "That mirror thing," he says. "Great idea. I like the way you're thinking, young lady. Where'd you come up with something like that?"

I just give him a dry smile. "I think I dreamed it."

I close the door as I leave, and instantly hear the tones of an argument. But I'm not sticking around to eavesdrop.

In my own room, away from the fight, I log on to Facebook out of habit and check my notifications.

Lizzie Kauffman has accepted your friend request.

I stare at the words for a good two minutes before I realize that my eyes are filled with tears. Apparently I don't blush in this world. I cry.

CHAPTER FOURTEEN

When I step out of my bathroom, fully made up and ready to dress for my big night, the funniest thought hits me a little too hard.

It's homecoming dance tonight at South Hills High, too.

I wonder who Shane is going with . . . and if Lizzie is still doing the *Degrassi* marathon. A little pull of something that feels like a mix of regret and longing squeezes me in the stomach.

I recognize it, of course. Homesickness. And I try to kick it out of my head and heart as fast as possible.

Honestly, who has time for homesickness? It's *home-coming*. And not only am I going with a guy who puts Shane Matthews to shame, I'm wearing *that*.

Hanging from my closet door, freshly pressed by Tillie,

is the most incredibly beautiful buttercup-yellow dress I've ever seen. I found it in my closet, still bearing the two-thousand-dollar price tag. That's right, two grand for a dress. Take that, homesickness.

Stepping into the gossamer silk, I run my hands over the exquisite beadwork, the strapless bust fitting perfectly over my boobs.

I twirl in front of the mirror, unable to take the smile off my face. I look like some kind of Disney princess. I step into four-inch sandals that I imagine will be kicked off for dancing, grab my bag, phone, some mints, and lip gloss, and I'm ready to go.

Oh, except I can't forget the adorable Louis Vuitton change purse that Jade and Bliss gave me, fully stocked with condoms and a "V-card" they made by gluing my picture to cardboard and writing *virgin* at the top. Tomorrow it can be shredded.

Because tonight I . . .

That funny feeling tickles again. That's not homesickness. That's fear.

Ryder's rose is just about dead now, but I pick up the card, taking a calming breath as I read his words.

A flower 4 u, since u r giving me urs.
Ryder

I look up and meet my own gaze in the mirror, no longer shocked every time I see my face. In fact, I'm getting really good at being Ayla now.

All I had to do was avoid overt contact with the invisibles (easy with Charlie, since he hasn't said two words to me since the hat incident), quit grilling my mom about ancient history, and log off Facebook, because Lizzie never says much of anything important about life back in Pittsburgh.

What could possibly be going on there that would be any better than this? More idiocy with Courtney Nicholas? I'm Courtney Nicholas on steroids, with a drool-worthy boyfriend who'll be punching the V-card tonight.

And why not? I've already learned there are no consequences for anything in Ayla Monroe's life, so what difference does it make?

Virginity's gotta go sometime, right, and sex is supposed to be so much fun. What better night to find out than the teenage dream of the homecoming dance?

He's picking me up in a limo any minute for a pre-party at Jade's, so I pause at the top of the Hollywood staircase, take a deep breath, and begin the slow walk down.

The house is very quiet.

"Mom?" The word practically echoes. Isn't she here? Doesn't she want to at least take a picture?

"Dad?" Not my first choice, but there's still no answer. "Trent?" I call, kind of desperate for someone to say, *You look pretty. Have a good time.*

Finally, I hear some footsteps, and by the solid stomp, I know who it is.

"Well, look at you." Tillie smiles—a rarity in itself—and nods. "Very nice, Miss Ayla."

"Thanks."

As if she can hear the little disappointment in my voice, she steps closer. "Your mother had to go up to Boca and see her friend, remember?"

No, I don't remember. Didn't she remember it's the homecoming dance tonight?

"And I really don't know where Dr. Monroe is."

Tapping some blonde, no doubt. "That's okay, Tillie."

Her smile falters, and I see pity in her eyes. Great. The staff feel sorry for me.

"Are you going to be the homecoming queen?" she asks.

"No, some dumb senior cheerleader is." Some really nice, sweet, beloved cheerleader who isn't quite in the above-popular crowd I'm in.

"Well, if you don't mind me saying so . . ." Tillie takes a few steps farther, her linebacker shoulders squared, her face reminding me of someone, but I can't place it. "If you'd been as nice as you've been lately, you probably would have been voted queen."

"I don't need to be queen," I say quickly, embarrassed. "It's for stupid losers." I turn when I hear a car door slam. "I'm going to meet Ryder in the driveway. See ya."

"Wait!" she says. "Let me take your picture."

I start to say no, but then realize how much I want her to. "Use my phone." I set it to camera and hand it to her. "Geraldine," I mumble as the name pops into my head.

Tillie frowns at me. "What?"

"You remind me of someone I know named Geraldine. A bus driver."

She inches her face around the phone to scowl at me. "As if you've ever been on a bus in your life."

Before I answer, she snaps the picture, hands me the camera, and stuns me with the closest thing to a hug I think she's ever given anyone. "Have a nice time."

I swallow an unexpected lump in my throat and nod. Tonight she's the closest thing I have to a mother in this house. "Thanks. I'm staying at . . . Jade's. So don't wait up."

Tillie angles her head, and I know she knows I lied. Before she can call me on it, I hustle outside to greet Ryder and skip any more chances for the maid to step into the mother role.

I don't need to bother hurrying. The driver's coming to the door for me. Ryder's waiting for me in the limo, and I consider getting mad at him for being rude, but he slams me with a kiss the minute I climb in, taking my breath and arguments away. He looks amazing in a tux, and tastes a little like vodka or gin or . . . I don't know, but it's bitter on his lips.

He mixes me a drink, and I sneak another at Jade's house, where her parents are a lot more into the event than mine were. They take a zillion pictures while a caterer gives us fancy hors d'oeuvres and the adults act like they don't know that all of the kids have put rum in their Cokes. The food clears my head, and I stop drinking, because, honestly, I don't want to miss a minute of homecoming.

Ryder hasn't let one inch get between us, his attention almost too intense. But I let it go, because, hey, it's a big night.

The best night of my life. Well, of this life, anyway.

There are six of us in the limo. Then we pick up two

more kids, and by the time we get to the Fontainebleau in Miami Beach, most of them are pretty toasted.

The ballroom is huge, lit with a million tiny white lights, and rocking with a DJ who calls himself the Inferno. The whole place is pulsating with earsplitting music. Shoes come off, kids are grinding, and I dive in for my first and only homecoming dance.

Everywhere I turn, someone is calling my name, giving me a hug, taking a picture, laughing. A lot of laughing, since, whoa and damn, some of these kids are fried.

I don't need booze to be buzzed. I've never been to a party like this. In fact, I've never been to a dance where I didn't spend most of the night in the back, on the sidelines, in a chair against the wall. Nothing like *this*.

"Hey, babe." Ryder wraps an arm around me when a slow song starts, his face close to mine. My heart hits quadruple time. I'm still not used to kissing him, even though we've been lip-locked plenty over the past few days.

During the dance, he kisses me so long and deep, my knees buckle.

"Let's leave now," he says.

I inch back. "No way," I say. "I don't want to go yet."

He gives me a pathetic look and pulls me closer, like I might have missed the boner pressed against me.

"Cool down," I tell him. "I'm not missing a minute of homecoming."

"What? You were here last year. The barfing starts in the next half hour."

The barfing? On cue, a kid blows on the dance floor, clearing it in an instant. When I hit the bathroom, there

144

are two girls passed out on the floor. By eleven, the whole event has disintegrated into small groups of kids, some loaded, some straight, and no one seems to be having "fun" anymore.

Is this what happens at all homecoming dances?

Ryder seems fine to see the party ending. His hand has spent the last half hour on my butt, and I can't stop thinking about that card in my bag.

Tonight is the night.

I fight the beginning of a low-grade panic with each minute that passes. I've never even seen a porno. Why didn't I watch the one Lizzie had? At least I'd know what I was getting into.

The thought sends me a little off-kilter, but Ryder's arm is strong and steady, and he glances down at me. "Let me go see what the transportation situation is," he whispers.

He leaves me by the table, and Jade and Bliss show up almost instantly.

"Marc's passed out in the limo," Jade says, referring to her date.

"Chad's about to be," Bliss says about hers, an expression of misery on her face. "He's an asshole when he's drunk. Thinks it's so hilarious to make fun of how I pronunciate words. Jeez, at least I have a vocabulary."

I bite my lip not to laugh, but can't resist a quick look at Jade.

"Oh, screw both of you bitches!" Bliss hisses, a little bit of spit popping out as she sways on her heels.

God, why did they all get so blasted on a night this special?

"Laugh at me all you want," she continues. "But Jade and I have been invited to a private party at Bianca Bloodsworth's house."

I've heard the name and know Bianca's an A-list senior who hangs out with Trent, who is probably there, because he pronounced homecoming a complete waste of time.

At this point, I'm starting to agree with him. I look around for Ryder, half wishing he'd pass out in the limo, too. Nerves like little steel needles scrape inside my chest as we get closer and closer to . . . it.

"You all right?" Jade asks, sliding an arm around me. "You're not having second thoughts are you?"

I give her a smile for being such an aware friend. "I'm okay," I lie.

"She's nervous," Bliss says, just as *aware* but not nearly as sweet. "She's freaking with Ryder tonight. Cherry popping is serious business."

As always, Jade comes to my rescue. "You go to Bloodsucker's house," she says to Bliss. "I'm going to stay until Ayla leaves."

Bliss's jaw loosens. "You'd stay at this puke fest when we can get into a private senior party? I've heard there are, like, yards of coke lines on every table."

I roll my eyes, so over Bliss.

"You know, Ayla, I've had just about enough of you," Bliss says, eerily echoing my thoughts with a little wobble and an inky black fingernail in my face.

"Whatever, Bliss. Go snort your brains out if you want."

"That's not why I'm going." She lifts her brow, adds a

hand to her hip, and wets her lip. "Trent texted me and asked me to come."

"Trent, my brother?" I half laugh the words.

"What, you think that's funny? That he might not like me?"

"I'm pretty sure he likes Bianca, but, whatever, knock yourself out. I'm sure he'll be thrilled to see you." And call you the queen of Skankovia.

She leans forward, a glint in her eye. "Something is so up with you."

"You know what's up with her," Jade says. "Lay off her."

Bliss stares me down, a tiny flare in her nostrils that reminds me of a bull. "I don't know what's gotten into you in the past week, Ayla Monroe, but I for one don't like it."

"What are you talking about?"

"I don't know. I just don't know, but you're different. You think you're better than us, like you are above approach."

Her wordkill isn't even funny anymore. "You're drunk, Bliss," I tell her, stepping away when I see Ryder out in the hallway talking to some kids.

"Maybe I am," she says, determined to follow me. "But I know you better than anyone. I've known you since second grade. Something about you is . . . different."

"It's the whole thing with Ryder," Jade insists, sliding her arm through mine in a touching act of defense. "Cut her some slack."

Bliss takes a step back, eyeing us both, then silently places a plastic cup on the table and takes off for the group in the hall.

"Remind me again why we're friends with her," I say to Jade, only half kidding. Why would I hang with someone like that—since second grade?

But Jade just tilts her head. "You two used to be inseparable," she says.

"Two peas in a pond, as Bliss would say," I reply.

She laughs. "If I didn't crack you guys up by giving the entire ninth-grade class nicknames, I don't think I'd have ever squeezed into the inner circle."

"I feel like she hates me half the time."

"Oh, it's more than half, babycakes." She nods to the hallway, where Bliss is inches away from Ryder.

"I know she's got the hots for Ryder." A blind man could see that. "But he's mine."

"And Trent's your brother, and if he's drunk enough tonight, Bliss'll be humping him like a dog in heat. In fact, if she could skin you and wear your flesh, she would. That's how bad she wants to be you." Jade shakes her head, her exotic features drawn in concern. "Unless of course she could ruin you and take your place at Crap Academy."

I lean back and take a new look at Jade. She's sarcastic and sharp and kind of painfully in love with fashion, but I like her. The question is . . . do I trust her?

She goes on with her little speech, also just drunk enough to say more than she normally does. "That's why since you've been acting so different, she's been really uptight. She doesn't feel right unless you stoop to her level. Which, I hafta say, you haven't been doing this week."

Oh, God, I want to confide in someone, anyone. Should I tell her? Would she believe me?

Not for the first time, I wonder why Ayla chooses friends she can't trust. Because if Lizzie Kauffman were right here with me, I'd tell her *everything*.

Before I can say a word, Ryder breaks free from the group and strides toward me. "I got a DD to take us home," he says. "The limo smells like five kids puked in it."

"Five kids did," Jade says dryly. "See you tomorrow, A-list. I'll have the scissors and champagne."

Ryder turns me around slowly in a move so criminally sexy, it has to be illegal. "What's that all about?" he asks, his words not slurred but definitely loose.

"Nothing." I look up at him, this golden god of gorgeousness who is about to rock my world. "You ready?"

"Yeah." He lifts one corner of his mouth and slides a single finger down my neck, dipping it in the top of my strapless dress, sliding it all the way into my cleavage. "Ready, willing, and way more than able."

I think I might die.

chapter fifteen

In the back of an Escalade driven by some kid named Justin, Ryder presses me against the door and barely comes up for air. Justin angles the rearview mirror away to give us privacy.

Ryder's a good kisser. I know I lack experience, but whatever he's doing, it feels pretty good. His mouth is open but not too wet. His hands are busy, but not all over me. His throat makes a sexy little catch that does something funny to my stomach.

Or maybe that was *my* throat, because we're too connected at the mouth for me to tell the difference. My head feels light, my arms heavy. I feel like I'm chugging up the rails of a roller coaster with no idea what's over the top, or maybe in a movie theater when the scene gets dark and creepy and you just know the girl's about to come face to face with an ax murderer.

My whole body is fired with anticipation and that sense of not being able to stop the inevitable, even though it's going to scare the holy crap out of me. But I kind of want to be scared. I *want* the inevitable.

Don't I?

"Hey, lovebirds," Justin says. "We have arrived at your destination." He fakes a GPS voice, and I laugh nervously as Ryder and I break apart.

"Thanks, dude," Ryder says, climbing out and pulling me down the high step.

The Escalade heads off into what looks like a tunnel of trees with branches that meet in the middle. For some reason, I stare at the brake lights until they're gone, rooted to the spot.

"You know, Ryder, I didn't bring any clothes."

He just laughs. "You aren't going to need them. Let's go, babe," he says, the endearment both grating and, well, endearing. "Time's up."

Is it? My time as a virgin? My time to hold him off? I follow him, barefoot, my shoes in one hand, my clutch in the other, to the side door of a very dark house. He moves by instinct, no doubt a pro at getting into his own house under cover of darkness.

"You know I gave up fishing in the Keys for this," he says, a little something in his tone that slows my step. Like he's warning me: You better be worth it.

Inside a dark laundry room, the air-conditioning instantly chills me. He takes my shiver as a cue for another kiss, adding a lot of tongue as he pushes me against a washer and his right hand crawls up my side, the palm pressing against my boob.

Palm. Against. Boob.

Wait till I tell Lizzie.

"Oh, shit!" he exclaims, jerking away. "The alarm."

He disappears around the corner, and I hear the digital beeps of him disarming the alarm. "Got it," he says. "With five seconds to spare."

"That would have been ugly," I reply, imagining a shrill alarm.

"Just what we need, the Gables cops showing up." He returns, holding out his hand. "Let's go to my room."

My stomach flips. "'Kay." But I don't move.

"Ayla." He tugs my arm.

"I'm sorry. I just . . ." Am having a bout of terror and second thoughts. Only, for me, they're *first* thoughts.

I've barely had a make-out session with him, just had my first hand-to-boob contact ever, and now I'm going to have full-blast sex? Yeah, I'm scared spitless.

"You want a drink?" he asks with a tinge of impatience.

"No, I don't need to be . . ." *Drunk.* But maybe that would cure my temporary paralysis. "No."

"Then, come on." He pulls me toward him, deeper into the house. "My balls are blue."

"Lovely," I say, curling my lip at the image.

He laughs a little, hustling me through a rambling dimly lit house, not nearly as nice as mine, but still reeking of comfort and cash. My bare feet tap on tile, a hollow sound that matches my heartbeat.

When we reach his room, he practically pushes me in.

I haven't even adjusted to the lack of light when he starts to kiss me, much harder now, tongue and hands and body everywhere this time.

I push away. "Wait a sec, Ryder. How about a little romance?"

"Jesus, Ayla. We've been talking about this since freaking September."

And it's what, November?

He backs me farther into the room, my knees hit a bed, and we tumble down onto rumpled sheets that smell vaguely of sleep. He's on me in an instant. Weight. Boy weight. It's so different from anything else I've ever felt.

"Just . . . go slow," I say.

He obliges me with a slightly less furious kiss, sliding his leg over my hip, getting me fully under him. I don't even want to think what this is doing to a two-thousand-dollar dress.

The true ludicrousness of that thought, along with world-class nerves, makes me laugh, and Ryder lifts his head.

"What's funny?"

"Nothing," I assure him. "I'm just nervous."

"Don't be," he says, tenderness in his voice for the first time. "It's nothing to be nervous about. It's fun. Believe me. Relax."

So Ryder hasn't saved his virginity for me. For some reason, that hurts a little. He kisses me again, tenderness gone, and suddenly both his hands are on my boobs, and I swear I can hear some beads popping off the dress as his hips rock against mine. The bulge on my stomach is . . . daunting.

I try kissing back, really getting into it, waiting for the

first tingle, the first burst of heat, the first little ache that makes me want to close my eyes and sigh and shudder and all that.

All I feel is . . . smothered.

"I can't breathe," I tell him, trying to push him off me.

I think I've read too many of Mom's books. Because none of that good stuff is happening. Right now it's just noisy breathing and heat, none of it too terribly exciting, especially because it feels like Ryder has twenty hands and definitely three legs, and he's panting in my ear.

He looks at me like I'm crazy, bunching the dress and pulling it up to my crotch, his hands greedy on my thighs, his fingers close to . . . me.

"Wait a minute." I fist my hand on his chest.

He groans. "Holy *shit*, Ayla. I'm dying."

The blood is pounding in my head, and my hands are sweaty and my legs are shaking for all the wrong reasons. "I'm . . ." In so far over my head, I really can't think straight. "I'm not sure . . . what to do."

He grabs my wrist and drags my hand between his legs. "Do this. Like you always do."

Panic pops inside me. Flat-out horror. I don't want to touch that. I don't want to do any of this. I yank my hand free and push his chest, my heart punching my ribs like a machine gun.

"Ryder, I don't know what I'm doing here," I say, the words tumbling out.

He balances over me on one straightened arm, looking down, looking scary, his face far less attractive than the first time, when I saw him and nearly melted at his hotness. "What the hell is that supposed to mean?"

"It means . . . exactly what I said." I wish I could explain this to him. "I really don't know what I'm doing here."

Here, in this world. And here on this bed.

"You're my girlfriend. That's what you're doing here. *Focus*."

I cringe at the demand, but my mind is sliding all over the place. Should I try the truth? I mean, if I can't speak the truth to my *boyfriend*, who expects me to give him my *virginity*, then who can I tell?

"I really don't know why I'm here," I say again. Pathetic.

"Damn," he mutters, sliding off my hips. "I told you I loved you. I got condoms. What the hell else do you want?"

"You told me you loved me." I say it as a statement, but really I don't believe him. No boy has ever said that to me, and for a second, I'm sorry this whole time/world/heaven/ dreamy thing has stolen that moment from me. Because knowing it might help me out here. "Can you say it again?"

"I love you." He says it so fast, it sounds like one word.

Still, I wait for the words to mean something.

They don't. Not any more than my first hand-to-boob action.

"Ayla, what the shit is going on with you?" he asks, searching my face as if he's seeing me for the first time. "You were totally, like, ready to go for it a week ago. You told me you couldn't wait to not be a virgin anymore. What was all that about it being a meaningless thing you carry around that you don't want?"

155

Virginity would be meaningless to Ayla Monroe. But it isn't to Annie Nutter, currently residing in Ayla's body.

How can I explain this to Ryder?

"Listen to me." I scoot up, decisions and words forming in my head. I have to tell someone or I'll die. Why not someone who professes to love me? Ryder's maybe not my first choice of confidant (which should tell me a lot about having sex with him), but he's right here. And he deserves an explanation.

As far out as this one is.

"Haven't you . . . noticed that I'm . . . different this week?"

"Oh, man. Are you on the rag?" He jerks his hand off my thigh like he's been burned. "I mean, that's cool, but—"

"No," I clutch his arm. "It's much deeper. It's much more confusing. See, about a week ago, I was a different girl."

He drops back onto the pillow with a disgusted sigh. "Jesus Christ, Ayla. Why don't you just tell me you want to break up?"

"I don't want to break up. I just want to . . . tell you what's changed."

"I don't care what's changed." He rolls over onto me, a sudden move that surprises me. "I want to get laid. You want to get laid." He sticks his hand right down my top, flat against my bare boob, like he's going to rip the whole dress off me. "Quit thinking so much and let me fu—"

"Hey!" I shove him off, set off by a fuse deep inside. Not the fuse I thought would explode when a boy touched my bare chest for the first time. A fury fuse. "Don't."

"Come on," he says, his voice shaking a little as he

switches tactics to open his pants, tearing the fly down. "Start with me, then. You like that."

"No," I say, alarm working up my spine into the base of my skull. "I don't."

"You told me you did last week, Ayla. What was that about in your pool?"

I have no idea. "I don't remember," I say honestly.

"Well, I do. You promised we'd do it on homecoming night." He's actually starting to whine. "You *promised*."

"*I* didn't promise."

"Like hell you didn't."

I take a shuddering breath and fight to stay calm, trying not to think of the position I'm in. Nearly naked, alone with a very pissed off and horny kid. I have to try . . . the truth.

"Ryder, I didn't promise. *Ayla Monroe* promised. And I know I look like her and live like her, but . . ." I manage to push him back far enough to look right into his eyes. "I'm someone else now."

"What the *goddamn hell* does that mean?"

"It means . . . that my soul has changed."

He's speechless. Jaw dropped, eyes wide, body frozen. "What?"

"Deep down, I'm different. Something happened. I woke up a few days ago and I was here, but this isn't where I belong. It's where Ayla Monroe belongs, and I know you think you know her, but I'm not her."

He's still staring, and my words are running together like melted ice cream on hot pavement.

"It's like I'm in a different universe or something," I finish weakly. "Like a dream, only it doesn't end."

Not a word, just a long, unbroken gaze of . . . nothing. I wait for an eternity before he finally speaks.

"You gonna do it or not?"

I blink at him. That's all he has to say? "Not," I whisper.

"Cock tease." He practically spits the words as he pushes off the bed.

"Ryder, I'm trying to tell you something very serious and very real and very scary to me."

"Yeah, well I'm trying to tell you something very serious too." He adjusts his pants, letting them hang open, boxers exposed. "I can have any girl in Croppe Academy. Shit, any girl in freaking Miami."

"I'm sure you can," I say softly.

He looks at me for a long time, then walks into the hall. "So get the hell out of here."

"Will you take me home?"

"No."

"Where are you going?"

I hear him snort. "To jack off."

I stay perfectly still, pressed into a lump of sheets, cold and sad and more alone than ever.

chapter sixteen

I try Jade. I try Bliss. I even try Trent. All I get is voice mail as I stand on a shadowy street near the University of Miami at one in the morning, my wrecked Vera Wang dress riding up my thighs as I walk toward lights and traffic. *Maybe I can call a cab*, I think, when a noisy car rumbles toward me, slowing down as I blink into a high, narrow-set beam of headlights.

Instinctively I back into the shadows, until I hear the driver say, "Ayla?"

I squint into the zipped-down plastic windows of an old Jeep and see the outline of a hat. "Charlie?"

"What are you doing here?"

Charlie. The homeless boy who I'm not supposed to talk to. "Can I have a ride?" It never occurs to me not to ask.

"Yeah, hop in."

I round the back of the Jeep, and the knot in my chest that was making it so hard to breathe loosens a bit. He reaches over to push open the door, an inviting move that touches me. "You okay?" he asks, his voice so kind I almost fold in half.

I didn't realize just how bad off Ryder left me. "Yeah." Although, I'm shaking.

"Need to sober up?"

I shake my head. "No, I haven't been drinking. I've been . . . I need to go home."

He gives me a funny look, and I know what's coming—some smart-ass comment about why don't I call my personal limo driver. Which I would totally deserve for the whole hat-drenching incident.

But he says, "You live on Star Island, right?"

I nod and pull on my seat belt.

"Think they'll let a ten-year-old dented Jeep Wrangler into that place?"

"If I tell them to."

He takes off his hat quickly, as though he just remembered he had it on, and tosses it into the backseat.

"Glad it survived the bath," I say.

"Me too."

There's a long silence as he pulls onto South Dixie and heads toward downtown and the causeway. After a minute, I rest my head and then close my eyes.

"I thought the dance was at the Fontainebleau," he says.

"It was. What are you doing out here?"

"Hanging out with some buddies in the physics lab at UM."

160

The physics lab? "Sounds like good times," I say with a little laugh in my voice.

"It was that or the party with the band nerds who don't go to homecoming. You have *no* idea what fun is until you've been to one of them."

"Actually, I do," I say softly. The second-rate, not-so-cool, average nobodies can have a pretty darn good time wondering what it's like at the cool kids' party.

"So, your boyfriend lives around here, doesn't he?"

"Ex-boyfriend."

That earns me a surprised look. "And he sent you out without a ride?" Charlie shakes his head in disdain as he changes lanes competently with one hand.

"How is it that you have an after-midnight license?"

"I'm seventeen."

"You are?" That doesn't make sense at all. "Why aren't you a senior?"

"I stayed out of school for a while," he says vaguely.

Maybe homeless kids can't go to school and advance grades. I drop the subject and study the scenery in silence.

"You wanna talk about what happened tonight?" he asks after a few minutes.

More than anything. "Not really."

The uplighted palm trees and storefronts of the Gables remind me that I'm a million miles and another lifetime from the tele-poles and autumn leaves of Pittsburgh. And if Ryder didn't get that, this guy certainly won't. So, no talking for me.

"You want to talk about anything?"

I let out a slightly overdramatic sigh. "I want to go home."

"You sound like Dorothy in Oz."

161

I manage a smile, an unfamiliar weight settling on my chest. "Yeah, sometimes I know precisely how she felt."

He stops at a light and looks at me. I turn to face him, taking in the angles and shadows bathed in reddish light. He really is a good-looking guy, even more so since he's being so dang sweet when I'm feeling all tender and bruised.

"Shame about the breakup," he says. "You two looked so . . . *right* for each other."

There might be a little sarcasm in that statement, but I ignore it. "Looks are deceiving."

He's still studying me, his skin turning greenish as the light changes. He doesn't look away. Behind us, a car honks. He still doesn't look away.

Neither do I.

"Green means go, Zelinsky," I finally say.

"So it does." Finally, he hits the accelerator, then shifts his attention to the road.

The car feels as cheap as a toy, but he cruises through the late-night traffic effortlessly, and soon we're on the causeway toward the beach. Outside, a few massive, majestic cruise ships are docked, bathed in white lights, enough to cast a glow inside the car and light up a stack of books in the well between the two front seats. Textbooks.

I pick up the top one, a monstrous doorstop that weighs about ten pounds. "*Introduction to Elementary Particles?*" I can't help but laugh. "Riveting."

He smiles. "Actually, it is. It's for my quantum mechanics class at Miami Dade."

I can't even spell *quantum mechanics*, let alone consider

taking a community college class on the subject. "So, you're like a real rocket scientist?"

"Not exactly."

"But you want to be?"

"I'm thinking about medicine."

It feels like he's creating a wall with vague answers again. Or maybe he just doesn't know what he wants to be—or is embarrassed that a homeless kid is thinking about being a doctor. Whatever, I'm kind of intrigued.

"What is quantum mechanics, anyway?" I open the book to a sea of incomprehensible words and diagrams. "Besides boring?"

"Part of quantum physics. Deals with atoms and stuff. You know, string theory, particle colliders, and cosmic catastrophes. You know what they are?"

"Cosmic catastrophes?" I give a dry laugh. "I'm living one."

He rolls his eyes. "Yeah, the beautiful rich girl breaking up with the hotshot jock. That would be a real catastrophe for the entire cosmos."

A jolt of resentment makes me slam the book closed. "You have no idea what you're talking about."

"Oh, I know. I can't possibly imagine what it's like to be you. Just like you can't imagine what it's like to be me."

"You're wrong about that, too." I return the textbook to the pile, right on top of another called *Light and Matter: Newtonian Physics*. "I know more about your life than you can imagine."

"I sincerely doubt that."

I open my mouth, then shut it. He's right; I don't know about . . . living in a box. And why am I dropping all these hints? He's the last person I want to confide in, despite how desperate I am to do so.

Fortunately, we've arrived at Star Island before I go any further. The guard steps out of the gatehouse when the Jeep approaches, an older man, frowning, hands on hips, no doubt ready to shoo the rattling bucket of bolts away.

"The help probably isn't allowed in this late," Charlie says to me.

"I hate to break it to you, but the help have better cars."

He grins at that, showing a decent sense of humor that I find surprisingly attractive. I shove that thought into the mental trash where it belongs and lean over to show my face to the security guard, whose expression brightens when he recognizes me.

"Good evening, Miss Monroe." He presses a button to allow the gate to open.

"Hi . . ." I spot his name tag and smile. "Bruce. Thank you. Have a nice night."

As Charlie drives through to the exclusive island, he's shaking his head like he's confused.

"It's easy to find the house," I say. "There's only one road around the island, and you're on it."

"That's not what I'm wondering about."

"Then what is it?"

"I'm just trying to figure out . . . What happened to you?"

I don't answer, but I have a pretty good idea where this is going.

"Did you find out you have a month to live? Make a bet with someone? Deal with the devil?"

"What are you talking about?" *Just play dumb, Annie. Don't let this cute, sweet boy steal any secrets from you.*

"Why are you being so nice to everyone?"

"Because I am nice."

"Mmmm." He's not buying it. "Which house?"

"Keep going, around the bend, toward the back."

He glances at the grounds and gates, which, for the most part, are all you can see of the mansions hidden along the edge of the island. "Everyone's talking about it, you know."

Oh, great. "Everyone?"

"Even the invisible people," he says, no bitterness in his tone. "Especially the invisibles."

The invisibles know that's what we call them? Of course they do. The nobodies know they're nobody at South Hills High. More universal laws of high school.

"You know what's sad?" I ask, trying not to sound scared, because deep inside, I know I'm messing with those laws. "What's sad is that people don't have better things to think about than my personality."

"Evidently not, but it's not just your personality," he says, slowing as he rounds the curve in the road.

"This gate," I tell him as we approach the wrought iron fence that surrounds our property. "What else has the invisibles gossiping about me at the band parties?" I try to sound condescending and disdainful, like I know Ayla would, but it comes out kind of pathetic. Like I *care* what they're saying.

Because I do.

He looks at me again, scrutinizing my face one more time. "You really are different." I don't know if he means different from what I was or different from what he expected or just different from all females. I don't want to ask.

"Maybe I'm getting more mature," I say. "You'll need a code at that box."

"You want to trust me with it?"

It's trust him or reach over him, smashing my whole body between the steering wheel and his chest to punch in the pass code. And while that idea doesn't strike me as being as horrific as it should, I've been pressed against enough boys for one night.

"It's ten-thirty-two," I tell him.

He opens the gate and heads up the winding stone drive until his headlights illuminate the house.

"Nice crib."

"Yeah." I reach for my door handle but can't find it, my fingers stabbing at torn leather and a rickety metal bar that might have once been a latch.

"Here, I'll get it." He reaches across me, his arm accidentally brushing my chest. I flatten myself against the seat to give him room. In the soft light I see color rise to his cheeks. "Sorry," he mumbles.

The door pops open, and I give him a smile. "Thanks for the ride, Charlie."

He nods, still a little embarrassed by the close encounter, I can tell. So different from Ryder. I try to ease the moment by putting my hand on his arm. "You go home now and read all about that quantum . . . stuff so you can be a doctor or rocket scientist or something amazing."

"I plan on it," he assures me, relaxing a little. "And don't you make any more deals with the devil."

For a flash of a crazy second, I wonder if that's what I've done. Is that how I got here, with my every wish come true?

"What's the matter?" he asks, reading the change in my expression.

Everything in me wants to tell him the truth. I can feel the words bubbling up, the ache inside me to share this situation with someone. Someone understanding. Someone who might actually believe me. Someone I trust.

And that wouldn't be this formerly homeless kid who probably hates everything about Ayla Monroe.

I gather up all my common sense and step out. Despite the fact that I know this guy could be the closest thing to someone like me—real Annie me—that I've met since I arrived, I'm not telling him anything.

"Nothing is the matter," I say. "Thanks again. You're a lifesaver."

A funny expression flickers over his face. "Not really."

When I slam the door, he waits for me to walk to the house. I glance over my shoulder to wave thanks, blinking into the distinctive round, high headlights of his beat-up old Jeep.

So, now I've been to a homecoming dance. And the best part was the ride home.

CHAPTER SEVENTEEN

Ryder changed his status to "single" on Facebook before I even got out of Charlie's Jeep, so I lie low to avoid the avalanche of calls and texts (like, twenty from Jade) until late Sunday afternoon, when she shows up in person, unable to take the suspense anymore.

"OMG! OMFG!" She throws herself into my bedroom. "Tell me every single word. Are you okay? Why haven't you answered my calls? Oh, my *God*, Ayla. I've been so worried about you."

"I'm fine," I insist.

"Fine? Look at you."

"What?" I haven't shed a tear.

"No makeup, your hair, and what did you do, borrow clothes from Loras?"

I glance down, not even sure which jeans and overpriced T-shirt I put on. Jade, of course, is wearing designer cropped pants and a rhinestoned tank top.

"What happened?" She drags me to the bed and forces me to sit. "I want to know everything. *Ev-er-y-thing*, Miss Ayla Monroe. No detail is too small."

I can't tell her everything. Can I? The temptation to confide in someone other than Ryder is burning, but I choose my words carefully. Jade will think I've lost my mind due to the breakup.

"There's not much to tell. I mean, about Ryder." I fall back on the bed. "I changed my mind about doing the deed, and he got royally pissed."

"That's not what he told Bliss."

My fury fuse gets lit again. "Why is he talking to Bliss about it?"

She pales. "He called her when you left, and she went over there."

"Jeez, at least wait until the body's cold."

"No, no," she says quickly. "Nothing happened. I know that, and she swears. He just wanted to talk about you. About how much you've . . . changed."

"Yeah, well, he could have talked to me about that." I can't keep the bitterness out of my voice. "I tried, but all he wanted to do was . . . it."

"Well, you did promise him sex, Ayla. I mean, it was *scheduled*."

That irks enough for me to give her a harsh look. "It's not a freaking cruise reservation," I shoot back. "I said I might, but that doesn't mean it's a binding contract, for God's sake. I just changed my mind. I changed . . . a lot of things. Which is what I tried to tell him. Did he tell Bliss a different story?"

"He just says you're whack." She fluffs some pillows and settles in for a chat. "What *is* going on with you?"

There. The door is wide open. All I have to do is walk right through it . . . *now*. I swallow and close my eyes. "I'm not whack, Jade. But I do have some . . . personal issues."

"Is it your parents' divorce?" There's a tenderness in her voice that's like a warm hand on my heart.

"No, not the divorce. I mean, I'm not thrilled about it, but I want my mom to be happy." I hadn't really thought about it, but as I say the words, I realize that's what's important to me.

But Jade looks stunned. "Your mom? Since when do you care about her?"

"Since, like, I was born?"

She coughs a laugh. "Okay, you *have* changed. Ayla, you hate your mom only slightly more than I hate mine." She pushes back a lock of thick black hair, her dark eyes pinning me. "Which is to say, a lot."

"I don't hate her."

"Ayla!" She practically falls over on the bed. "How many times have you been in this room ranting about her nonstop desperation to be good enough for your dad and how she never can be?"

I stare back in disbelief, then take a deep breath and say, "That wasn't me, Jade. That was some other girl who just looks like me."

She kind of smiles, obviously not sure if I'm making a joke.

"I'm serious. I'm not the same girl you knew a week ago. You see, I woke up . . . different."

"Different, how?"

"Inside. In my soul. I'm not Ayla Monroe. I'm . . ." *Annie Nutter, painfully average and unpopular band geek who lives in relative poverty with a hoarder dad.* "Different."

She clearly doesn't get that. "Like you come from a different place, and have a different perspective?"

"Yes!" I scoot toward her. "Exactly. Inside." I tap my chest. "I'm not the same girl. I don't even look the same. And my family is all different. I don't really know what happened, but . . . Listen, Jade, this is going to sound really bizarre, but I went to sleep as one girl and woke up as another. Something *changed* me."

"Oh, I totally know what you mean!" She leaps from the bed, her eyes wide. "Like, last year, remember when I tripped in front of Brock Easterhouse? I was so mortified, I was never the same. I changed, Ayla."

I can merely blink in disbelief. "Um, no. This is a little deeper than that."

"That was deep!" She's painfully sincere. "I, like, legitly fell on my freaking face right outside the cafeteria. No one comes out of something like that the same."

"Legitly? Now you sound like Bliss."

"I'm serious. Like, one second I'm walking, I catch his eye. Oh, my God. You remember what a mad crush I had on him? Well, there he is, totally checking me out, and I'm

walking . . ." She walks. "I look at him." She sends a flirta-
tious glance to thin air. "Then, *wham*." She trips herself,
arms flailing, then looks at me. "I was never the same after
that, Ayla."

She drops to her knees in front of the bed, practically
begging me to share. "I've never told anyone how the Brock
fall changed me. Now something happened to you. What is
it? You can tell me."

No, I can't. I can't tell anyone. "This is my burden to
bear," I say, sounding a little melodramatic, but feeling that
way.

She sighs in sympathy. "There's really only one thing to
do to ease your burden, my friend."

"Shop?" I can't even fake enthusiasm for that. "I'm so
over shopping."

"Nah. You need a new man." She pulls out her phone
and gives me a sly smile. "Remember that guy that Bliss and
I were talking to at Mynt the other night?"

"You were talking to twenty guys at Mynt."

"I know, right?" She gives a self-satisfied grin. "He's having a party on his yacht tonight, and we are so going. It's
going to be wild. I heard the guys are all, like, male models.
Everyone gets a line of coke the minute you board."

"Oh . . . fun."

"Come on." She's already off her knees and headed to the
closet. "Bliss is going with her Gulliver friends, and they'll
pick us up. Let's dress like the rock stars we are."

When she disappears into my closet, I just stay on the
bed, digging for enthusiasm.

I've never been on a yacht. I've never met a male model.

I sure as heck have never done a line of cocaine. So, where is my sense of adventure?

I pick up my phone, grasping for an excuse not to go. What's wrong with me that I don't want to go? My fingers flick over the pictures, landing on the close-up Tillie took of me last night when I was walking out the door.

My finger grazes the screen and accidentally pulls up my apps, and one of them jumps out at me.

Famous Faces. I have that app my dad used to create that image of me in his mirror invention thing?

My finger slides down the list of names, to some faces I've never even seen, with names that mean nothing to me. These might be famous faces, but not all are perfect. Some are kind of ordinary.

I start picking some features that feel "familiar" and sliding them over my image until I've created a face that looks a lot more like Annie than Ayla. And the dumbest thing happens. My eyes tear up and that homesickness thing starts again.

I don't miss my friends and family and home. . . . I miss *me*.

"Ohmigod, you're crying!" Jade's in front of me, armloads of clothes tumbling to the floor as she reaches out. "You're really upset about losing Ryder."

Not in the least, but I'll take the excuse. "You go tonight, Jade. I'm really not up for it."

She's totally understanding—but not about to give up the yacht party—and an hour later, she's off with Bliss and her friends, and I'm on my bed looking at my old pal Annie.

*　*　*

Later that night, the weirdest thing happens. I'm on Facebook and Lizzie Kauffman pops up in a chat box.

LizzieKauffman: i know we're friends, but do I know u?

I stare at the screen, inching back like she has actually walked right into my room. I can hear her voice in my head, see her freckles as she scrunches up her face, imagine her in that T-shirt with the monkey she got at Justice when we thought it was cool to shop there, and she refused to stop wearing it even when it was too small. I can picture her dark hair falling out of a sloppy ponytail, hear her easy, happy laugh.

I actually ache for her as I read her question over and over.

I know what she means, of course. She accepted my friendship but doesn't have a clue who I am. The words swim a little as my eyes tear.

"Yes, Zie," I whisper, using my secret nickname for her that I made up on some sleepover in another lifetime. "We're friends and you know me." Better than anyone.

I type slowly, but I know what I'm going to say. I've already imagined this conversation, but didn't want to initiate it.

AylaMonroe: We've never met, but I found your profile.

LizzieKauffman: why?

AylaMonroe: Might be moving to Pittsburgh and searched South Hills High kids.

174

I wonder if my capital letters and punctuation will give me away. Lizzie always teased me because I used them in texts and chats.

But then I remember. How can they "give me away" when I don't exist? At least, not as Annie, Lizzie's BFF. Her response takes a second, and I find myself on the edge of my desk chair, a physical ache to reach into the computer and pull her out.

There's no one on earth I trust more or need more at this very minute.

LizzieKauffman: cool. u live in miami, right?

That's on my profile, of course.

AylaMonroe: I do now.

"But I haven't always," I whisper to her name on the screen. "Zie, do you remember me?"

LizzieKauffman: and u r going to SHH if u move here?

AylaMonroe: Maybe. Is it a good school?

LizzieKauffman: u will probably like it

A long minute passes with no text, and my chest clutches a little. I don't want her to go away. But I don't know what to say. It's not like I can come right out and say, Hey, I know you. We were friends in . . . another . . . life.

But I have to say something.

AylaMonroe: You're in orchestra, right?

Seriously lame, but it's all I've got.

LizzieKauffman: yeah violin

AylaMonroe: I'll want to join the orchestra at SHH.

Where did that come from?

LizzieKauffman: really???

Of course, she doesn't believe it, either. She's read my profile, looked at my pictures—at concerts, on yachts, at the beach—so she knows what I look like, what kind of friends I have.

AylaMonroe: Thinking about it. Who do you hang out with?

LizzieKauffman: other band kids mostly—how about you?

Popular girls who shoplift, smoke pot, and are mean to people like you.

AylaMonroe: Just . . . the usual crowd. Who's your best friend?

Like, who replaced me?

LizzieKauffman: got a couple

She doesn't want to name names, in case I'm some kind of stalker. I could check her friends list. Again.

LizzieKauffman: so let me know if u r moving here, k? gotta go

No!

AylaMonroe: Ok—can I ask you another?

LizzieKauffman: sure

I have to type fast. I don't want to lose her. But I don't know what I want to ask. *Do you miss me? Do you remember me? Is there a big fat hole in your life where you used to have a really fun best friend who you laughed with all the time and knew since kindergarten and shared a band stand with and kept a joint journal with since seventh grade full of nothing but our private inside jokes?*

AylaMonroe: Can we talk again sometime?

LizzieKauffman: sure! shoot me a message gtg

And she's logged off.

I hear footsteps outside and jump up, anxious for company. I push open the door to see my mom in baby blue pajamas, her hair pulled back, her face, I think for the first time since I've been here, completely washed free of makeup.

She looks so much like Old Mom, as I've come to think of her, that my heart aches. "Can you come in?" I ask, a little hesitant.

"Is something wrong?"

God, does something have to be wrong to talk to my mother? "I just . . . I'm lonely," I admit.

Her eyes flicker, then shift to behind me. "Are you on Facebook?"

"Yeah." Talking to a girl you once loved like your own daughter. "But I can talk to you." I step aside and gesture for her to come in, and actually breathe a soft sigh of relief when she does.

She sits on the edge of the bed, giving me a chance to see how expensive and beautifully made those pajamas are. Mom's favorite pj's were Target sleep pants with hearts on them and an AT&T sweatshirt Dad got for selling the most phones in one month at RadioShack.

For a second, I wonder what Old Mom would think of these silky things that probably cost as much as Dad's commission that month.

"How was homecoming?" she asks, leaning closer so that

I get a soft whiff of a sweet and spicy perfume that doesn't fit this pulled-tight woman. Old Mom would wear something like that, though.

Homecoming? Craptastic. "Fine."

She searches my face. "What's going on with you?"

"It's kind of hard to explain." I feel something slip in my chest, and realize what's happening. I'm homesick. I'm *momsick*. I want that lady who smelled like this and came into my room to talk with me on the bed. I want . . .

I want to go home.

"Oh, my God. Are you crying, Ayla?"

Am I?

She lifts a hand to my face, then pulls back before she touches me. "What's wrong?" she asks.

The fact that she cares so much kind of puts me over the edge, but I manage not to drop a tear. "Really, you don't want to know."

"Yes, Ayla, I do."

Does she? How would she even deal with this story? But I avoid her gaze, so direct and familiar, and instead pluck on a thread on my comforter.

"I'm just not myself," I finally say, my voice cracking like a twelve-year-old boy's.

"Oh, Ayla." She collapses a little and reaches for my face again, the gesture full of yearning, but still tentative. She doesn't make contact, at least not with her fingers. But our eyes connect. "You never cry."

"I do lately," I say softly.

She inches back. "And you never show any kind of vulnerability. I guess that's what everyone is talking about."

More of everyone talking? Why don't they all talk to me instead of to each other? "Who's everyone?" I ask.

"Trent and Tillie."

"Trent says I'm vulnerable?" I find this hard to believe.

"He says you're acting weird, and I heard Loras telling Tillie that you said thank you."

"That doesn't make me vulnerable, Mom. That makes me human."

"But it's so strange, so out of character for you."

"Well, it shouldn't make headlines in the staff newsletter that I said the two most common words in the English language. Loras practically breaks her back picking up my shoes."

Mom glances around and shrugs. "Not anymore."

"I can't see the point of making a room this pretty all messy," I say. "It's like . . . out of a *magazine* or something." I eye her for a reaction, but there is none.

Instead, she just shakes her head, a smile tugging. "No wonder Tillie thinks you've lost your mind and Trent says you were abducted by aliens. Who's this girl and what did they do with Ayla?"

She laughs at her joke, but emotion erupts like a volcano in me. I have to tell her, I have to. She's my mom. Won't she understand?

How do I start? Will she believe me? How can I prove I'm not crazy? I have to know something that only Annie would know. Something that would connect me to her past.

The answer is kind of obvious. I go for it. "Does the name Melvin Nutter mean anything to you?" I say.

179

For a moment, all I get is a blank stare, a hint of disbelief. Then all the color drains from her face. "What?"

"You do know him?"

Her body stiffens as she leans back. "Where are you going with this?" The softness in her tone has hardened to ice.

Is the memory of Dad—of Mel Nutter—too much for her to take? For some reason, that gives me weird hope and happiness. I scoot up on my haunches a little, ready to finally open up.

"It's complicated, but I need you to tell me the truth. Do you know a man named Mel Nutter?"

She stares at me, her whole body suddenly quivering, waves of something dark rolling off her. I decide to take that as a yes. I still have to prove I know something from her past with him.

"And do the numbers one-four-three make any sense to—"

"God damn you, Ayla!" She launches off the bed, her fists clenched as if she's trying to fight the urge to strike me. "What the hell were you doing? Going on my computer? Reading my private stuff? You *are* your father's clone—a conniving little spy who'll do anything for money. For his empty promises. That's all he can make. Don't you know that yet?"

"No, no, Mom. You don't get it. I—"

"Oh, I get it. Is that why you've been so nice? Is that part of your strategy to butter me up and get me talking about old boyfriends so your father can claim, I don't know, that *I'm* having an affair, not him?"

"Mom, I—"

She pushes the air with two hands, symbolically shoving me away. "Stop! Just stop it, Ayla. I don't know what you found. Well, I *do* know, but trust me, it was nothing. Nothing at all. I looked up an ex-boyfriend on Google, and we exchanged an email. I barely told him anything about me. And he lives in—"

"Pittsburgh."

She looks horrified. "You did read my email! Why? Did your father put you up to it?"

"Mel Nutter *is* my father." It's out before I can stop myself.

She opens her mouth to speak, but the only sound that comes out is a strangled, choking cry. "Is that what he's going to do?"

"Who? Mel?"

"He's going to do some . . . some *paternity* thing? Try to get out of paying child support by claiming you are some other man's child? Because considering the history and why we got married, well, that is just . . . ironic." She has lost it now, with full on shaking and quaking. "Oh!" She balls her fists and punches the air in frustration. "I hate that man. I hate him. And I hate yo—"

"No!" I shout. "Don't say it! Don't say that to me!" The tears are pouring now, and I don't even bother to fight them. "Please don't." My voice breaks. All I want to do is reach out and hug my mother, because I *need* her to understand. But how can she? *I* don't understand.

She's already backing out of my room. "Stop, Ayla. Or I will say something I regret. You've made your choice. You and your father—together forever. You know, you two deserve each other. I'm through with you."

"No, Mom, please. You really, really don't understand what I'm trying to tell you. I'm different because I'm not who you think I am!"

"No." She freezes at the door, turning slowly. "You're not who I've *wanted* you to be. Big difference."

The words hit as hard as if she'd slapped me. All I can do is stare, the golf ball strangling my throat ready to crack into a sob, but I fight it.

"When I had a girl, I thought we'd be friends," she says. "I thought we'd shop together and laugh. I thought we'd have some kind of, oh, I don't know, connection." She sniffs the last word, embarrassed and broken.

"We do," I whisper. "We *did*. We shopped at Walmart and ate at Eat'n Park." I'm choking on the words, knowing I sound crazy, but if I could just get her to see . . . "On your birthday we got manicures together, and one time in the snow you accidentally got lost and drove down four steps in that South Side graveyard, and I swore I'd never tell Daddy, and I didn't."

"What in God's name are you talking about? How have you heard of Eat'n Park? You've never even been to Pittsburgh."

"Yes, I have."

"Not since you were two! Your father hates to go there."

"No . . . Mom." I can't stop crying or talking, and she's just shaking her head. "Don't you remember, Mom?" Oh, God, this hurts so much. I want her to remember. I want her to remember me—Annie Nutter—the girl she wanted. I want somebody to remember me—not this Ayla Monroe I don't even know or like.

"No, I don't." Her voice is as cold as the car that day we drove down the graveyard stairs.

How can this be? I remember sitting in the car, waiting for AAA, laughing at what a bad driver Mom is. We pinkie-swore never to tell Dad.

How can she not remember?

Because it never happened. Not in this life, not in this bizarre, weird, inexplicable vacuum of a real world where I now live.

"It was . . . another life," I say softly. And this is a waste of time. No one on earth will ever believe me or understand. "So just forget it."

I'm alone in this. Completely, utterly alone.

Mom's face is a reflection of how gutted I feel inside, but she fights for composure, wiping her cheek, squaring her shoulders under the silk of her pretty pajamas. "You have a few choices, Ayla."

"What are they?" I ask.

"Rehab for whatever drug problem is giving you these hallucinations about graveyards."

I exhale softly. "I've never done drugs in my life."

I can tell by the raised eyebrow that Ayla has, and Mom knows it. "Or you can set up an appointment with a psychiatrist to discuss your mental health, or . . ."

"Maybe I'll just head back to whatever planet I came from." Not that the option is even a possibility.

She doesn't smile, not even close. "Whatever you do, Ayla Anne Monroe, you stay the hell out of my personal life and tell your father to talk to my lawyer. I'm leaving."

She closes the door, and I just collapse to the floor in a heap. I know I have to figure out exactly how I'm going to live in this life, but all I do is cry for everything I've lost.

CHAPTER EIGHTEEN

Bliss is leaning against the brick wall outside the cafeteria the next morning when I arrive at school. She's on the phone, and gives me no more than a cursory finger wave, turning to block me out of her conversation.

My first thought is that she's talking to Ryder, but I can tell she isn't using her phony boy voice, so this must be a girl.

A few kids walk by and look at us—at me—which is nothing new anymore, but a slow burn of embarrassment rolls over my skin as Bliss makes a point of blatantly ignoring me.

"I know, right?" she hoots. "And someone call the ripped-jeans police and send them after Alexis Carillo. So last year."

She pauses, and I give her a nudge. "Hey."

She turns away, snorting into the phone. "OMFG with the Uggs already. It's Miami, people."

"Where's Jade?" I mouth to her.

She shrugs and shoulders the phone, letting her hair fall over her face as a barrier to me. "Hey, listen, sweetie, I gotta go," she says in a whisper, finally looking at me through her strands. "I've got some eavesdroppage, if you know what I mean."

I almost choke. "Who knows what you mean, Bliss?" I hiss at her. "You barely speak English."

She taps off and makes a show of putting her phone away, then finally looks at me. "Well, somebody had a rough night."

So all that MAC and Bobbi Brown makeup doesn't cover the puffy purple circles of my sleepless night. "You look nice today too," I say, undaunted. I may have had an endless night, but I came to some serious conclusions and worked out a plan for going forward. "Is that skirt DKNY? It's completely adorable."

She gives me a dubious look, a little longer than is comfortable, then pulls out her phone even though I didn't hear it vibrate.

I dig deep for the strength I thought I'd found in the middle of my long night of thinking. The only way to handle this whacked-out world is to live in it as best I can. I can't change a lot of things, like my parents' pathetic marriage. I can't make my two best friends stop doing dumb stuff. But I can change who Ayla Monroe is on the inside, all the while enjoying the fruits of who and what she is on the outside.

I am determined to have the best of both worlds.

"Where's Jade?" I ask, since she declined a ride this morning.

After a moment's hesitation, Bliss says, "She's cutting today."

"Why?"

"The history test," she says like it's the most obvious thing in the world.

"Oh, crap! I forgot to study."

She laughs. "Funny, Ayla. This'll be a cinch now, since your buddy Flute Fly is in our class. She salivates whenever you breathe on her, so tell her you need her to keep her answers easy to see, then you give me the finger signs, since Guerra only gives multiple choice tests." She taps out a text, smiling. "OMG. My friend who goes to Gulliver got back-stage passes to the Bruno Mars concert. Win!" She starts to walk away, texting.

I don't have much choice; I follow, and eventually we separate for first period. But the whole time, I'm feeling a weird vibe in school, and am aware of enough whispering to know I'm the center of gossip.

I don't care, and head to English lit holding tight to my plan to be Annie in Ayla's body.

It made so much sense in the middle of the night, but the strategy feels tougher in school. For one thing, every time I say or do something that feels "right," I get a look like I'm being some kind of phony or disappointing these kids somehow.

Ayla has a rep, and changing it isn't going to be easy.

But I have to, I tell myself as I slide a glance to Charlie when I pass him. He's given up the hat—thank God—and looks up through thick lashes and dark locks to give me a slight smile.

My heart kind of tumbles around, and I bump right into the empty desk next to him.

A low murmur goes around the room, and my gaze follows everyone else's to Ryder, who's slouched lazily in his seat.

He coughs loudly, "PT." Then coughs again.

Prick teaser. I ignore the comment and take a seat, and Mr. Brighton launches right into a lecture about the use of light and dark imagery. My thoughts are spinning, my heart is racing, and, frankly, I'm kind of sick of being the center of attention. Especially now, because I know what that kind of scrutiny is going to do to my plans to convince everyone this *new* me is the *real* me, and then I can *be* me.

There's no unassailable law of the universe that says Ayla Monroe has to be a bitch who steals and gets high and has sex with boys she doesn't even like that much, I tell myself while Mr. Brighton drones on.

When a guidance counselor comes to the door, Mr. Brighton steps out with orders for us to read a passage and be prepared to find an example of dark imagery with a message. Hell breaks loose almost immediately.

Phones come out, voices rise, and Ryder's up in seconds, slowly walking the aisle, making a show of balling some paper. His hip brushes my shoulder as he passes. I keep my head down on the page, refusing to take the bait.

He tosses the paper ball into a wastebasket across the room.

"He shoots and he scores," someone in the back says.

Ryder pivots and comes back toward me, stopping at my desk. "He doesn't always score," he says, just loud enough to be heard over the room noise. "Sometimes he just gets teased."

I finally raise my head to stab him with my darkest gaze. It has zero effect.

"Then she gives it to a geek," he adds, slyly reaching behind to knock Charlie's book off his desk.

"Grow up, Ryder," I say softly.

He leans over, his face inches from mine, his backside in front of Charlie. "Heard you got picked up on Red Road the other night."

I don't know how he knows that, but I won't take his bait. "Because someone was a jerk and kicked me out."

"Because someone is a cock-teasing little bitch."

"Get away from her," Charlie says.

Ryder just leans into my face, his rear end even closer to Charlie. "Did someone say something to my girlfriend—er, I mean, my ass?"

"Sit down," I tell him through clenched teeth.

"Did he take you home to his cardboard box under the causeway?" Ryder goes on.

"Shut up, Ryder," I say.

He lets out a long, loud fart in Charlie's face, and the room explodes with screams and laughter, but I feel like I'm underwater and can barely hear it through the blood pulsing in my head.

Charlie backs away, or maybe he jumps. I can't tell, because everything is in slow motion for a moment. Just as

Charlie raises his fist to slam Ryder, the lights flicker on and off.

"Mr. Zelinsky!" Brighton booms, and the room falls mostly silent.

Ryder just grins and holds up his hand. "No problem, Mr. B. Charlie's fine." Voices erupt again, and Ryder slinks back down the aisle as Brighton scowls at Charlie, and then at me.

Charlie avoids eye contact with me or Mr. Brighton. When class is over, he's gone before I get a chance to say a word to him.

And no one says a thing to me, but Ryder is surrounded by an adoring crowd, taking high fives and looking all kinds of smug.

"Oh, my God. The entire school is talking about Ryder." Bliss practically skips to our locker bank right before world history. "He's, like, a hero!"

"A hero?" I slam the door with so much force, it jolts my arm. "He's a complete douche."

A bunch of kids pass us and make farting noises, then erupt in laughter. "Hey, Ayla. It was the fart heard round the world!" one kid yells.

"Cute." But their laughter drowns out my dry response.

"Take back Crap!" another kid shouts. "We're not the home of the homeless!"

I keep my head in the locker, biting my lip.

"Ayla, no one wants Charlie Zelinsky in this school," Bliss says, getting close and lowering her voice. "What's the matter with you? He's an embarrassment to Croppe Academy."

I've never heard her call it anything but Crap. "Get off your high horse, Bliss. He's on a scholarship," I tell her. "That doesn't make him unworthy to go here. It certainly doesn't mean he deserved . . . that."

She stares at me, her mouth in a little O of feigned surprise. "It's true," she says softly.

"What's true?"

"Did you do it with that loser?"

I close my eyes, not sure if I should even respond. She's casting like crazy for something to use against me, and no matter what I say, she can twist it around. I finally settle on the plain truth. "No, I didn't do it with him."

"But you like him, don't you?"

·"I don't—" But I *do*. "I don't like anyone to be treated the way he is."

She snorts. "Like, since when? You live for that shit."

"Maybe I did, Bliss, but not anymore."

She takes a step back, then lifts an interested brow. "Can I count on you to get the answers from Flute Fly in history?"

I don't respond, repositioning my books and looking anywhere but at her.

"Can I?" she demands.

Ayla would say yes, of course. Cheating is nothing, really. A small price to pay for popularity and approval that I can feel slipping like sand through my fingers. But Annie? Annie never cheated in her life.

"We'll see," I finally say.

"WTF, Ayla?" She pushes past me. "Never mind. I'll handle the flute player. Good luck with the test."

"Bliss." I grab her arm as she starts to walk away. "Listen to you. Are you or are you not, like, my best friend? Is this the way we talk to each other?"

She searches my face. "I don't even know you anymore."

"Why?" I demand. "Because I don't want to make fun of kids or throw stuff I can pay for into my purse or cheat to pass a class? You don't want to be friends because I follow some rules?"

She frees her arm from my clutch with a dark look. "You're breaking the rules, Ayla. You're doing irrepairable damage to us."

I just stand there and stare at her as she disappears into a group.

Do I really care about a girl who says *irrepairable*?

No. And I'm determined to stick with my plan. And that will not include cheating on a history test. Even if I didn't study for it.

CHAPTER NINETEEN

"I hope you are all ready to show what you know about the fall of the Roman Empire." Ms. Guerra speaks with a soft Cuban accent, but there is something commanding about her. When she stands at the front of the room and crosses her arms, everyone shuts up and listens.

Well, almost everyone.

"Ms. G., I'm confused," Bliss says, sticking her hand into the air.

"Yes, Miss Tremaine?"

"I was in Rome this summer, and the place was rockin'. And, ohmigod, the shopping was to die for. How can it have fallen if it's still there?"

Some kids laugh, a few others turn to give admiring glances to Bliss, and props for having the nerve to delay the test, but Ms. Guerra is not amused. She begins to hand out test forms, walking up and down the aisles.

Bliss has placed herself strategically behind and to the left of Candi Woodward, her mark. I'm sitting one row away from Candi, wondering just how much of the test is from what we covered in class, because I seriously did not think I'd be around this weird world long enough to have to take a test. But grades are really the last thing on my mind as I watch Bliss reposition herself to see Candi's test.

Ms. Guerra reaches me and puts the paper facedown; no one is allowed to look until she calls time, like we're taking the SAT or something. The room is quiet except for some gum cracking, pencil tapping, and seat adjusting.

Finally, the teacher is in the front again, and she claps her hands and says, "Begin!"

Papers flutter and chairs scrape. An old familiar tightness grabs my belly as it always does when I take a test.

I read the first question quickly. *The Roman Empire lasted from* _____.

Before I can even process the four possible answers, I hear Bliss let out the softest grunt.

Some kids laugh in sympathy, but I look over and see exactly why she's grunting. Candi Woodward is left-handed, and there's no way Bliss can see one word of her page. But I can pretty much follow along with each question.

My eyes automatically go to her page and see that she's already colored in the answer: B. I look at my page. B is *27 BC to 476 AD*. That sounds about right.

I color B, and swallow the fact that I just cheated.

No, I would have known that. We talked about it in

class, I rationalize. The next question is *What was the praetorian guard?* I have no clue. It could be (A) the wall around Rome, (B) the emperor's bodyguard, (C) a centurion's headdress, or (D) an ancient form of birth control.

A little bit of laughter tells me that most people have caught Ms. G.'s joke and safely eliminated D as the answer. I stare at the options, but my eyes have a mind of their own, and my gaze moves to Candi's paper.

B. The emperor's bodyguard.

Shoot, I just cheated again. I feel my palms sweat as I mark the answer. I hear Bliss clear her throat softly. Again. Unable to resist, I slyly look at her.

Her face is pink with fury, her eyes narrowed as she moves them from Candi's desk to my test. *Share*, she silently screams.

My pulse kicks up. I just cheated for me, and am already feeling a little angsty about it, but should I help her, too?

She drops her hand and uses her index finger to make a "one" and lifts her eyebrows in question. I know what to do, I know this technique. I've seen it done.

If I scratch my face with one finger, the answer's A. Two, B, and so on. I study my paper, glance at Ms. Guerra, who is making a show of trust by working on her computer, profile to the class. I could give the answer to Bliss, easily.

Ayla would.

But I don't want to be Ayla. I have to start somewhere, right?

Swallowing hard, I look back at my test, the words to the third question swimming around. Something about Constantine the Great.

Bliss sighs audibly, loud enough to get Candi to look over her shoulder, then re-cover her page.

"You owe me, Flute Fly," Bliss whispers so softly that only a few of us hear it.

Candi ignores it, coloring in another circle. I see the answers to the next four questions, and, like it or not, they register in my brain. A, D, A, C.

I stare at my page, squeezing my pencil hard enough to crack it.

"We're nearing the halfway point," Ms. G. announces.

Halfway? I'm on number four.

A, D, A, C. If I color those in, I'll be on number eight. And there are only twenty questions.

I hold my pencil over the circle, and see my hand is shaking.

"Ayla." Bliss's whisper is desperate. A few around us look up, glancing from her to me. "Help." She mouths the word and flips two fingers. "Number two?"

I just stare at her.

"Ms. Monroe, is there a problem?" Ms. Guerra's question resonates through the silent classroom.

"No," I answer, heat stinging my skin.

"Then finish your test."

I nod and return my attention to the page, reading a question six times before the words even resemble English.

"Psst." I hear the sound and don't even want to look, but then realize it's Candi, not Bliss, trying to surreptitiously get my attention.

When I look up, she has completely shifted in her seat,

leaving her test wide open for me to copy. Partially turned to me, she adds a tight smile, and I read the message in her eyes.

She thinks she owes me for being nice to her and defending her to Bliss in the cafeteria.

A row away, Bliss stares me down.

The only thing I can do is turn down the offer. I shake my head at Candi, ignore Bliss, and read the next question, taking a shot at the answer.

"Five minutes!"

I skim the test, answer three that I know offhand, and Christmas tree the rest. I don't look at her, but I sense Bliss doing the same random marking, smashing her pencil over the circles like they're my head and she's holding a hammer.

"Pencils down, please. And you are free to socialize for the remainder of the period."

As though the conductor has nodded to the string section, twenty-five arms reach for cell phones and iPods, but Bliss stands, gathering her books and bag while she stares at me.

I say nothing, making a show of getting my own phone.

"Call your friends now," Bliss says as she nears me, her voice low and menacing. "Because by tonight, you won't have any left."

She walks out of the classroom without even glancing at the teacher.

CHAPTER TWENTY

I wish there were some way to avoid it, but I have to go to lunch. Several unanswered texts to Jade confirm my suspicions; if she has to pick sides, she'll go with Bliss.

Guess Jade knows which way the wind blows.

I cruise through the cafeteria line, reaching for a Styrofoam bowl of fries.

"French fries, Miss Monroe?" Charlie is right next to me, a sly grin on his face. "I think that might be taking this whole cool-girl-goes-rebellious thing too far."

I laugh easily, the first time in hours. "I know, right?" I pop one into my mouth and make a *nom-nom* sound. "I've already broken every unspoken rule the school has. Why not enjoy some forbidden calories while I'm at it?"

We slide our trays and our knuckles brush against each

other, sending an unexpected jolt up my arm and into my chest. I sneak a look at him to confirm he got the same charge.

I can tell by his smile he did.

"There's a lot of talk about your bad behavior in world history, too," he says.

I shake my head. "I'm completely out of control." I reach the cashier, a heavyset Latina woman who smiles at me and then glances at Charlie.

"Are you paying for both lunches, Ayla?" she asks.

"Uh . . ." I'm not sure what to say.

"I have my card," Charlie says, his voice tight as he pulls his wallet out.

Lunch Lady just gives him a pitying look. "The payment didn't clear yet, Mr. Zelinsky," she says. "I told you that on Friday."

"Try it again," he says, holding his student ID.

"Your name wasn't on the list I received this morning," she says coolly. "So you can't get that lunch."

I don't know what list she means, but I can practically feel the heat of shame rolling off him.

"Just put it on this card," I say quickly.

"No, Ayla. That's not necessary," he says, leveling a dark look at Lunch Lady and getting nothing but scorn in return. She hates him too, I realize, just like everyone else in this school. "If you swipe the card, Mrs. Alvarez, you'll see that money was deposited this morning."

"I don't have time for that, young man."

There's a line building and some unhappy grumbling behind us.

"Let's move it up there," someone calls out. Lunch is short, and line delays cost precious time. I stick my card into the machine. "Put both lunches on here."

"Ayla." Charlie puts his hand on mine, but there's no electrical charge this time.

"Don't sweat it," I tell him while I swipe the card to escape his grip. "There's a chem test next week. You can pay me back in—"

Charlie stumbles a little as a kid passes behind us, bumping into him. It's a pack of populars, with Ryder in the middle.

"Chump charity," Ryder chokes between fake coughs.

I glare at Ryder, but Charlie ignores them all. "Let's go, Ayla. There's a line."

Ryder gets a few steps ahead of us, but turns at Charlie's words.

"'Let's go, Ayla,'" he repeats, a sniveling mock in his voice. "What is this, a community service project for you, Ay?"

The boys around him snort with laughter, but I walk to the side. Instantly Ryder steps out and blocks me. I'm gripping the plastic tray so tight, I can feel the rim making a dent in my palm. "Get out of my way, Ryder."

"Are you headed back to his cardboard box to hump the homeless?"

Charlie moves forward. "Shut the hell up, Bransford."

Ryder looks down at Charlie's tray, and a cold chill goes through me. I'm not even sure what Ryder is capable of. Swinging a punch? Spitting? I don't want to find out.

"Charlie." I put my hand on his arm. "Let's go."

Time freezes for a minute as the two of them stare at each other, but Charlie steps away first, and we walk side by side, with every eye in the cafeteria on us.

"Find a seat," I say softly to him.

"You can go to your table," he says. "You don't need to stay with me."

But I do. I want to. "I'm not welcome at that table anymore," I say, slipping into the first empty seat I see. "Sit with me."

He avoids my gaze as he takes the chair across from me, silently opening a milk container. None of the kids at my regular table drink anything but soda or energy drinks, and I find his choice oddly endearing.

"I'm not going to let him ruin my french fries," I say, attempting lightness when I feel anything but.

Charlie eats in silence, his shoulders squared with tension, and all I want to do is reach over and put my hand on his to somehow reassure him.

A huge eruption of laughter from the far side of the cafeteria pulls our attention to a long table under the window. My so-called friends are raucous, forced to eat inside because it's raining.

"He's a jerk," I say, vaguely aware that a door has opened across the cafeteria and two of the janitors are rolling a dolly full of boxes and supplies toward the bathrooms.

"No kidding." Charlie gulps his milk.

"I wouldn't let them bother you."

"They don't bother me," he shoots back. "That freaking lunch lady does."

"Oh, that? That was . . ." But I can tell by the look on his face, it wasn't nothing. "A misunderstanding, obviously."

He closes his eyes, finishes his sub, and rolls up his trash. "I gotta go. I need to make a call."

I swallow a fry, which has lost any appeal whatsoever. "Okay," I say weakly.

"Sorry to leave you sitting here alone," he says, and I believe him. But he's grabbing his tray and books. "Thanks for lunch," he mumbles.

"Charlie." I look up at him, and he finally holds my gaze, his eyes angry and fierce. "I understand how you feel."

"Really, Ayla, I appreciate your kindness. I get you're not what or who I thought you were. But there's no way in hell you understand."

An ache washes over me, and without even realizing it, I close my hand over his. "There's a lot about me you don't know."

"Yeah? Maybe I can find out sometime."

For a wild instant, I want to tell him. But then I'm aware of an eerie quiet in the cafeteria, and I don't have to look around to know what's going on. Once again, Ayla Monroe is providing the school entertainment, and I sure as heck am not going to add to the swirling rumors with a confession like the one that's on my lips.

"See ya." Charlie slides his hand out from under mine and walks away, and the soft buzz of students rises again. I watch him cross the cafeteria and pause at the door to the boys' bathroom. He holds it open for the janitors who are leaving, then goes in.

Feeling ridiculous and alone and foolish, I look down at my fries, which are cold and dry by now. I stare at them for a long minute. When I look up again, Ryder and two of his friends are on their way into the bathroom.

No. Oh, God, *no*. Did Charlie get out? Every muscle in my body wants to do something, to stop them, to call out, but I freeze, just staring at the door as it closes behind Ryder.

This can't end well.

I glance around, aware that some kids are getting up to leave. Others are watching the bathroom like I am, but most are clueless about what's going on. Off to the far side, the table where I would have sat is emptying. I see the back of Bliss's blond head as she leaves, already surrounded by what used to be my posse.

I'm immobilized, alone at my table, waiting. The bell rings, and the rest of the students are up, shuffling, laughing, talking, texting. But the bathroom door is still closed.

I glance around for a teacher; there's no one but Lunch Lady, who's oblivious, refilling a napkin holder. Not that she'd do anything for Charlie, anyway.

Slowly I stand, willing the door to open, and willing Charlie—safe and whole—to come cruising out.

The cafeteria is almost empty, just a few band kids gathering up their instruments. I see Candi Woodward talking to a boy, and I wonder, could one of them help me? Could I ask that boy to go into the bathroom and see if Charlie is okay?

Ryder wouldn't hurt him, would he?

But the band kids leave without even looking at me, and I'm the last person in the cafeteria.

Finally, the door swings open with a vicious push from the inside, and Ryder's two friends stumble out, guffawing and high-fiving.

"Total ownage!" one says, giving knuckles to the other.

What did they do to him?

Ryder is behind them, urging them out, darting glances around the cafeteria. He stops when he sees me, and gives me an ugly smile.

When he and his friends walk out of the cafeteria, I don't even hesitate. I go right to the boys' bathroom.

CHAPTER TWENTY-ONE

I see the urinals as I inch the door open, and some stall doors are open. "Charlie?" I call tentatively. He has to be in here.

"Mmmm!" The sound is muffled, coming from the last stall.

I head back to the wide handicap door. It's locked and all I can see underneath is one of the large paper towel boxes that the janitors just delivered. "Charlie?"

The box scoots to the left. Oh, God. He's in it. I stick my head farther under the door to see duct tape securing every crack in the box. Those stupid jerks taped him into the box.

He grunts again.

And they taped his mouth. And probably his hands and feet, or he would have—

The box shudders again, as if Charlie is shimmying and kicking with all his might. I consider getting a teacher or the custodian, but before I give that much thought, I'm pushing myself under the locked stall door, turning my face so it doesn't accidentally brush the floor as I force my way in to help him.

Without saying a word, I start ripping the tape, popping the top in less than a few seconds. He's curled into a ball, arms, legs, and mouth covered with duct tape.

The juvenile bastards.

He looks up at me, his eyes damp. My heart just about collapses, and I help him out, whispering something encouraging and soft, but not really certain what I'm saying because my hands are shaking and I just want to get him out and be sure he can breathe.

I get the tape off his hands, and he rips the one from his mouth. "Assholes," he mutters, yanking at what's left of the tape.

"I'm sorry." I reach for the lock to open the door and give us air and space.

He grabs my arm. "It's not your fault."

"Yes, it is, Charlie. He's after you because we're friends."

He searches my face, all sign of his tears gone, but his eyes are still bright. Irate, embarrassed, stinging with emotion. "Are you my friend?" he asks softly.

"Of course." I feel heat crawling up me, completely unexpected and unnerving. "I don't brave boys' bathroom floors for just anyone."

He almost smiles, that kind of half smile that I noticed the first time I saw him. It does something to my pulse. His hand still on my arm, I give the lock a push to slide it open, but that just makes him grip me tighter.

"Are you?" he asks again.

"I just told you—"

"Prove it."

I back up, not at all sure what he means. "How?"

"There's someone . . . something . . ." He takes a breath, closing his eyes, corralling his thoughts. "I want to take you somewhere."

I don't even hesitate. "All right."

"Now."

I try to swallow, but my throat is bone-dry. All I can do is stare at him, aware of something magnetic and warm in the air, like static electricity, only there's nothing static about it. It's alive and real and zipping all over my body.

"Okay," I manage to say. "Let's go."

He finally releases my arm and nods toward the door. "Wait for me outside."

I walk out slowly. Lunch Lady is wiping down a table and looks up at the sound of the door opening. Her eyes widen when she sees me emerging from the boys' bathroom.

I ignore her and walk to the first table, and pull out a chair to wait for Charlie, his strange request still echoing. Where does he want me to go? Why am I shaking? What was that feeling I just had?

Do I have a crush on Charlie Zelinsky? Maybe a little. But no crush I can remember ever made me feel so . . . connected. Liking a boy usually makes me feel silly and excited. It makes me dreamy and lost. But this . . . this . . .

"You shouldn't talk to him."

I jump at the sound of a woman's voice next to me, and I spin around to face Lunch Lady.

"I don't think this is any of your business, Mrs. Alvarez," I say, copping my best Ayla-dissing-the-staff tone.

"You're better than him."

"Really." I choke softly. Even the school workers are opposed to him. "And you know this how?"

"The same way everyone does, Miss Ayla."

A shot of irritation pushes me to my feet just as the bathroom door opens and Charlie walks out. Fueled by a need to smack down the cafeteria worker, I slip my arm through his and tuck myself close to him.

"Let's go," I whisper.

He just gives me that beautiful one-dimpled smile and ignores Lunch Lady completely.

I see enough signs for Hialeah on our way out of the Gables that I kind of know where Charlie is taking me. Home. His home. I dig up in my memory what I've heard from around school.

He used to live under a bridge in a box. Now he lives in Hialeah. His mother cleans offices. That's it. That's the sum total of what I know about this boy who is taking me out of school in the middle of the day.

He's pretty quiet on the drive, not talking about the incident. I don't want to, either, so I pick up one of his books, a tome on organic chemistry.

"I thought the college class you're taking was a physics class," I say.

"Both."

"Are you going to graduate early?" I ask.

"Next year," he says. "In January. After I took a year and a half off, I crammed in a bunch of summer classes, and I have all the credits I need to get out of the happy place we call Crap Academy."

"Then what? College?" I check myself, a little sorry I mentioned it. He likely can't afford college.

"Probably Duke, although Johns Hopkins and MIT are options."

"Whoa," I say, with a whistle. "You've already applied?"

He throws me a look. "I'm already accepted with a full ride."

My jaw drops. "Then what are you doing at Crap Academy? Why not go to a public school and not have to deal with the grief?"

He takes a deep breath through his nose, his lips tight as he stares ahead at traffic. "I have my reasons."

"Like you're a masochist? You wouldn't get treated like this at public school."

"How do you know?"

"Because I've gone to one."

He shoots me a sideways look. "Yeah, right. In another life."

"You have no idea," I say vaguely, looking out the window as the Spanish villas and exclusive shops of Coral Gables morph into a seedier section of Miami. Something deep in my belly squeezes, and I hear words in my head.

Tell him. Tell him. You can trust him.

"Ayla, there's actually a lot you don't know about me."

It's like he's reading my mind. "There's a lot you don't know about me," I say softly, keeping the irony out of my voice.

"I mean, you heard I lived in shelters with my mom."

"I heard, and I don't care."

"And some news reporter interviewed me after I won a science fair, and a pharmaceutical company wanted to use my research."

I shake my head. "I didn't hear that. Just that you were on the news and the people at Croppe thought they'd get good press by giving you a scholarship."

He slides a look at me, questioning.

"What?" I ask. "I don't think that's anything to be ashamed of, seriously. You don't live in shelters now, do you?"

"No, we rent a house. Right around here," he says, jutting his chin toward some run-down residences.

"It's not bad," I say, sensing that he expects me to curl my lip at the houses, but this neighborhood is just a few steps down from Rolling Rock Road. Not exactly living in squalor, just not Star Island.

"Well, I thought you should see it, just so you know. Before . . ." His voice trails off.

I turn to him, adjusting the seat belt that feels like it's crushing my chest. *Something* is crushing my chest. "Before what?"

"Before our friendship goes any further."

"You think if I see that your mom doesn't have much money, I'm going to run screaming into the arms of Ryder Bransford? Seriously, Charlie? I think you know now that I'm really, really not that girl."

"I do." I expect him to smile, to lighten this up, but he doesn't. "We're almost there."

"Anybody going to be home?" A funny feeling creeps through me. Is he the same as Ryder? Taking me home for sex? If so, I know I'm going to be kind of interested . . . but wildly disappointed in him.

"Someone is always home."

"I thought your mom works."

"At night." He pulls into the driveway of a wee little gray house, with a carport and a tiny front porch. The grass is cut neatly, and there are some flowers under one of the windows. "There's more to the story than the TV news reported."

The way he says it sounds ominous, so I just wait for more.

"You're about to meet her."

"Your mom?" I ask.

"My sister." He gets out of the Jeep, and I do the same. As I round the car, he reaches way down into the backseat and pulls out his Frank Sinatra hat, setting it on his head at a jaunty angle.

"Sorry about that fountain incident," I say sheepishly. "I noticed you don't wear it anymore."

"Well, don't tell my sister," he replies. "She gave it to me and thinks I wear it every day."

"Sorry," I say again. "Is she older or younger?"

"She's my twin."

I slow my step toward the front door. "You have a twin sister? Where does she go to school?"

"She doesn't." He shoots me a very serious look. "That's why I want you to meet her."

He opens the door to a small entry that somehow seems brighter than outside. I recognize the strains of a Schubert piece we did in orchestra last year, a tough score with a beginning vibrato that always challenged me.

"Is that your sister playing?" I ask.

He kind of laughs softly. "No."

"What are you doing home this early?" a woman calls out.

"I brought a friend, Mom." There's a serious warning in Charlie's voice.

"Oh?" A woman appears, petite and dark, a wary expression on her tired but not unattractive features.

She looks hard at me, then lifts an eyebrow toward Charlie like he's done something wrong.

Aren't friends welcome? I reach out my hand. "Hi, Mrs. Zelinsky. I'm Annie."

Next to me, Charlie kind of chokes, and I realize the mistake I've made.

"Ayla," we both correct at the same time.

"Ayla Monroe," he adds quickly, giving me a funny look. How will I explain that?

"Ooooh," comes a low noise I think is a girl's voice from the room behind Mrs. Zelinsky. "A-list Ayla! Are you serious, Charlie?"

His mom's brown eyes, so much like Charlie's in color and shape, narrow to slits as she shakes my hand. And despite the sunny house and happy music, she's blocking the room's entrance with her body.

"It's fine, Mom," he says. "I want Ayla to meet Missy."

"And I want to meet Ayla." That's definitely a girl's

voice, but kind of . . . weird. Low, stiff, and strained. "She's like the celebrity queen bitch of the school."

I glance up at Charlie, not sure I heard that right, but he gives me a rueful smile. "Just a warning," he says softly to me. "My twin has no filter. None."

Slowly Mrs. Zelinsky steps aside to allow me into the living room. "Come on in. She's in rare form today."

A girl looks up at me from a chair. I'm riveted by her looks at first, by a heart-shaped face that is far too sweet-looking to have called anyone a bitch, and cropped black hair that sticks out in four different directions, reminding me of an elf. She looks much younger than Charlie, more like thirteen than seventeen. She doesn't move or reach her hand out or get up to greet me.

Charlie pops his hat off and puts it on her head. "Worn almost all day," he says softly. "As promised."

The hat tips to the left, and she makes no effort to right it but smiles at me. A beautiful, bright, blinding smile.

Only then do I realize she's in a wheelchair.

CHAPTER TWENTY-TWO

"Wow, you're right, Charlie," the girl says. "She's hot! Even prettier than the yearbook picture."

I'm speechless.

"And that's a good picture," she adds with another winning smile. Nothing has moved but some muscles on her face. Everything about her is completely still.

Everything is . . . paralyzed. And so is my brain. "I didn't know Charlie had a twin," I say, still trying to process what's going on.

"I'm Melissa, the family secret."

"Stop it," Charlie says, taking his hat back. "You can call her Missy," he says to me. Then he turns to his sister. "You need to get up?"

Can she? I feel my chest squeeze with hope. Maybe she just broke her leg. Maybe this chair is temporary.

"Nah, my bag isn't even full yet." She looks down toward her lap, that strange, strained voice clearly a part of her physical problem, her eyes doing most of the work while her head stays relatively still. "And Mom has tonight off, so I'm getting a shampoo. Woot!"

"But I might run an errand now that you're home, Charlie," Mrs. Zelinsky says, crossing the room to put both hands on Missy's shoulders. "You okay if I'm gone for an hour?"

"Of course. I can talk to Ayla Monroe!" Missy says my name like I'm some kind of movie star. "Will you sign your picture in the Croppe Academy yearbook?"

"But you were just about to nap," her mother says.

Missy turns her head slightly, not more than an inch, but somehow it's comforting to finally see her move. "I can stay awake for a few more minutes, Mom," she says. "This is a special occasion."

Mrs. Zelinsky kisses her cheek softly, closing her eyes as she does. "I'll be back in a little." She straightens and looks at Charlie. "I have my phone if you need me."

"We'll be fine, Mom," he says.

"What happened at school?" his mother asks, searching his face and reaching out to touch a bruise on his cheek. I didn't notice it before, but I guess that's Ryder's handiwork. "Is everything okay?"

For a moment, I wonder if he's going to tell her about the bathroom incident. "Yeah, it's cool. Just a light class load today."

"You sure?" She's frowning at him, then at me, as though I should cough up more information. I take my cue from Charlie.

"Yes," I tell her. *Except your son was taped into a box an hour ago.* "Fine."

"Then I'll be back in an hour." Mrs. Zelinsky scoops up a handbag, and Charlie digs into his pocket and holds out his keys.

"You're welcome to it, Mom. In fact, if you fill 'er up, I'll love you forever."

His mother just shakes her head, her expression a mix of sadness and appreciation. "No, baby. But thanks. I'm just headed down to the market, I'll walk. I'm glad you're home, because now I can pick up some things I'd rather not ask you to buy."

He rolls his eyes. "Mom, nothing bothers me. Even lady stuff."

She smiles and nods to me. "It's nice to meet you, Ayla. Please, have a seat and make yourself comfortable."

"Thank you," I reply, perching on the edge of a sofa, still facing Missy, who hasn't taken her gaze from me.

"Did you cut today?" Missy asks me as soon as her mother is out the door.

"Well, yeah," I acknowledge. "Charlie wanted me to come here."

She beams at her brother, her eyes bright. "You're the best, big guy."

"Then you better let me win Scrabble tonight," he says easily, heading toward the kitchen. "Want a soda, Ayla?"

"Okay."

216

"How 'bout you, Missy? Chocolate or strawberry?"

"Ugh. I want a Coke."

"You're getting Ensure, bones. Chocolate or strawberry?"

"Whatever is handy," she says, then slides her eyes back to me. "Have you ever tasted that crap? Like they put chocolate sauce in Elmer's glue."

I laugh. "Never had the stuff," I admit.

"No, you wouldn't," she says, drinking me in with her wide ebony eyes. "You're perfect."

"Far from it," I say quickly.

"I've read every word about you in the yearbook and when Charlie brings home the *Cropper*."

She reads the school newspaper?

"Isn't Ryder Bransford your boyfriend?" she asks.

She reads *more* than the newspaper. "Not anymore," I say.

Charlie comes back in, sticking a straw into a pink can. "Don't grill her, Missy. She'll never come back."

Missy manages a little smile, but I can tell it takes concentration to move those muscles. "I think she'll come back. Won't you?"

"Not if you scare her off." Charlie holds the can to Missy's mouth, carefully placing the straw between her lips. "Suck it down, Georgia Brown."

I'm mesmerized as she works to drink and I see the liquid rise in the straw. Little more than a bird's-size sip reaches her lips. She makes a grunting sound, and he moves the can away and a trail of pink liquid dribbles down her chin.

"Charlie," she says, mortified.

He's quick with a paper napkin I didn't even see him

holding, dabbing at her chin. Color rises to her face, and she averts her gaze.

"So much for being normal," she says, her slightly unnatural voice tight in her throat.

"Hey," Charlie says. "You were doing good. Wanna try again?"

She shakes her head, but not vigorously. Slowly, from side to side. "Ayla doesn't want to see me slobber. Maybe I'll go watch TV in my room."

"But I want to talk to you," I say, surprising myself with how true that is. "Relax."

She looks up and smiles at me. "Wow, you really aren't a bitch at all."

"I can be," I tell her with a laugh. "Just ask my brother."

"Trent? He's really hot."

I snort softly, realizing that I was thinking about Theo. In fact, since I walked into this house, it feels like I've forgotten I'm Ayla. I have to be careful. "Trent the Tool? Not hot," I tell her.

She laughs so hard, she starts to choke, and Charlie's by her side instantly. "You okay?" he asks.

The coughing spell lasts a few seconds, but it shakes her thin body in a weird way, and while her eyes are closed, I take a moment to look at the chair and the coverlet over her. She's completely paralyzed, I decide. Neck down.

My whole body sinks in sympathy for her.

"Trent the Tool," she finally says, working not to laugh. "You are too funny." She turns slightly to Charlie, giving me the impression that moving her head is tough. "No wonder you adore her."

He just gives one of those partial Charlie smiles, like he isn't going to deny it, but he might be humoring his sister too. "I think you adore her more," he says.

"I admit I spent too much time on your picture in last year's yearbook," she agrees.

"Like an hour."

"Charlie holds the book for me," she says.

"That's really nice of him." Like everything else he does for his sister.

He tries to get her to drink again. "Have some more, Missy."

"I don't want any," she protests, but he patiently waits for her to change her mind, then helps her take another sip, more successful this time.

After she finishes, he takes the can back to the kitchen, and Missy's eyes move to meet mine again. "He's the best brother in the world."

"I see that," I say, unable to imagine Trent *or* Theo doing that for me. My throat tightens up. What I'm really unable to imagine is what it would be like in that wheelchair.

"You know, don't you?" she asks.

I look at her, wondering how much of my thoughts are all over my face. "Know what?"

"How much he likes you."

"Um, we're just friends."

Her smile says she thinks differently. "He wants to kiss you so bad. That's all he thinks about since you saved him in literature with the whole *Lord of the Flies* thing."

"I—I . . ." Have no idea how to respond to that.

She has no filter. No kidding.

"You're not going to break Charlie's heart, are you?" she asks in a soft whisper.

Am I? The question throws me. "I don't plan on it."

"You're not going to disappear and leave me to pick up the pieces, are you?"

"I—"

"'Cause I'm not very good at picking things up."

I laugh softly at the dark humor. "I won't disappear."

"Do you promise?"

I stare at her. Can I promise that? "Well . . . I . . ."

"Because a promise is a promise. Just ask Charlie. When you make one, you can't break it."

"No, I realize that, but . . ."

"So, you're not going to disappear."

"Why would I?" I ask. "We're friends, and . . ." I pretty much sealed my permanent outcast status at school this morning. "I don't disappear on my friends."

Except for Lizzie, but she doesn't know I disappeared.

"Good, because the last girl ran screaming when she met me."

"Really?"

"She's full of shit." Charlie comes out of the kitchen and hands me a soda. "That's what you need to know about my twin sister. She loves to exaggerate and take all the credit for everything in my life."

I feel a little like my head is spinning. They are acting so normal.

"You can't possibly last with Charlie," Missy says as I take a drink of soda. "You're the queen bee of Croppe Academy. A-list Ayla. The most popular girl in the school."

"You're not getting the latest news," I tell her.

Charlie falls back onto the sofa next to me, draping one arm along the back. "Sorry to break it to ya, Miss," he says, "but Ayla's coolness factor is on a serious downslide, probably because of me."

I turn to him and actually have to work not to suck in a soft breath. He looks so cute right now, so completely comfortable in his own skin, and so different from the science nerd in the Frank Sinatra hat I first met.

He's lanky and thin, but broad enough to look like he'd be a great hugger. He crosses his long legs, looks at me from under thick lashes, and gives me that half smile, and all my insides just melt. A great hugger *and* kisser.

He wants to kiss you so bad.

Missy's words echo around in my head . . . and I can only think of one response: The feeling's mutual.

"Aw, Ayla's got a big bad crush on you," Missy announces with a giggle. "She blushes when she looks at you."

Am I blushing? Really? I hadn't felt the dreaded red face since I stepped into Ayla Monroe's life.

But Charlie laughs. "I warned you."

"I'm homeschooled," Missy says suddenly, the unexpected change of subject like a cool drink of water to a parched throat.

"Oh?" I reply politely. "What classes do you like?"

"Music," she says quickly. "That's what I was doing when you got here. I live for music. It's really the best medicine for . . . me."

"I play the violin." Jeez, why did I say that? Speaking of no filter. *Ayla* doesn't play the violin.

But Missy's eyes are saucer-wide. "You do?"

I can tell by the way he shifts forward that Charlie thinks I'm lying, and doesn't know why.

"I used to," I say quickly. "Not so much anymore."

"I have a violin!" Missy says, her gaze glittering and excited now. "Will you play it?"

"Oh, it's been forever. I couldn't remember anything."

"Even a scale?"

"No, I shouldn't have said that. I don't—"

"Oh, come on, Ayla." Her plea just rips at my heart. "Get my instrument, Charlie. I know she'll play for me."

He gives me a warning look, like if I let his sister down, he won't be happy. Then he pushes up and says, "If I can find it."

"It's in my closet," Missy says. "Top shelf."

He disappears down the hall without a word, but Missy is still on fire.

"I used to play the violin," she admits. "I loved it. Before . . ."

Before whatever happened to put her into a wheelchair. I know my face is registering sympathy, and the question I don't have the nerve to ask.

What happened?

"Charlie didn't tell you, I take it." She might be paralyzed, but her brain is sharp, as is her ability to read people. Either that or I am totally obvious.

"No, he didn't tell me anything. Just brought me here to meet you."

"I made him promise he would let me meet you, as soon

as he said you two were getting to be friends." She smiles sweetly. "He never, ever breaks a promise. That's his super-power."

"That's a good one."

"Well, that and his IQ, which is respectable, but not as good as mine."

Then she must be really smart. "So," I say softly. "Will you tell me what happened?"

"It was a car accident, four years ago. Four years ago in less than a week, on November seventeenth. We were on our way home from my soccer game, which had gotten called on account of lightning. The storm was getting bad, and Mom was in a hurry 'cause she wanted to get home to unplug the computer in case of a power outage." She works to swallow, closing her eyes like it hurts her. Or, oh, God, maybe she's going to cry.

"That's okay, Missy."

But she continues, and I get the feeling she wants to tell me the whole story. "We were on Old Cutler Road. You know that really winding one down south? We were just turning onto 168th Street, and . . ." She takes a ragged breath. "Mom always says she wishes she'd just let the computer fry. But anyway, she ran a yellow light making a left, which is totally legal, but some truck driver was barreling through the inter-section, and . . ."

"I'm sorry," I say, feeling like those have to be the two most useless words in the English language.

"Mom was always scared of left turns, too. Now she won't even drive anymore, she feels so guilty."

"Oh, Missy." I glance down at her body. "Can you . . ."

"No. I can't do anything." She swallows visibly. "But I will. I know I will."

"I'm sure there's hope." But I'm not sure of that at all.

"I know I'll walk again." She sounds entirely confident. "Charlie promised. My spine will be fixed."

A chill tingles my own spine just as Charlie returns and hands me a violin case, a dubious look on his face. "This I gotta see," he says.

"Me too!" Missy is far more certain that I haven't lied.

I slowly open the case and take out the instrument. It's a three-by-four, so a little smaller than the one I played in my other life, probably because Missy last played four years ago. This one hasn't been touched in a while, I can tell by the little bit of dust gathered on the strings. I take the soft cloth and brush them, and check the rosin on the bow. Someone rosined it in the last few years. Charlie?

I don't know, but I have to play this thing now, because if I can't, I know I'm going to let them both down. And I don't want to. God, I don't want to. I pick up the neck and stare at it.

It feels strange in my hands. Ayla has never played a violin, I'm willing to bet. She . . . I . . . won't know the first thing to do or how to hold it.

I might have Annie's moral compass and soul, but I still have Ayla's body and fingers. Can I play a violin?

I look at Missy, who smiles expectantly. And then at Charlie, who's wearing a serious expression.

I'm shaking a little as I lift the instrument and tuck the chin rest under my jaw. It still feels unfamiliar, and my heart is hammering. "I'm afraid I've forgotten everything," I admit. "It was . . . another lifetime when I played."

"Please," Missy says. "Try. I'll tell you what you need to know. Move the bow."

Taking a breath, I pluck first, and we all make faces at how out of tune it is.

"Tighten the A string," she suggests.

Which one is that? I take a guess on which key that is at the top. I get it right. And then the next string. And the next. In a minute, I'm tuned, completely on instinct.

I hope that keeps working.

"There," Missy says happily. "Now play something."

I raise the bow and hold my breath, shifting my gaze to Charlie. I stare at him and hope he's not too mad when I can't do this.

I move the bow, press a string, and play an A.

Missy lets out a soft cry of delight.

The reaction spurs me to play another note. I close my eyes and let myself be Annie for a minute, a shaky bow moving across the strings to play the first few bars of some really dumb French folk song we played in eighth-grade orchestra. It's all I can dig out of my subconscious.

"Oh, that's beautiful," she says.

I open my eyes to see Charlie's expression. That is probably the way I looked a few minutes ago when I was bowled over with a blast of affection. He looks like he cares for me. Deeply.

He leans closer and puts his hand on my leg, burning me with his touch and his relentless gaze.

"Who *are* you?"

I am Annie Nutter.

And right then, I decide. I'm going to tell Charlie the truth.

CHAPTER TWENTY-THREE

I play one more simple piece and by the time I finish, Missy has fallen asleep. Her head slips slightly, and Charlie is up in a flash behind her chair.

"Let me take her back to her room," he says softly. "The meds usually hit around this time and she gets tired. Especially when there's good music. Actually, great."

I feel another blush coming on—why now, after a week of no red face?

"Not great," I correct him, but actually, it wasn't horrible, considering Ayla Monroe had never picked up a violin in her life.

Where the heck did *that* ability come from?

By the time Charlie returns, I've put the violin away and mentally prepared my speech. I'm scared, I admit to myself.

But I can't go through this alone any longer, and Charlie—a boy who makes and keeps promises, holds the yearbook and an Ensure can so his sister is able to drink in the nutrients she's missing, and endures the second level of hell at school—Charlie is the right person to tell.

"I think I've figured you out," he says as he comes back to the living room. "You have a secret life you hide from the kids at school so you'll stay popular."

I let out a relieved breath. "You know, you're not far from the truth."

"I like it." He drops down onto the sofa. "Maybe you could teach me how you've done it, so I don't have to get boxed up in the bathroom every few weeks."

My eyes open wide. "That wasn't the first time?"

"I used to carry a penknife but got suspended for it, and I didn't want to screw up my college career. Someone always finds me, but . . ." He smiles. "Usually a guy."

I shake my head as the question I asked him in the car resurfaces. "Why don't you go to a public school? You wouldn't get treated like that."

"Can't. I have to stay at Crap for Missy."

"I don't get the connection. Why?"

He looks at me like he's not even sure where to begin.

"She told me a little about the accident," I offer, to help him out. "And I know that you guys—well, you and your mom, like you told me—were on the news and that's how you got your scholarship. But how does Missy fit into Croppe?"

"After the accident, my mom pretty much lost everything trying to take care of Missy. Before that, we lived in an apartment in Cutler Ridge, and my mom taught sixth-grade science. Then . . . everything changed in an instant. Insurance covered a lot of it, but still the medical bills wiped us out. We got some help here and there, but eventually we couldn't stay in the apartment, so we found a few shelters—you have to move after a certain amount of time—that could accommodate Missy's special bed." He pauses for a minute, rolling the Coke can in his hands. "I stayed out of school as long as I could before some government agency made me go back. When I did, I won the Miami-Dade County Science Fair, competing against seniors in high school, and I was basically in eighth grade. And I also won state."

"Wow. No wonder they did a news story."

"Yeah, and that's when Croppe got involved."

"Offering the scholarship."

He shrugs. "That's just a little side PR benefit for them, but it's part of the whole deal."

"What deal?"

"John J. Croppe isn't just the name of a private school in Miami, Ayla. John J. might be the granddaddy who built the school, but Croppe Pharmaceuticals and Medical Devices is an international company, and research—like what they're doing with Missy—is where they mine for money in the future."

"What are they doing with her?"

"Missy has a rare kind of spinal cord injury. Before, she needed a ventilator to breathe, which is the worst thing imaginable, believe me. But Croppe is testing this device that provides electrical stimulation to the muscles in her diaphragm, and it allows her to breathe on her own. Her voice is funny, but before, she could hardly talk at all."

"Really? I would never have known something was help-ing her breathe."

He leans forward, excited. "It's a huge medical break-through, but they don't want the competition to know how far along they are. The FDA knows, of course, and they are constantly sending people here to check on her. And she gets all kinds of attention from doctors and scientists from Croppe, and they've made it possible for us to have a home and live without my mom working full-time, although she cleans offices at Croppe Pharm because she hates feeling like a charity case."

"Not a charity case if they're going to profit from the research," I say. "But why do you have to go to Croppe?"

"For the good PR they get about how they're helping this 'homeless' family." He puts the word in quotes, but that does nothing to erase the ugly way it sounds on his lips. "They want me there as part of the deal. I can't take a chance they'll back down and stop providing the medical treatment for Missy. So, I endure the homeless jokes."

"But you weren't homeless," I say. "You had extraordinary circumstances."

He smiles and shakes his head. "God, Ayla, I had no idea you were such a . . . sweet girl."

"Ditto," I say. "Except for the girl part. You're an awfully good brother."

He shrugs modestly. "She's my twin. My other half. I'd be in that chair if I hadn't been a jerk and insisted on the front seat. The air bag saved me from any serious injury. She wasn't so lucky." Guilt drips off every word.

"Are you ever going to forgive yourself?"

"Probably not, and neither will my mom. It was our fault," he says simply. "She made a dumb move, and I should have been in the back."

"You can't second-guess history," I say. Then I shift on the sofa and turn to him, ready. "Although, sometimes, life can surprise you by doing that for you."

"What do you mean?"

I bite my lip and realize I'm squeezing my hands together. "I have to tell you something, Charlie."

"Okay."

"It's big."

He laughs and points at the violin. "After that, nothing could surprise me."

"This will. But you have to make me a promise . . . and I understand keeping promises is your superpower."

"I do what I can," he says. "What do you want me to promise? To keep it secret? You don't even have to ask."

"I need you to promise not to tell me I'm crazy—"

"No problem."

"Or lying or an alien or manipulating you or making this up in any way, shape, or form." I'm rushing the words because it is so important to me now. "I want you to promise that."

"I promise."

I believe him. How can I not? I've seen what he's made of, I've heard his sister's testimony. And I've never felt more comfortable or, oddly enough, more like Annie than since I walked into this house.

"I'm not Ayla Monroe," I say quietly.

His head angles a little, like my dog Watson when I used to ask him a question he couldn't possibly understand. "Is that why you called yourself Annie?"

Relief rolls through me. "Yes. My name is Annie Nutter, and about a week or so ago, I was in my house on Rolling Rock Road in Pittsburgh, Pennsylvania, just as ordinary as I could be. Then there was a lightning strike and I woke up living and breathing in Ayla Monroe's world. In her body, actually."

He pales a little. "You did?"

Encouraged by a response that doesn't include wild accusations or running from the room screaming, I power on. "I did. I was one girl, living one life, not perfect by any stretch of the imagination. But everything was completely normal. Then I was in Walmart, and my mother—who is the same mother I have now, by the way—was crying about Jim Monroe's house in *Architectural Digest,* and we got home and my dad had invented some bizarre mirror thing where you can put perfect features together to create a new you, and my mom broke it and they had this big fight and I had pancakes for dinner and there was a storm, and I think lightning hit the house or something, because I woke up here."

"You just woke up in a different world." He cuts off my word spew with a statement, not a question. A glorious, reasonable *statement.*

"You believe me?" I can see he's having a little trouble. At least, he can't quite catch his breath or form a word. "I knew you wouldn't be—"

"Of course I believe you," he interjects. "Holy crap, this is the most exciting thing I've ever heard."

I laugh a little, like someone has shot endorphins straight

into my brain. Charlie believes me! I barely realize I'm holding both his hands, gripping him, and he's gripping back. "Exciting?" I repeat.

"Oh, my God, beyond exciting."

"It's crazy, though, right?" I say. "But it happened. It really did. And I have no idea what's going on or how this happened."

He pulls me a little closer. "I do."

My jaw drops. "You do?"

"Of course I do. This is my passion. This is my *real* superpower."

"What is?"

"Quantum physics and particle theory. Atomic collisions and multiverses."

"*What?*"

He laughs and squeezes my hands. "You did the most amazing thing a person can do, Ayla. I mean, Annie." He thinks about that for a second, searching my face, a slow smile breaking across his. "Annie Nutter." Oh, my God. I love the way he says it. Like it's the prettiest name ever. "'Annie' fits you, somehow. Much better than 'Ayla.'"

"Thanks, I think." I curl my fingers through his, my pulse jumping like crazy. "Can you please tell me what this amazing thing I did is?"

He leans closer. "You made the ultimate journey from one universe to another."

"I did?" I shoot back, reeling. "How?"

"Well, we'll have to figure that out. My guess is the Heisenberg uncertainty principle and hyper-dimensional physics in a level three or four parallel universe."

What? The only word I got in that was *uncertainty*. My life has been nothing but uncertain since this happened. "What are you talking about?" I say. "Parallel universes?"

"Yes!" He's as excited as Missy was when I said I could play the violin. In fact, at this moment, I can see they're twins. "Of course, we'll need to do some research to figure that out. You'll need to tell me exactly what happened, when, and how. I know a quantum physics genius at UM who's involved with some major particle colliding projects. He might—"

"You can't tell anyone!"

"How else are we going to help you?"

"Help me? Help me what?"

He finally lets go of my hands, easing away, the first real confusion registering on his face. "Help you get back."

I collapse a little, staring at him. "I can go back?"

"Unless, of course, you don't want to."

"Oh, Charlie." I cover my mouth as the possibility washes over me. *I can go home.* I can give up this perfect world, this lucky life, this wonderful boy . . . and I can be Annie Nutter again.

"You want to go back, don't you?"

I have to answer honestly. "I don't know."

CHAPTER TWENTY-FOUR

A few hours later, I'm leaning back in the Jeep as we cross the causeway to Star Island, with the canvas top stripped off to let the warm Biscayne Bay breeze blow our hair. Charlie is holding my hand over the stack of science books between us, and jazz music plays on the car radio.

I close my eyes, but behind my lids all I can see is universe bubbles, images of stars, wormholes, laser lights, dancing electrons, photons, and something I've never heard of, a graviton.

My master course in quantum mechanics and cosmology did little but confuse me.

"Everything makes so much sense now," Charlie muses, letting go of my hand to turn the music down.

"You're kidding, right? Nothing makes sense, Charlie. I

still don't understand the four levels of parallel universes or how there could be one right here"—I grab a handful of air—"and we can't see or smell or hear it because it's in another dimension where laws of physics don't apply."

The corner of his mouth lifts, the dimple appears, and my toes curl like they've been pulled on a string. "I mean about you," Charlie says. "Everything makes sense about you now."

I don't answer but bask in his glance, fast but full of admiration.

"You were never Ayla Monroe, not from the minute you walked into school that day you were late. I could just sense it."

"But I am," I insist. "This is Ayla." I point to myself, then to the entrance of Star Island. "And that's where she lives."

"This is Annie." He taps my breastbone, a few inches above my heart. "And *that's* where she lives."

How is it that he got that already? Just knowing that makes me feel better.

The Star Island guard gives the Jeep an evil eye, but lets us by when he sees me.

"It's not a bad way to live," I say, somehow feeling I have to defend Ayla's lifestyle. "And, except for the idiots like Ryder, being popular and pretty instead of an invisible nobody doesn't suck."

"You're not serious."

"Of course I'm serious, Charlie. You can't tell me you wouldn't like to wake up in a luxurious house, a whole improved you, and not have to be bullied and treated like crap by the likes of Lunch Lady."

He slows down in front of the gate to my house but doesn't

press in the numbers. Instead he stares straight ahead, that amazing brain of his whirring, I can tell.

"Lunch Lady doesn't exist for me, luxury doesn't matter, and the assholes can't hurt me if I don't let them." He turns to me. "You know the only thing I'd barter with the devil to change."

Missy. My gut twists. I guess I'm being ridiculously shallow for worrying about money and popularity when his sister . . .

"I didn't barter with the devil," I say softly. "I just had a few fantasies, pictured a perfect life, and a lightning bolt took me there."

Without answering, he taps in the code just as a car pulls up behind us. I look in the side mirror and recognize my mother's silver Mercedes.

"That's my mom," I say, a whole bunch of mixed feelings stirring inside me. I don't want or need to tell her the truth anymore, but I do want to straighten out her misconception that I read her email.

And I *really* want to know what she said to Mel Nutter, and what he said to her.

"Want me to pull over so you can drive in with her?" he asks, seeing me look longingly at Mom's car in the side mirror.

"No, I'll catch her inside. Do you want to come in with me?"

He shakes his head, heading into the wide paved drive and pulling over to let my mom pass. I catch her eye as she drives by; she looks pensive and sad—and worried. I give her a little wave, and she attempts a smile in return.

"She was happier in that other universe," I say as Charlie

parks next to a cluster of palm trees. "I mean, she cried that day in Walmart, but most of the time, my mom would sing when she cooked or talk to the fish when she fed them." I feel that homesick lump building in my throat, a semipermanent resident lately. "She didn't fight that much with my dad, either. I wish she were happy now. I wish she didn't want a divorce or drink in the afternoon or act like I don't want her in my room. I wish . . ."

My voice cracks, and Charlie puts his hand on mine, turning in the seat to face me. "You cry a lot."

"I didn't used to. I blushed. How do you explain that? Not all the particles that blasted through the wormhole came through right?"

"Blushing and tearfulness are inherited traits," he says, all scientific and serious.

"And playing the violin?"

He brushes my cheek, wiping a tear. "From the soul or whatever indefinable part of you makes you Annie. I like that part." The pad of his thumb circles my cheekbone, and I can't take my eyes off his. "Yes, you are pretty, and when you pictured perfect, you came damn close, but the part of you I like the most is inside."

Oh. *Oh.* "That could be the sweetest thing anyone's ever said to me," I whisper.

He smiles and leans close enough to let our foreheads touch, and I feel connected to him like this is a Vulcan mind meld or something.

"I'm going over to UM right now to talk to Doc Pritchard. I'll call you tonight when I find out more."

"Is he going to want to meet me and experiment on me?"

Charlie smiles. "No testing on Annie, I promise." He takes my chin and lifts my face toward his. "Just so we're clear on this, I like Annie a lot."

I almost nod, but I'm pretty paralyzed with affection for him at the moment. Our lips are close, and I know he's going to kiss me. I want him to so badly that my lips actually hurt.

When he doesn't, I ask, "Do you want me to go back, Charlie?"

"I want you to be happy. If you're happier here, then you should stay."

"I promised your sister I wouldn't disappear. If I go back, she might think she scared me off."

He looks at me, his eyes so warm and dear. "I'll take care of her."

"You already do," I say, unable to keep the admiration out of my voice. "You're a good brother."

"I'd be a better boyfriend."

I smile at him. "Charlie Zelinsky, are you asking me out?"

"Yep."

"Even though we're from . . . different universes?"

"Yep."

I smile and give him a quick peck on the cheek, saving a bigger, better kiss for somewhere other than my driveway. "Yes, you can be my boyfriend. In this or any universe."

"Deal." He gives me a warm hug, and then lets go so I can climb out of the Jeep. While I watch him drive away, I realize that for the first time since I woke up in wonderland, I'm truly happy. So, why would I want to leave?

*   *   *

I stop in the kitchen for a snack, hoping to talk to Mom, but she has already disappeared upstairs. Tillie tries to make conversation with me, but after a while, I drift away. When I hear Mom talking on the phone, I head toward her room. Just as she hangs up, I tap on the open door.

"Hey, Mom."

She turns and meets my gaze, and then I see that her room is covered with open suitcases and clothes.

"Who was that boy?" she asks.

"Just a kid from school. We're . . . working on a science project together." For once, my age-old excuse is true.

She gives me a rare smile. "Well, it looked like some definite chemistry going on out there."

I nod and indicate the suitcases. "Looks like some definite packing going on in here."

"I'm going away," she says quietly.

Oh. I feel the impact of that in my stomach first, then all the way down to my toes. Moms don't *leave.* "Where?"

"I'm staying with my friend Deirdre at her condo in Boca for a while."

"And then?"

She shrugs. "I'm still deciding."

I take a step inside, studying her, trying to determine her mood. Like always, she seems closed up, protected, and . . . tight. Like always, I can't believe how much marriage to the wrong man affected her.

It's a lesson to me: marry wisely.

The image of Charlie—my sweet, caring, smart boyfriend—flits through my brain, but I put him away for now, concentrating on what I want to say to Mom.

"Listen, about that question I asked you about Mel—"

She waves a hand to silence me. "I'm sorry I lost my temper with you, Ayla."

"Well, you thought I was snooping—"

"You were snooping."

"But I wasn't." I can't stand it. I have to know where history changed in this universe. Encouraged that she hasn't kicked me out yet, I prop myself on a silk vanity bench. "Mom, can I ask you something?"

She nods, but her attention is on another top she's taking off a hanger.

"If you could do it all again differently, would you?"

That gets her to look up, her expression surprised. "Why?"

I shrug. "Just curious. If you could have chosen a different path, a different . . ."—*husband*—"life, would you?"

"I don't know. I can't."

"Would you have married Mel Nutter?"

She closes her eyes, the fight that was in them when I mentioned his name the other day gone now. "I never got a chance to figure that out," she says.

"Why not?"

She swallows and turns, disappearing into a closet. "I had my reasons."

I have to know. I follow her into a clothes cave that makes mine look like a kitchen cabinet by comparison. "What were they?"

She's way in the back, around a corner, in a shoe store. "None of your business."

"It is my business."

241

Scooping up an armful of shoes, she lets out a bitter laugh. "No, Ayla, it isn't. Your job of spying and digging for my missteps is over now. Dad won; I'm leaving, and I won't try to take one dime more than the state of Florida or the board of Forever Flawless deems appropriate."

"What were your reasons?" I ask again, not interested in her divorce settlement at all.

"Do the math," she finally says, clutching the shoes to her chest as she looks at me. "Trent was my reason."

Just like . . . my real mom. Only she got pregnant with me. This mom got pregnant with Trent, and me a year later. "You got pregnant?" I state the obvious, hoping it will get her to explain more. "But . . . you already knew Mel, didn't you? So how did that happen with Jim?"

"The usual way. Which is why I wanted you to protect yourself with Ryder."

"That's not what I mean. How did you end up with one man when you were seeing someone else?"

"I came down here to tell your father that I'd made a decision and I wanted to completely end things. He was very good at stringing me along. Still is. Anyway, I'd met Mel and . . . and, well, Jim talked me out of it. He's persuasive like that." She brushes by me, dropping a shoe as she goes. "My mistake."

I pick up the fallen stiletto and follow her. "What was your mistake?" Dropping the shoe? Getting pregnant? Leaving Mel?

"Marrying your father. I've never been good enough for him." She dumps the pile of shoes onto the bed and then systematically begins to smash them into corners of a suit-case one by one.

"I've never been young enough." She stuffs a shoe. "Pretty enough." And another one. "Smart enough." And another. "Witty enough."

I hand her the last shoe. "You're all those things, Mom. And if Jim Monroe doesn't realize that, he's an idiot."

She looks at me, and I see a world of pain in her tear-filled eyes. A world I never saw before. "Thank you, Ayla. I never thought you noticed."

"Of course I notice," I tell her, watching a tear fall just like it did that day in Walmart, when she cried because she wasn't rich enough, or whatever *enough* she longed to be. "You're a fantastic mom. You know that? You are patient and funny and loving."

She makes a soft, strangled sound, blinking more tears over her face, smearing her expensive makeup over her polished cheeks. "Why are you doing this, Ayla? You haven't had a kind word for me in ten years. You've always been . . . his. Daddy's girl and Mommy's enemy."

My insides shrivel up like a raisin for how wrong that was. "I'm sorry," I say softly, reaching for her without thinking.

She stiffens at first, then relaxes into my arms, wrapping hers around me, too.

"I wish I could make it up to you, Mom."

She strokes my hair, the way my real mom always did, the affection creating my own waterworks. "You can't do anything to change history, Ayla."

Really? That's where you could be wrong, Mom.

"But you can do me a big favor," she says, leaning back to look at me.

"Sure. What do you need?"

"Dad's having that dinner party here on Wednesday for the latest Forever Flawless franchise owners. I need you to stand in for me."

"Like, as the hostess?"

"You can do it," she assures me. "Just greet people, make sure the caterer and staff are on time, and keep the party going. That'll be easy for you. And you know how hard Dad works to give the image that we have a happy family. It's important to him."

I snort softly. "Then, he ought to make it real."

"Ayla, please. All you have to do is make small talk. Be nice to the new franchisees. Ask them about their plans and their facilities. That's all. That way, I won't be missed."

She'll be missed by me. But I agree reluctantly. "Okay, but can I invite a friend?"

"I don't know. The last time we had a party, Bliss got drunk."

"I was thinking of my, um, science project friend. Charlie. He's a good guy, really." So, so good. I almost add that he's my boyfriend now, but resist the temptation.

"He should hide that hideous car. Otherwise your father will have a fit."

I laugh softly. "I'll tell him. And, Mom . . ." I steal a glance at the suitcases. "Will you be back?"

"I don't know." She picks up a sparkly silver top, then discards it as if it won't fit in wherever she's going. "I guess it depends on what the universe has in store for me."

The question is, which universe?

She turns to me and pats my cheek. "I was wrong about you, Ayla."

"Wrong about what?"

"You really *have* changed recently. Where has this girl been all these years?"

I smile. "Living in her own world, I guess."

CHAPTER TWENTY-FIVE

Should I stay or should I go?

The eighties tune I heard when Mom (real Mom) forced me to listen to those obnoxious oldies stations in the car has been playing in my head for two days, and it still is as I dress for Dad's dinner party.

An earworm is better than my swirling thoughts, anyway. There are so many things in my brain, I can't seem to settle on anything but that musical question. And, OMG, what a bad, bad song.

I feel like I should be mature in my hostess role—which consists of pretty much nothing, I've learned. Still, I choose a simple black dress (if anything in its price range could be called simple) and strappy high heels.

Mom really did jettison out of here, and the only person

who seems remotely upset about it is Trent, who hasn't said anything in two days that didn't include an F-bomb. Really, Theo's burping back in the home universe is so preferable. Jimbo has been more visible, too, and I've got a weird feeling he's going to have a "friend" here tonight. How gross is that?

And speaking of friends, I haven't seen Charlie at school—where I've kept a seriously low profile—but we've talked and texted a jillion times, and all I know is that he has a lot of news from his conversations with the University of Miami physics professor. News he's going to give me as soon as he arrives.

My cell phone vibrates with a text that says he just pulled in, early as promised.

Charlie always keeps his promises.

And that is the other thing on my mind—Charlie and Missy and the lessons they've taught me already. Surely if he's able to figure out a way to get me from one universe to another, he can discover the cure for his sister's paralysis.

After a quick check of my makeup, I look around to see if I've forgotten anything. But everything's just as it should be—orderly, beautiful, perfect—in my room.

My room. When did that happen? When did this expanse of turquoise and lime green, chocolate and pink, with all its fabric and clothes and exquisite furniture, become "my room"?

The song lyrics torture me again. *Should I stay or should I go?*

First I have to find Charlie, and find out if I *can* go.

I hear his voice as I come down the hall, low and hardly

audible over the sound of the catering crew and dishes. But he's exchanging greetings with Tillie, and I notice I'm walking faster, my heart rate higher, my head buzzing like a million bees are in there.

Yes indeed, I have it bad for this boy.

Should I stay or should I go?

When I walk into the kitchen, he turns, and I suck in a little breath of surprise and pleasure. He's wearing a collared long-sleeve dress shirt, a tie, khakis, and the Sinatra hat tipped at a downright sexy angle.

He touches it. "I promised Missy," he says in an apologetic voice. "You know it was her Christmas present to me last year, and when I wear it, I—"

"Shhh." I stop him with a single finger to his lips. "It looks cute."

He places the lightest kiss on my fingertip and steps back to give me a very admiring once over. "Pretty," he says.

And the best part of that compliment is that I believe he would say the same thing if he saw Annie, with braces, no boobs, no butt, and a Ross Dress for Less outfit. That's what is so special about Charlie Zelinsky.

Should I stay or should I go?

"Can we talk for a few minutes?" he asks.

Tillie flicks her fingers toward the open doors that lead to the patio. "I'll holler if I need you, Miss Ayla."

Charlie follows me outside, taking in the infinity pool and waterfall and the spectacular view of the bay. On the lawn, three long tables are already set like we're having a wedding rather than a corporate dinner for thirty. It's not dark yet, but white lights flicker everywhere, and my father's giant boat—aptly named *Floating Flawlessly*—bobs at our dock.

"This place looks like a country club," Charlie says, turning to me. "And you sure look like you belong in it."

I wave off the compliment. "I'm dying here, Charlie. What did you find out?"

"A lot." We walk toward the dock, seeking privacy from the waiters and caterers milling around.

I open the gate, and we cross the dock, the breeze lifting my hair and carrying the scent of exotic flowers and salt water. I inhale it and the closeness to Charlie. It all smells so good. Nothing like I ever smelled in Pittsburgh.

Should I stay or should I go?

"It was the mirror," he says, yanking me from my reverie.

"What do you mean?"

"The mirror invention of your dad's. That's what put the image of you on the phone and transferred it to your computer. How did he make that? What parts did he use? How were they connected?"

I have to laugh. "I have no idea. He said he had PIN diodes and . . . rec . . . somethings."

"Rectifiers. Okay, I can get those. What else?"

I shake my head. "I don't know, Charlie. But I wasn't looking at the mirror when the lightning flashed and hit my window."

"But the image from the mirror was on your phone in your hand."

"Yes, that's true. That's the last thing I looked at before the lightning strike."

"Do you remember how you felt?"

"Tingly. Electrified. Numb."

He nods like a doctor considering symptoms before making a diagnosis. "What were you thinking about?"

"About . . ." I turn to the house, seeing it at an angle precisely like one of the pictures in the magazine. "This perfect house. And, of course, being the perfect girl who lived in it . . ." My voice trails off as I look at Charlie. "You think I somehow wished myself over the rainbow?"

He shakes his head. "Nope. There's a far more scientific explanation, but I've no doubt your thoughts guided you to this universe. The electrons that make up your body, every atom of *you*, had some sort of massive and sudden particle collision caused by the refraction of light, just at the instant that the membranes of two different dimensions crashed, transferring you from one universe to another."

Huh? "Are you saying I exploded and went through space?"

"Remember, you have to think of the universe not as *one* place with black holes and stars and planets, but as an infinite space that contains many, many individual universes, like giant bubbles that scientists call multiverses."

"I understand," I say, even though, come on, I don't have a clue what he's talking about.

"It's a growing theory of quantum physics," he adds, as if that will explain it to me.

"How many universes are there?"

He lifts his brows. "They're infinite, and you understand what that means, don't you, Annie?"

All I really understand is that I love it when he calls me

Annie. "That there's no end to how many universes there could be?"

"Yes, but more critical, there's no end to the possible combinations of time and events in those universes. Because they are infinite, one or even many of them have, in essence, replicated our universe, with the same history, or maybe slightly different. Maybe a universe where Rome didn't fall or Shakespeare never lived or—"

"Emily Zimmerman married Mel Nutter instead of Jim Monroe."

"Bingo."

I lean back on the dock railing, the realization finally settling over me. "But, Charlie, of all those infinite universes, what are the chances of my old universe bumping into this universe at that very instant?"

"The chances are good," he says. "Because of this." He taps my forehead. "Not only did the lightning bounce electrons—which is what light does when it hits a reflective surface, like, say your window, or even the screen of the computer you had open—it shot photons and electrons to many different places. The fact that you—your particles, which is all we're made of—traveled from that universe to this one was no coincidence at all. You were thinking about this life. Maybe you didn't realize it, but this universe, where your life is rich and perfect, that's where your particles went."

"But we're made up of more than just particles, Charlie."

"That's right. We've got that special something that makes us who we are. Your conscience, your self, your *you-ness*."

"My soul," I whisper, the first real understanding finally dawning of why I could be Annie on the inside and Ayla on the outside.

"I'm happy to say that your soul made the trip with you."

"What happened to Ayla? The one who lived here before me?"

"She didn't go anywhere. She's you."

Oh, confused again. Still, the fact that there is a science behind my situation is reassuring. "You're sure she's not living in that other universe?" I ask. "We didn't switch places? She's not running around Rolling Rock Road demanding that my parents give her non-strawberry yogurt while my brother Theo burps in her face?" Because, whoa, if this is heaven, poor Ayla must think she went straight to the other place.

"Well, to be honest, I'm not sure of anything, but, no. We—the physicists who study this kind of theory—don't think that's how it works. The physical 'her' hasn't gone anywhere."

For some reason, that's also reassuring. I don't want her being me—anywhere. "But what's happening in my old life, in my old universe?" I ask. "Who is controlling the decisions made by Annie Nutter back in that world?"

"She's probably still there, living the same life. But you—your consciousness—is here. Annie Nutter's probably going through her life with no idea that she's lost a piece of herself."

I shake my head, not understanding this at all. "So all that really came here in that . . . that particle collision is my consciousness?"

He places his hands on my shoulders, warm and strong and so competent that I just want to lean into him. "I know this is tough to understand, but it's the best Dr. Pritchard and I could come up with. He's excited, though, about the possibilities."

"The possibilities?"

"Of getting you back."

For a long, heart-pounding few seconds, I just let this thought settle over me. *Should I stay or should I go?* If both Annie's and Ayla's lives are going to continue, where do *I* want my soul to live? Here, or there?

"How would I go back, if I wanted to?"

Charlie lets out a slow exhale that pretty much tells me that whatever it is, it won't be easy. "To start with, we'd have to re-create your dad's invention," he says. "Only he knows exactly how he put that thing together."

"Yeah," I say, echoing the impossibility in his voice. "So what are the chances of that?"

He shrugs. "If you could find Mel Nutter living in this universe, and could convince him to make that mirror, you might—"

"My mom knows him!" I exclaim. "She's been communicating with him on the Internet. Maybe I can contact him."

"You could. But then what? Ask him if he happens to have invented a mirror that you could borrow during the next thunderstorm so you could be his daughter? He's going to think you're crazy."

I just smile. "You've never met Mel Nutter. He lives for crazy." At least, he did.

"So what do you want to do?" He gives my shoulders a

squeeze, and I know that whatever my decision is, he'll support it. How can you not adore a guy like that?

"I want options, Charlie," I tell him. I want to know where Mel Nutter is and if there's any chance of ever finding him. "Do you think you can hack into my mom's email? I mean, if I know the email address, is it possible?"

He laughs.

Twenty minutes later, he's sitting on my bed with my laptop, opening up my mom's email like it's his for the taking. He's wildly clicking keys, but I can still hear some voices and laughter floating up from the patio.

"Hurry," I tell him. "I only have a few minutes before my hostess duties begin."

"I'm in the email program. Help me look for his name."

I scoot over to get next to him, scanning the list of names, looking for Mel Nutter. No one in her email in-box or saved mail has a name remotely like that.

"Can you get into the deleted mail or sent messages?" He does, with ease. "You're a handy tool to have around, Charlie Zelinsky," I say with admiration in my voice.

He smiles, that not-quite-whole thing that lifts one side of his mouth and all of my heart.

"Nothing," he says, scrolling through a dozen or so messages. "She must delete and then delete the trash, too."

"What about the saved messages?" Surely something as special as communication with her ex-boyfriend would be in a saved file.

He slides the cursor over to the side and down the few files. They're named: doctor's hospital fund-raiser; book club; school communication.

"She communicates with the school?" Who knew she was that interested?

"That's all there is," Charlie says. "Except for this one, called one-four-three."

I gasp. "Wait! That's it!"

He stops the cursor on the three numbers. "One hundred and forty-three?"

Like music to my ears. "That's their code. One-four-three. The letters in—"

"I love you."

I know he's just finishing my sentence, but the words trip my heart anyway. "That's . . . right. That's what it means. Open that file, Charlie."

He does, and there's only one email saved in it. Without waiting for me to give the word, he clicks it open.

It's from Mel Nutter to Emily Monroe. Dated a month ago, with a subject line *Hello, old friend.*

Charlie glances at me. "You sure you want to read it?"

I nod, unable to stop myself.

But he doesn't scroll down to read the message. "Remember, Annie, this isn't your dad, at least not in the old universe where you used to live. This is Mel Nutter, here, in this world. Can you separate the two?"

I know he's gently warning me so that whatever I read doesn't upset me. But I nudge his hand so he'll scroll down. "Let me see what he says."

Hello, Em . . .

I can't tell you how great it was to
hear from you, however briefly. I could
have used some more information about
your life and family! But I understand
you were just saying hello to an old
friend after all these years.

My eyes start to tear so much that the words swim. I feel so close to my dad, but so far away. I lean back from the screen.

"Can you read it to me, Charlie?"

"Sure. He says, 'Things are good for me up here in Pittsburgh. I have to admit, it took a long time to get over you (ha ha), but I eventually got my engineering degree and have been working for Process Engineering for almost fifteen years.'"

"He always wanted to get that degree but never could afford to do it. That's good."

Charlie continues reading, "'It's a good job, but there's a lot of management now that I've moved up the ranks, and less time to fool around with my secret projects. Yes, I still have them! Got one I'm working on now that's sure to be a winner.'"

"He's still an inventor!" I'm so glad that some things never change, in any universe. "So maybe he can re-create the mirror." Just this tiny connection to a man I miss so much makes me happy. I lean on Charlie, closing my eyes. "Go ahead. Keep reading."

"'But what I'm most excited about, Em, is that I've finally found the perfect woman and I'm getting married.'"

Oh. I bite my lip and let him read on.

"'She's a single mom named Barbara, and I'm just crazy about her. I love her daughter, too, which is nice, since I thought the fatherhood ship had sailed without me. We're taking our vows on November seventeenth.'"

Charlie's voice has a funny hitch when he says that, but then I realize I'm squeezing all the blood out of his arm. Because my dad is getting married.

"That's this Saturday," Charlie says softly.

"I know." I just don't quite know how to feel about that. "Does he say anything else?"

"Yes. 'Funny how life works out the way it's supposed to, isn't it?'" Charlie reads on. "'I would have gladly given up my engineering career for you, but if I didn't work at Process Engineering, I'd have never met the temporary secretary for our department, who stole my heart. I love her very much and can't wait to be her husband, and can't wait to be a father to her girl. I'm going to adopt her, so when her mom takes my last name, so will her daughter, which is sweet. She'll have to endure all those bad jokes about being a nut when she goes from Lizzie Kauffman to—'"

"What?" I shoot up, the word caught in my throat. "He's marrying Lizzie's mom?"

"Do you know Lizzie Kauffman?"

"She's my best friend!" I can barely breathe. No, I *can't* breathe. Emotions I don't even understand are like sharp nails scraping over my heart. "That's not fair. He's my dad."

"Annie," he says softly. "Not in this world, he's not. And it sounds like he's happy."

Shame washes over me, trying its best to wipe away the

jealousy, and only partially succeeding. "And I bet Lizzie is, too," I manage to say. "She's wanted a father for as long as I've known her."

He looks at me, understanding and sympathy in his dark eyes. "I know it hurts to think about him in love with someone else, but at least you know his daughter will be someone you care about."

"But I'm his daughter," I say, my voice breaking a little.

He takes my face in his hand and holds it. "I told you, not in this universe."

I nod, more tears threatening. "He's getting married on Saturday."

"But he also says he's working on something exciting," Charlie points out. "You know, if that's the Picture-Perfect mirror and you could get it, you might . . ."

He lets his voice trail off.

"Stop that marriage?" I finish.

"I was thinking you might find a way to go live in the universe where that isn't happening."

I close my eyes. "I can't change what's going on in this universe, and I don't want to," I say to him. "But . . . if I have the chance to go back . . ."

He gently wipes my infernal tears. "You have to decide where you belong now, Annie."

"I like when you call me that."

"You know what I like?"

I shake my head.

"You." He places his cheek against mine. "I like you. That's one-four-three too, you know."

I smile. "One-four-three back at you, Charlie Z."

With that half smile in place, he kisses me. His lips are warm, tender, and tentative. But I angle my head and take the kiss, letting it send sparks all through me as he wraps his arms around me and deepens the connection.

Maybe this is where I belong. Right here, in Charlie's—

"Ayla!" The door pops open like a firecracker, jolting us apart.

"Dad . . ." I feel a whole different heat creep over me.

"Our guests have arrived," he says, his voice dark, his eyes locked on Charlie like he's an escaped convict. "You may leave now, young man."

"Dad, why?"

"Because you have work to do." He indicates for me to follow him out the door.

Slowly I get off the bed and give Charlie an apologetic glance.

"It's all right," he whispers, quietly closing the laptop and sliding it away. "I can show myself out."

Jim is still glowering. "Downstairs. Right now," he orders me.

I follow him out of the room, aware of Charlie behind me. At the bottom of the stairs, a couple is talking by the fountain.

"I found my daughter," Jim says, trotting down the stairs, his voice all bright and phony. "Let me introduce you."

The two people look up at me and smile, no doubt already informed what a *perfect* family Jim Monroe runs.

Fighting the urge to set them straight, I plaster a smile onto my face.

"Ayla, I'd like you to meet the newest Forever Flawless franchisees, Dr. Jack Passarell and his wife, Cynthia."

I step off the last step, extending my hand, knowing my duties. "So nice to meet you," I say. "Welcome to the Forever Flawless family." I wonder if Jimbo hears the sarcasm in my voice.

Evidently not, since he beams with pride.

"Where is your clinic located?" I ask.

"This is our second," Dr. Passarell says. "Both near Pittsburgh."

"*Pittsburgh?*" I can't keep the utter disbelief out of my voice. Still on the stairs behind me, I can hear Charlie's soft intake of breath. "You have got to be kidding me."

"Don't be so surprised," Mrs. Passarell responds defensively. "We do have cosmetic surgery in Pittsburgh."

"But *Pittsburgh* . . . Pennsylvania?" It can't be possible.

"It's not the steel city it once was," her husband replies quickly. "There's a lot of money in Pittsburgh, and a lot of need for this brilliant walk-in cosmetic surgery concept."

Mrs. Passarell raises a sharp eyebrow. "You should visit before you pass judgment, young lady."

Jimbo is scowling at me, no doubt thinking I've made the ultimate hostess faux pas by insulting the doctor's hometown.

"And you can see it," Jim adds. "I'm flying up to Pittsburgh in the company jet on Friday morning for some meetings, then the grand opening on Saturday. You should come to represent the family."

"To Pittsburgh? On Saturday?"

Should I stay or should I go?

I glance over my shoulder at Charlie, and he looks as torn as I feel. But something, something *down in my soul,* tells me the answer.

"I'd love to go."

CHAPTER TWENTY-SIX

The party eventually dwindles down to the Passarells, several noisy Forever Flawless employees, and one extremely attractive young woman named Sierra—not the same girl from Mynt, I might add—who has kept her balloon boobs within inches of Jimbo at all times.

I watch from my seat at the kitchen table, more content to stay inside with Tillie than with the guests. All of them, with the exception of Jim—he remains as sober as a judge— have deteriorated from somewhat relaxed to outright drunk. A few guests have stripped and gone swimming. One is dancing under the waterfall. Two more have a bottle of tequila, limes, and salt. I know enough about drinking to know that duo will be naked and in the pool after a few shots.

It's like homecoming, grown-up style.

Done with my hostess duties, I am antsy to figure out a way to get to Charlie. He texted me that he has something major to share, but he doesn't want to risk getting kicked out of the house again.

However, the limo driver is on a run, so I'm stuck for the time being. At the long granite-topped island, Tillie pauses in the nonstop act of cleaning the always immaculate counter, her eyes on the same woman I'm watching.

"You think that's the one who sent my mom packing?" I ask her.

Tillie exhales out a sizeable nose. "I think it was the one before her that really did Ms. Emily in, but, if you ask me, they're interchangeable."

"Sad," I say, resting my chin in the palms of my hands. "What's his problem, anyway?"

Tillie raises both eyebrows in surprise. "Miss Ayla, you know him better than anyone. You tell me."

"Peter Pan syndrome?"

She snorts. "Nah, he's plenty mature. I think . . ." She stops herself and swallows, as if she suddenly remembers who she's talking to. "That you should go find yourself something better to do than watch these people make fools of themselves."

"Finish your sentence," I urge softly. "I want to know what you think."

"Since when?"

Another person I still have to convince that I'm really different. "Since I became the new me, and have developed a genuine respect for your opinion. What do you think is wrong with him?"

She rounds the island, her attention fully on me now. "I think, Miss Ayla, that if you had been acting for the last sixteen years like you've been acting for the last week or so, this might have been a happier home."

My jaw slackens. "You think that Jimbo and the bimbo is *my* fault?"

"You've made it too easy for your mother to leave."

The accusation stings. "Me? What about him?" I point toward the patio. "And Trent! There are two kids in this family."

"But your relationship with your father has always hurt Ms. Emily. You shut her out. Until recently, anyway."

I think about that. If I stay here and live this universe as my life, can I change the course of this marriage? Can I get Mom to come back home? Can I get Jim to stop cheating?

Can I do more good here than there?

"Food!" Trent comes clomping into the kitchen. "Tillie, tell me there are mountains of leftovers." He lets out a burp that would bring Theo to tears of envy.

"You're disgusting," I say, more out of habit than anything else.

He looks at me like he has just noticed I'm here. "Well, if it isn't the laughingstock of Crap Academy. Listen, I'd really appreciate it if you'd wait until I graduate before you wreck the family name."

"What did she do?" Tillie asks.

"Just acted like . . . like . . ."

"Like a person with a heart and soul," I fire back.

"As if you ever had a heart and soul in your life." He

takes a container of milk out of one of the fridges and holds it up to his mouth. "I'm the one with those around here."

"You wouldn't dare." Tillie practically growls at him.

"I'm going to waterfall it, Tilster. No worries." He raises the bottle an inch from his open mouth.

"One drop, and you're dead."

He freezes just before the milk pours into his mouth. "Tillie, don't deny a thirsty man his milk."

"Dead."

I watch the exchange, aware of a dizzying sense of déjà vu. This is exactly how Theo and Mom interact. That tight longing seizes my throat again, the scene sucker punching me with homesickness.

On the table, my phone buzzes with a text.

Charlie: Hey, if you can get over here, I might have some answers for you. That is, if you want to go "home." Let me know. 143

I stare at the message and the numbers. *Our* numbers now. *I like you.*

"Don't kill Trent, Tillie. I need him to drive me to Hialeah."

Without moving the bottle, Trent slides me a sharp gaze from under thick lashes. "Why the hell would I do that?"

"Because you have a heart and soul."

Very slowly he lowers the milk without having taken a sip. "All right, I'll take you. But only because I got a new babe who lives near the Doral, and when I tell her I'm such a great big bro, she'll invite me and my guns . . ."—he flexes a bicep—"over for a ride."

Even Tillie has to snort at that, but I scoop up my phone. "Whatever it takes, big boy. Just drive."

Trent spends most of the ride on the phone arranging a booty call, so while he makes caveman conversation with some girl, I think a lot about what he said, what Tillie and even my mom said. And of course, Charlie.

Some people in this alternate world are starting to depend on me. If I leave, will the old Ayla return? Or can I leave enough of my soul behind to be sure things go the way I want them to go here on Planet Perfection?

I don't know, but I hope Charlie can give me some answers.

"Dude lives in the armpit of Miami," Trent says after he hangs up with his late date and cruises into Charlie's neighborhood.

"It's not that bad."

"So, you seeing this homeless kid?"

"He's not homeless, you jerk. Can't you be better than those kids?"

"Of course I am. I take after Mom, remember? You're the one who's all Monroe."

"Not all." I look out the windows at the flickering lights of a Cuban sandwich shop, unable to read almost any of the Spanish signs.

"You can have the business, by the way," he says. "I got another plan for my future."

Where did that come from? "I don't want the business," I tell him.

He gives a dry laugh. "Well, ain't that rich? Dad's bribing us with promises of power, and neither one of us wants it."

"I thought you were being groomed for the top spot."

"Mom and I are talking about starting a little real estate business. She's getting her license. Bet you didn't know that."

I didn't, and it tweaks me. "She'll be good at real estate," I predict confidently. "She has a knack for it."

He throws me a look of total WTFery. "How would you know?" he asks.

"Just an educated guess. Turn here. Third house on the left."

He follows the directions, tapping the steering wheel in time with the classic rock on the radio. "You know what, Ay?"

"What?" I brace myself for insult *and* injury. After all, this is Trent.

"This guy's been a good influence on you. I'm giving him all the credit for the new and improved, highly tolerable, and almost likable Ayla Monroe."

Charlie doesn't deserve the credit, but I let him have it. "I'll tell him you said so."

Trent slows down at the driveway, and I see Charlie on the side of the house holding a mirror and a flashlight.

"What the hell is he doing?" Trent asks, leaning down to look out the passenger window.

"Science experiment. He's a total geek."

Trent gives me a smile. "Whatever blows your skirt up, I say."

"Enjoy your, um, date."

"I plan on it, Sister." As I open the door and climb out, I pause, kind of expecting some kind of brotherly advice.

He burps, and I just laugh. I miss Theo in the worst way.

"He gonna bring you home?"

I look over my shoulder at Charlie. "Home is exactly where he's going to take me."

Trent narrows his eyes at Charlie, then nods approval. "Use protection, shit-for-brains."

"Screw you, dirtbag."

"Ah. There's the Ayla I know and can't stand. I knew she'd be back."

I'm still looking at Charlie and the mirror that reflects some moonlight. "Don't be too sure of that yet."

Because I'm not sure where I'm going, if I'm going . . . or why. Not anymore.

CHAPTER TWENTY-SEVEN

Charlie's so engrossed in what he's doing, he doesn't even look up when I approach.

He's kneeling over the mirror, surrounded by tools and circuit boards and multiple flashlights. On a stack of text-books, his laptop is open and a YouTube video is playing with no sound.

I drink in the scene, my knees almost buckling with the impact of still more homesickness. Will it never stop?

I suddenly want my family so much, it steals my breath. My mom—the one with a wrinkle in her brow and a little too much width around her waist. My burping exclamation-pointed brother, because Trent the Tool isn't as evil as I thought, but he isn't my obnoxious little brother.

And Dad. I miss Dad so bad because Mel Nutter kind of *belongs* in the middle of this all-too-familiar tableau of miscellaneous junk gathered together for an "invention." In a freakish twist of irony, he'd love this.

Charlie melts me with that smile. "How was the party?" he asks.

"Pretty lame, but I am flying to Pittsburgh on a private plane Friday morning."

"Cool."

Is it? Hard to tell how he feels about that. "What are you doing?" I ask.

Charlie doesn't answer immediately, adjusting the mirror a little and angling the flashlight, which is super bright, like a halogen bulb. "I did some more research, and decided to attempt an experiment."

"What kind?"

He fiddles with the electronics some more, moving wires on a circuit board. "I thought we could test the arrangement of matter and energy."

"Good times," I say with a laugh.

"It could be. I have a Geiger counter that can help detect the movement of quarks and gluons."

"Gluons? I take it you don't mean fake nails."

He chuckles softly and flicks the flashlight back and forth, adjusting the mirror. "He must be smart, your dad," he says.

"He is smart. And funny, and kind, and makes the best chocolate chip pancakes in the world." I sigh, and can't help adding that other bit about my dad. "He's also . . . a collector."

"What's he collect?"

"'What doesn't he collect' is a better question." I settle on a strip of stiff Florida crabgrass, a cloying honeysuckle smell hanging in the air just like the word I don't want to say. "I think there's another, less flattering name for him." I pluck at a sturdy blade that doesn't want to come out. "He's kind of a hoarder."

Charlie gently rests the mirror against the side of the house to give me a quizzical look. "Like on the TV show?"

"Not quite as bad. But . . ." Our house had been getting close. "Still, it's embarrassing."

Charlie looks hard at me, considering that. "Were you upset about it the night this all happened?"

"I don't know if I'd call it . . . upset."

"Was it on your mind?"

I try to go back in time—and space, evidently—and remember exactly how I felt that night. "I was more upset about my parents fighting, I think. Why?"

"Because what was on your mind, like exactly your emotional state, seems to be key to getting you back to that universe."

"So you said. But even something like that?"

"Here. Watch this." He guides me over to the laptop, and we sit in front of it while he starts that YouTube video from the beginning. It's a quantum mechanics physicist talking about parallel universes on some shaky home video taken in a college classroom, with particularly bad sound.

Charlie turns it up, and we lean close to listen.

Honestly, I don't get half of what the lecturer is saying. Until he gets to the part about the power of thoughts—

powerful enough to move us between two universes if all the other external factors happen to be lined up.

"In the instant when you have a fleeting thought, your whole body makes a quantum leap into a whole different dimension," the guy says.

Charlie pauses the video. "I think if we can somehow figure out how to spark the right light over the right mirror at the right time, you have to cooperate by having the right thoughts. That's why what you were feeling that night is so important."

I drag my legs up to wrap my arms around them and rest my head on my knees, thinking hard. "I had a lot of emotions going on that night," I admit. "I was feeling . . . cheated."

He waits for me, giving me some time to gather my thoughts and put them into words.

"I wanted a better life," I finally say. "Kind of like my mom, when she saw the magazine article about Jim Monroe. I wanted my life to just be . . . better."

"And is it?" he asks softly.

"In some ways, it is," I say. "Obviously, on the outside, it's better. I've got money and looks, and all the kids want to be me. Who doesn't want that?"

Charlie lifts an eyebrow, the minuscule gesture saying it all for him.

"You're different," I say quickly. "Most teenage wannabes crave more of that stuff."

"And that's what you were thinking, when the lightning struck? I guess it would make sense that you landed here, then."

"You mean, if I'd been thinking of something totally

different, I might have gone to some other universe? Like, if I'd been obsessing over . . ." I try to pull something out of the air. "My grades?"

"You might have landed in that universe where you have a one-hundred-and-eighty IQ."

"Getting bumped to fifth chair in orchestra?"

"You'd arrive in virtuoso universe."

"My pathetic love life?"

He grins, which sends a shower of chills all over me. "Maybe that would have dropped you into my lap." Before I can answer, he adds, "All I'm saying is, what's going on in your head is as important as where the electrons fly. Now look at this."

He reaches for a penlight on the ground and flicks it on. It emits a thin red beam. "Low-beam laser," he says. "Hold it and shine the light onto the mirror."

I do, and a few other red dots appear around it. "What are they?"

"The same particles of light going to multiple places at the same time. And some of them we can't see." He looks up at me, the red lights casting a soft glow on his face. "They're in a different dimension."

"I can't believe you figured all this out already."

"Not that much science involved, and I had help from Dr. Pritchard and the Internet. Now let's make this more complicated and add you to the mix. Get in front of the mirror."

When I do, of course, I look like Ayla. And I have an idea.

"Let me show you something," I say, sitting back down

next to him. I take out my phone and flick to the photo I changed with the Famous Faces app. "Will this help?"

"Is that Annie?"

"Not exactly. But closer than . . ." I gesture toward my image in the mirror. "This."

He studies the picture for a long time, and I realize I'm biting my lip. I'm so used to being pretty around Charlie. What will he think of the "real" me?

"You looked like that?" There's no judgment in his voice.

"Worse. Add braces."

He looks up at me. "I think I would love Annie."

For a moment, I can't speak, because everything in my body is up and running around doing a little happy dance. "You would?"

He smiles, a beautiful, sweet, honest smile. "Can you email this picture to me? So I have it?"

"Sure." I take the phone and send the photo as an email to his address. "She's kind of . . . plain. I mean, compared to this." I gesture vaguely toward my face. "So it might be a bit of a disappointment for you."

"Annie, it's not the outside of you that I like." He inches closer. "When are you going to figure that out?"

"Sometimes I still feel like the girl who gets asked to homecoming as a joke." I laugh softly. "I was, you know. Right before I came here. Some jerk said, 'Hey, homecoming's Saturday. Maybe you'd want to go with me.'" I close my eyes. "And I was the laughingstock of my bus because, you know, I thought . . ."

"Hey." Charlie puts his finger on my lips. "He didn't deserve you."

I'm frozen in the moment, in Charlie's eyes, near his mouth. I've never wanted anything as much as I want to kiss him.

"So forget that clown, and think about me," he says.

That's all I think about. "I can't believe this."

"Believe what?"

"That I finally meet a really, really great guy and I'm considering leaving him."

For a long moment, neither one of us says a thing. I can hear crickets and cars, wind in the leaves, and his next slow breath.

"You don't have to leave . . . Ayla." Reaching over, he puts his hand along my cheek and lightly runs his thumb over my lower lip.

Deep inside, things flutter around. All those things that were dead on the night with Ryder are very much alive and well and . . . fluttery.

"I like it better when you call me Annie."

"I know you do. And you know where Annie belongs."

Yes, I do. "No way I can go back and forth for a few years, is there?" I ask.

He laughs softly. "I hate to break it to you, but I'm not even sure you can go back at all. You may end up in some weird half-alive, half-dead state."

I suck in a breath and back away from his touch. "Are you serious?"

"Dead serious. Or you might have some random thought

about the queen of England and end up in London. But really, place is not the only variable that worries me."

"What is?"

"Time. Time is so critical. You know those red light particles that we don't see? They aren't just in another place; they could be in another time. That's what's really important about this experiment—that you get to the right moment of time."

I frown at him. "What do you mean?"

"I mean that for this to work, I think, you have to go back to that very moment when you were in your room, or at least the next morning, so that not too much could have happened without you in that universe."

I shake my head, unable to look away from him, my stomach tight and my limbs heavy and my mind so completely boggled by it all. "How?"

"Time is a continuum," he says. "So, for you to get to the right place, you have to more or less mentally erase everything that's happened to you since then. Just wipe it out of your mind. This life, this experience, this new family and school. Me."

"I could never do that," I say quickly. "I could never erase you."

He smiles. "Mind over matter, Annie. You can do anything."

All I can do is sigh. Trying to get back to who and where and *when* I was seems more daunting than ever. "I don't know," I say skeptically. "What if I think the wrong thoughts and go flying back to Timbuktu five years ago?"

An expression flickers over his face, a hint of darkness. "I wouldn't mind going back five years," he says softly. "But this is about you."

I know why he wants to go back five years, but don't know how or what to say. "What about Lizzie?" I ask instead.

"What about her?"

"If I go back, does it take away her chance of having a dad in this universe? 'Cause I can't do anything to hurt her, not in any universe."

"I don't know," he admits. "But going to Pittsburgh might make a difference in the scheme of things."

"How?"

"You're messing with the universe."

"Yeah, well, the universe messed with me."

Charlie's hand is still on mine, and he squeezes, pulling me closer. "You know, you might be one of the luckiest people in the world. You get to see both sides and make a choice."

I feel so close to him, so connected. Have I ever felt like this about anyone before? "Charlie . . ."

He leans closer, and our faces are inches apart. "I don't want to complicate your decision," he whispers.

"You already have."

He kisses me so softly, it's like a breeze on my mouth. Then I close my eyes and reach for him, letting him ease me back to the ground. His hands close over my face, holding me as we kiss, my heart beating so hard I can feel all my pulse points throbbing.

This is so different from Ryder, so different from anything

I've ever imagined. I just want to lie here forever, holding him, trusting him.

I smell fresh-cut grass, and the scent of something soft and musky that will always remind me of Charlie. Closing my eyes, I wrap my arms around his neck and sink into our kiss, dizzy with the pure bliss of it.

An alarm bell screams so loud, we both jump a foot.

"Oh, my God. What is that?" I ask.

He's up in an instant. "Something's wrong with my sister." He takes off toward the back of the house, and I push up and follow, hustling to keep up as he throws open the back door and charges to the bedroom hallway. On the way, he slaps a white alarm pad on the wall, silencing the screaming buzzer.

"Coming, Missy!"

He sails into a room, barely lit by a night-light. Right behind him, I come to a complete stop when he reaches her bedside. It's not a regular bed but very high and angled, like a hospital bed.

"Oh, Charlie, Charlie." She's sobbing. "I dreamed about the accident again, and it hurts. Everything hurts!"

"Shhh. Don't cry, Missy." He reaches over and holds her, and my heart—the one beating with a crush a minute ago— is breaking into a million pieces. "It doesn't really hurt. It's just your imagination. It's just your memory."

"It hurts," she cries. "In all the places I can't feel. I want to forget that day, but I can't."

"I know," he says tenderly. "Neither can I."

My hand is over my mouth, holding back my own sob of sympathy. I step back into the hall, away from a scene that seems so private that I shouldn't be here.

"Why did it happen?" she croaks in a husky, broken voice.

"I don't know, Missy." His voice is as defeated as hers. "Why does anything happen?"

I back farther away, a tsunami of shame drowning me.

How could I possibly be so selfish? So small? So wrapped up in whether I'm A-list or invisible, rich or poor, pretty or plain?

Melissa Zelinsky can't *walk* in this universe. And her brother, who loves her so much, is in as much pain as she is. If anyone should get to a better place, it's them, not me.

Is there any way I can do that for him?

CHAPTER TWENTY-EIGHT

I have one day left at Crap Academy before I leave for Pittsburgh, and two things to accomplish on this last day. I almost skip school completely because, well, no one really cares if I go or not. Jimbo isn't around, and my mom is living in some condo in Boca.

But I do go, mostly because I need to see Charlie. I haven't heard a peep—not so much as a text—from Bliss or Jade, but there's part of me that wants to say goodbye to them. Because what if I do find Mel, and he has a mirror, and I somehow travel through time and space and never come back here? The more I think about going to Pittsburgh, the more I think about not coming back here again. Maybe I'll just talk to Mel . . . or maybe lightning will strike twice. I have to be ready for anything.

When I get to school, I don't see Jade or Bliss outside by the fountain, so I head to their lockers, and on the way cruise by the eleventh-grade girls' bathroom. I'm just in time to see a few girls hustling out, mumbling unhappily, then sliding distrustful glances at me.

"Your friends probably want you in there," one says.

"Maybe not," someone else says. "Ayla's off the A-list."

"Yeah, she's one of us now."

"I wouldn't go that far," someone says snarkily.

But Candi Woodward steps out of the pack toward me. "Ayla's in a class of her own," she says, giving me a wide smile. "She's different."

The compliment warms me. "What did they do, kick you guys out again?"

"They think they own that bathroom," Candi says wearily.

"The whole school," another girl says.

Irritation slams me. "They only own it if you give them the power to."

"Easy for you to say," one girl whispers from the back. "You don't know what it's like to be us."

"No?" I fire back. "Well, that's where you're wrong. And you know what? They have nothing on you but some luck in the gene pool, street smarts on how to work the system, and attitude."

"So, what are you saying, Ayla? We can be like them and not be invisible?"

"Who wants to be like them?" I challenge. "They're mean and miserable, and they don't even trust each other. And you are *not* invisible."

Candi kind of laughs. "To them, we are."

"If you were really invisible, then who would treat them like royalty? Believe me, they need you to be very visible. Without you, they'd be center stage with no extras, no audience, and no props."

They kind of look at each other and laugh. "Right, Ayla."

"I mean it. If you didn't stare at them and part the hallways to let them by, they'd notice in a hurry, believe me."

"Maybe we should try it."

"Yeah!" a dark-haired girl says as she comes forward. "Let's treat them like *they're* invisible."

I shake my head, putting my hand out to stop her. "Then you're stooping to their level. Let's just take back our bathroom and not give them any power."

A couple move to the door. "Like the storming of the Bastille."

I laugh. "Without the guillotine."

They gather round me, and I realize I'm the de facto leader, which is fine with me. "You ready to go in?" I ask.

"Ayla," Candi says, holding me back, "are you sure? If you do this, you lose your queen bee crown for sure and certain."

"I don't want it." I link my arm with Candi's, feeling the first flicker of *true* friendship with another girl since I got here.

Together, we give the door a solid push, and the group of seven or eight follow, all of them laughing and whispering nervously.

Jade's hand shoots out of the last stall. "What part of 'You need to leave' don't you understand, Flute Fly?"

"I don't understand anything about you, Jade."

At the sound of my voice, Jade slowly steps out, taking in the minimob behind me. "What do you want?" she asks.

"We want to use the bathroom."

"Find another one," Bliss calls out from inside the stall. "You made your grave, Ayla, so sleep in it."

I roll my eyes, but Jade is looking hard at me. "She's with a bunch of invisibles," she says under her breath to Bliss.

Finally, the blond head leans out of the stall. "I'm serious, Ayla. We're not amused by your escape-ades."

"Oh, my God," one of the girls behind me says, and laughs. "She means 'escapades.'"

"She's an idiot," another whispers.

Bliss's blue eyes narrow at her. "And you're ugly."

"Really?" I demand. "How can you tell? I thought she was invisible."

There are snickers behind me, but Bliss is slowly stepping out of the stall. When she does, about six small handbags thump to the floor, tags visible.

"Get out of here, Ayla," she grinds out.

"We're using the bathroom, Bliss." I turn to my little posse. "Do what you need to do, girls. We have a few minutes before first period. Nobody owns this place."

Bliss just stares, and Jade shakes her head. "Why are you doing this, Ayla?" Jade asks.

"Why are you?" I take a few steps closer and glance at the purses, then bend over to pick up a satiny clutch that's been ruined by water—or worse—on the floor.

"Hey!" Bliss swipes it away, knocking it back to the floor. "You're not getting any of this."

"I don't want your stolen crap," I say, leaning against the

cool metal of the stall and crossing my arms. "And you don't need to shoplift to prove you're cool."

Jade immediately assumes peacemaker position, stepping between us. "Ayla, you've made some really bad decisions lately—including this latest stunt today—and we're just trying to figure out what to do with you."

"You don't have to do anything with me, Jade. Friends don't think about what to do with their friends! You like them. You support them. You have fun with them."

Bliss inches closer, still barely at my chin, even with high heels. "You got that right, Ayla. And you totally broke that code. You are acting like a complete tool, hanging out with nerds and geeks, and risking our position at this school so you can get some kind of social services award."

"That's not why," I say softly, a twinge of sympathy for her because I can tell she's choosing every word very carefully, not wanting to make a mistake and look stupid(er) in front of the very people she claims she can't see.

"Then, why did you change?" Jade whines. "What brought this on, really?"

I can't answer, so I shake my head. "I tried to see all this from both sides." I gesture toward the girls who are in front of the mirror, pretending to comb their hair or put lip gloss on, but listening to every word we say.

"And what'd that do for you?" Bliss challenges. "Make you all happy and whole and . . . and . . . *happy* inside?"

I smile at her. "It made me blissful. And you should try it. You'll find Bliss."

She rolls her eyes. "Oh my God with the Oprah crap."

Jade takes my hand. "Come on, Ayla. Just go back to

normal. This . . ." She nods toward the girls. "This isn't the natural way of things."

"That"—I point toward the fallen handbags—"isn't the natural way of things, either. Why shoplift when you have more money than most of the free world, or torture kids who are already living in hell, or cheat when you're smart enough not to? Why? Just because you can?"

"Because we're supposed to," Bliss says firmly. "That's our role in this place, and we do it better than anyone else. For that, we get into the best parties, treated like royalty, and respected."

"Respected?" I throw the word back at her. "Fear is not respect, Bliss."

"Get out of here, Ayla." Bliss tries to drag Jade back into the stall. "You don't belong in our world."

"I don't belong in a bathroom stall, that's for sure."

The girls at the mirror laugh softly, but I didn't say it to be funny. Bliss disappears, but Jade stays rooted to her spot, looking at me with sad eyes.

"I can't fight Bliss on this."

I shrug. "You have to make your choice. Listen." I reach for her hand. "I need to say goodbye."

"You're leaving?"

"For a while," I say vaguely. "I'm going to a clinic opening with my dad, and then . . ."

"You'll be back on Monday?" Jade actually sounds worried. She leans very close and whispers, "I bet we can work this out."

"I don't know. I can't make any promises about who—er, how—I'll be when I get back."

She gives me a weird look, but nothing I haven't become pretty used to over the past few weeks. "Maybe a little time away will be good for you. Especially with your dad. He always makes you see things the right way."

The right way. His way. Not *my* way.

"Yeah," I say, aware that the bell is ringing. "Now I gotta go find Charlie."

"Box boy?" Bliss chokes.

"His name's Charlie Zelinsky, Bliss, and he happens to be my boyfriend."

"Jeez, Ayla." Jade slips into the stall. "You are too far gone, even for me."

I turn and catch Candi's surprised expression in the mirror. She doesn't look away, though, and I see a glimmer of approval. I leave the stall and get next to her, leaning over to pick up her flute case.

She gives me a tentative smile. "Charlie Zelinsky is your boyfriend?"

"Yeah, he is."

"I know he gets a lot of grief, but I always thought he was kind of cute." She tucks a tube of lip gloss into her purse. "You know, kind of in a young Ashton Kutcherish kind of way."

"Exactly!" I say.

"It's going to be rough for you, Ayla." She puts her hand on my shoulder. "He's an outcast."

"They're my specialty. Anyway, it's going to be way worse for me when I make my next announcement."

"What?"

"I'm signing up for orchestra."

Her jaw flaps open. "What do you play?"

"Violin."

She gives me a squeeze and holds it. "The soul of the orchestra, I always say."

"So it is."

I'm still smiling when I head to English lit, but that grin disappears when I see that Charlie's seat is empty. I don't know why, but I have a very bad feeling about this.

CHAPTER TWENTY-NINE

By Friday morning, I'm a mess. I haven't heard from Charlie since the night of Jim's dinner party. He never came to school, he's not answering his texts or calls, and he hasn't been on Facebook.

If I had time, I'd go to his house, but Jimbo is on a tear to get to the executive airport and fly to Pittsburgh. He finally notices I'm upset when I climb into the backseat of the limo.

"What's the matter, Ayla?"

"Nothing," I assure him, settling into the cool leather of my favorite seat, already used to the family limo.

"You're not apprehensive about flying, are you?" He glances up to the always clear blue skies. "It's a good day for flying. I'll let you take the controls if it's smooth."

"No, thanks." Is he nuts?

"Is it that homeless boy?"

God. Him, too? "He's not homeless," I say without emotion. "I wanted to say goodbye to him before I left, is all. I don't suppose you'd swing by his house in Hialeah before we go."

"You don't suppose right. Hialeah?" He curls his lip. "Well, your mother had a weakness for losers, too."

"Evidently. She married one."

That gets me a dark, dark look. "Don't be a smart-ass. I meant her other boyfriends."

Does he know Mel Nutter? I don't want to get into it. I turn toward the window, hoping he'll just shut up.

"I Googled that boy's name after I saw him with his tongue down your throat."

Oh, boy. Here we go. "I'm sure you found lots of interesting information," I say.

"And I know about his sister."

I whip around to him, a sudden and fierce defensiveness rising. "What about her?"

"She's a—"

"Don't." I hold my hand out, no idea what he's going to say, but I know I have to stop it. "Don't say another word."

Fortunately, his cell phone buzzes, and someone else is the victim of his sarcasm and condescending attitude. I can just sit here and think about my plan.

Except, I have no plan. I was going to make one with Charlie, but then he disappeared on me. I couldn't find a street address for Mel Nutter in Pittsburgh, but I know where Process Engineering is, so I might go there as soon as I'm away from Jim, who says he has meetings all day today. Or go to South Hills High and pretend to be a new student, and check out my old lunch table. Or cruise by my old house on Rolling Rock Road.

I don't know what I'm going to do, because I wanted Charlie to help me figure that out. I really want Charlie to come with me, but now, considering Jim and his Googling, I decide this is better.

Still, I pull out my phone to check my text messages again—nothing new—and send one more to Charlie.

Am on my way to Tamiami airport. Leaving soon.

My fingers hover over the keyboard. Should I add 143? Make it more personal, more urgent?

I just hit send, and put my earbuds in to drown out the sound of Jim Monroe barking business into his phone. I watch Miami roll by, not so enamored of the palm trees and sparkling water now, bracing myself for the heavy skies and old brick buildings that make up so much of Pittsburgh.

Morning traffic is slow, but Marcel finally pulls us into the small airport out in the suburbs, and I see a row of private planes on a tarmac. I'll be getting on one of them in a matter of minutes.

Without having said goodbye to Charlie. Without a plan.

I climb out, and Marcel gets our two bags. Jim says he'll meet us at the plane and strides inside the tiny terminal, presumably to do whatever paperwork has to be done before flying.

"This way, Miss Ayla," Marcel says, gesturing with Jim's Louis Vuitton bag.

I start to walk toward the row of planes. The sun is already hot enough to warm the pavement under my feet. *This is a waste of time,* I think glumly. What am I hoping to accomplish here? The chances of getting to my universe are slim to none without Charlie's help.

All I'm going to do is—

"Annie!"

I spin around to see Charlie climbing out of his Jeep, waving.

"Charlie!" Flooded with relief, I run toward him, leaving Marcel behind. "Where have you been?" I ask, fighting the urge to throw my arms around him.

I don't have to fight long. He hesitates only a second, then reaches for me and holds me close, squeezing me so hard he takes my breath away. "I thought I'd missed you," he admits, his voice husky.

"Why haven't you answered my texts? Where were you yesterday?"

"Locked at UM, working on something with Dr. Pritchard." He clutches me tighter, and despite the fact that exhaustion has made his eyes red and a little swollen, I can see the joy and excitement all over his face.

That expression is eerily familiar. Mel Nutter, moments after an invention has been completed.

"What are you working on?"

"This." He reaches into the back of the Jeep and pulls out a backpack, handling it carefully. "For you to take to Pittsburgh." Slowly he pulls out a mirror, about the size of a laptop. "It's Picture-Perfect, and, Annie, it works."

He holds it in front of me and I see my reflection. Then he reaches behind it and presses a button, and . . . there's Annie. The picture I emailed him, but even more accurate.

"How did you do this?"

"Long story, but I haven't slept for two days." Even so, he beams, his smile sending a bolt of energy right through me. "It works, Annie. I mean with the light. It breaks particles up and sends them to a million different places."

My jaw loosens. "How do you know? You traveled to another universe?"

"I didn't," he says. "But we sent a few rats somewhere."

Now my mouth drops and basically hits my chest. "How?"

"Light, angle, and good thoughts. What you need to do, we think, is get as close as possible to the place where you were before. Even in your old house, in your old room. Even better if you can go at night and re-create the moment. Can you try?"

"I guess. I was thinking about going to my house."

"Here. I made a special padded case." He slides the mirror into the backpack. "It might work. It really might."

What if it does? I may never see him again.

He places the bag onto my shoulder, then runs his hand down my arm, giving me a squeeze. Looking up at him, I know I have to say what I've been thinking for the past day and a half.

"Come with me."

He doesn't react, but looks into my eyes.

"Please, Charlie. I can talk Jim into bringing you. We'll come up with a reason why you have to go. Please. I need you."

"Then I'll come home alone."

"Not if you travel to the other universe with me."

"I can't. I might be doing some traveling of my own."

"Really? Where are you going?"

His smile is sly. "I made two of those mirrors," he says.

"Meaning . . ."

"Figure it out, Annie. If I can get us to the right place at the right time . . ." His voice trails off, and I can finish the rest. He wants to leave this universe for a better one, too. A universe where Missy can walk.

I swallow hard. "But what if we're not in the same place together?"

"We might not be," he says softly. "But if we are, we'll know."

"You think so? How?"

"We'll need a secret code. Next time we see each other, we'll know who the other one is . . . or isn't, if only one of us knows the password."

For a long, long minute, we look at each other, the connection between us as intense as the blistering sun.

"What's in the bag?" Jim Monroe's voice makes us jump; neither one of us heard him approach. (Either because he's a sneak or because we were lost in each other's eyes. Or maybe both.) He's pointing at the backpack.

"It's nothing, Dad," I say quickly. "I'm trying to convince Charlie to come along on the trip to Pittsburgh."

He ignores that, reaching for the pack. "You're not taking anything on that plane I haven't examined," he says.

I step back. "It's personal. And you haven't seen what I packed, so that's just ridiculous. You aren't the TSA."

"My plane, my rules. Open the bag."

"It's noth—"

He grabs for it, yanking the bag off my shoulder.

"Hey!" Charlie yells, a hand up to stop him. "You can't do that."

He shakes off Charlie's touch. "I can do whatever I want. Open the bag, Ayla, or you can go home right now."

Ten minutes ago I'd have jumped at that offer, but now—with the mirror, with a plan, with *hope*—I don't want to give up this chance. What would it hurt to show him? With a quick shake of my head to Charlie to tell him to back off, I slide the pack over my arm.

"It's a mirror," I say. "Charlie invented it. He's a scientist. A physicist. A quantum . . . mechanic."

Charlie laughs softly. "Not exactly, but I doubt you'll be interested in my . . . discovery, Dr. Monroe."

"Let me see it," Jim says coolly.

I unzip. "It's just a mirror that changes the way you look." I take it out to let him see it. "He's giving it to me for . . . good luck."

Jim is staring at the mirror, his fingers reaching around the back to press the button. For a second it catches the light, almost blinding me. I gasp as I shut my eyes, half-terrified that I'll open them and we'll all be somewhere else.

But that doesn't happen. Instead, Jim Monroe's eyes are bugging out.

"Is this what you were talking about the other day in the exercise room?" he asks.

"Not exactly, but . . . a little bit." I hate that he has stuck his nose into this business, but there's nothing I can do right now.

"You made this?" he asks Charlie, unable to take his gaze from the mirror. He must like the version of himself he created.

"I had some help at the physics department of the University of Miami."

"Whoa." Jim angles the mirror back and forth. "This is sweet." He lowers it. "Are you some kind of inventor?"

"It was a class project."

At Jim's skeptical reaction, I add, "Charlie takes classes at the community college. He's a genius."

"I see that," Jim says, flashing a surprising smile. "It's good." He slides it into the backpack with far more care this time. "I'll take it to the plane for you, Ayla. Say goodbye to your friend. Sorry you can't come along, young man. Weight limit on the flight. Hurry up, now."

He marches away with the backpack in his arms. For a moment, we both look after him, then at each other.

"He's unpredictable," Charlie says.

"Yeah, and a whole lot of other things I don't like."

"Where were we?" Charlie asks, reaching out to me again.

"Saying goodbye." Leaning close, I put my head on his shoulder and wrap my arms around him. "I can't believe this might be the last time I ever see you . . . as me."

He nuzzles into my ear. "One-four-three, Annie."

"One-four-three," I repeat in a whisper.

"And four isn't 'like.'"

Oh. I close my eyes as he puts a gentle kiss on my lips, so softly, I barely feel more than a breath.

And then he's stepping away, his face blurry through my tears. I stand there for a minute, watching the red Jeep

Wrangler drive off before I jog toward the plane and up the stairs to board.

Then I turn to take one more look at Charlie Zelinsky, the boy with the heart of gold. He sticks his hand out the window of the Jeep, and even from fifty yards away, I can see him hold up one finger, then four, then three.

And four isn't "like."

I love you, too, Charlie.

"You've never seen anything like this, Frank. It's a freaking gold mine."

At the words uttered by my father, I turn to see him in the pilot's seat, a cell phone in one hand and the mirror in the other.

"We could put this in every clinic in the country and make a fortune. It's like magic. You just look better, damn near perfect."

I feel the hair on the back of my neck rise, hating him for seeing Charlie's effort as something commercial. It's my passport back to my real life.

"I'll take that," I say to him.

He shoots me a look. "Sit down and buckle up, Ayla. This thing is *mine*."

CHAPTER THIRTY

One thing I learn about Jim Monroe on the flight to Pittsburgh: He gets what he wants. Oh, and he's a really good pilot, but the flight is bumpy, so we don't talk much. When we land, he refuses to give up the mirror, and I give up the fight, planning to get it back from him later. At least he's letting me use the limo while he's in his meetings, so I know exactly where I'm going to start.

Rolling Rock Road.

Everything looks pretty much the same in this universe. Dreary and gray, as the 'burgh often is, weathered and blue-collar in parts, a chill in the air, some potholes in the roads. The 1950s houses and nearly bare oak trees all seem so lackluster after Miami. There's no vibrancy in this town, no sizzling culture, no over-the-top cruise ships, no stately palms, and no heartbreakingly blue skies.

And there's no Charlie.

I'm clutching the buttery leather seat as the limo turns the corner to Rolling Rock Road, and I peer down the hill, a wave of familiar longing washing over me as the memories do.

I've given the driver my old address, but as he pulls up to 4628 Rolling Rock, I have to look hard to be sure it's my house. It's painted a soft yellow, and the windows are different. There are flowers everywhere, and two giant oak trees that were never there in my universe.

But the general size and shape is the same, including a little dormer upstairs that I know makes a really awesome fort, and the window on the first floor looking out to the side is in a pretty snazzy girl's bedroom. Not turquoise, lime green, and chocolate, but *mine*.

As we slow to a stop, I notice that the garage door is open and a woman in a pink suit is walking out to the driveway. She's looking up the street when her attention lands on the limo.

She looks so familiar, but I can't quite place her. Then another person runs into the driveway, and I almost scream.

Lizzie! So that's her mom, who looks totally different—brunette, slender, and fit. Lizzie and her mom live in my old house!

I tap on the privacy screen, not giving myself a moment to think this through. "Stop now," I tell the driver. "I'm getting out."

He brings the limo to a halt, and I can see the disbelief on Lizzie's face. Limos don't cruise Rolling Rock Road in *any* universe.

I grab the door before the driver can even get around to help me.

"Do you think the girls sent a surprise limo for the shower?" I hear Lizzie ask her mom.

"Or we just won Publishers Clearing House."

"Neither," I say as I climb out. "I came to find Lizzie."

Lizzie takes a step forward, her mouth in a little O shape, her forehead all squished up like she gets when she totally doesn't understand something.

"Do I know . . . Holy guacamole! You're the girl from Florida on Facebook. Ayla?"

I beam at her, ridiculously happy she recognizes me. "My dad had to come to Pittsburgh on business, so I decided to join him and, you know, check it out." I'm walking toward her, my arms aching to hug her and do our little dance of joy after we've been apart for a while.

But she doesn't exactly look joyous. "How'd you find me?"

"Lizzie, you didn't put your address on Facebook, did you?" her mother asks, equally skeptical about my arrival.

"No, no," I assure them both. "I just . . . have this really amazing software"—called my life in another universe—"and, like I told you, I might be moving here. But I'm not a stalker or anything. I thought it would be fun to meet."

Lizzie gives me a shaky smile. "Yeah, it is. Um, Mom, this is Ayla. . . ."

"Monroe," I supply, the name feeling so false on my lips. I reach my hand out to Lizzie's mom. "It's nice to meet you, Ms. Kauffman."

"About to be Mrs. Nutter," Lizzie says brightly.

I feign happy surprise. "Really? You're getting married?"

"Tomorrow," she replies with a smile. "In fact, we're on our way to a little wedding shower luncheon some friends are having for me. And we're late."

"Oh, I'm sorry."

"Too bad we can't take that," Lizzie says, pointing to the limo.

"You can!" I almost grab her arm to pull her closer to the limo. "It's mine for the day, and you are more than welcome to use it."

"That's not necessary," Ms. Kauffman says quickly. "My fiancé is on his way here to take us there."

Her *fiancé*. Mel Nutter. I have to see him. I *have* to. "Are you sure?" I ask them. "He can come, too."

"Mom!" Lizzie says. "We could arrive in style!"

But Ms. K. just shakes her head, then points over my shoulder. "Here he is now."

The limo pulls up to give some room to the approaching car, and I realize my whole body is shaking a little as I turn to see the man climbing out of the driver's seat. *Please don't be different, Dad*. Please don't be changed. Please be . . .

Dad.

Oh, he is! He really is. Okay, this universe has been a little kinder to his hair—or maybe Ms. Kauffman is a better haircutter than Mom—and he's wearing contacts or had that eye surgery, because Mel Nutter is bat blind. And he definitely has more money and better taste in clothes—or he's totally overdressing these days for RadioShack. Oh, that's right. He's an engineer in this universe.

"I know I'm late, Barbara," he says as he closes the door. "But you didn't have to call a limo."

"That's mine," I say.

Lizzie jumps in and makes the introductions, telling him I might be moving here, giving me a chance to shake his hand, too. He's stronger, this new dad, maybe hitting the gym more or saying no to those Polish sausages he loves so much.

Then he heads right to Barbara Kauffman and lays one right on her lips. "Hello, gorgeous."

Gorgeous? She isn't . . . Well, she is also a vastly improved model. Lizzie, I'm happy to say, looks exactly the same. Freckled, pretty, grinning at her new dad.

Dad.

Jealously pinches, and I work it away. "I'm offering my limo, Mr. Nutter," I say. "My father let me have it for the afternoon, and you are more than welcome to take it to the luncheon."

He shakes his hand and gives Lizzie a wink. "Well, la dee and la dah, the girls can go in a limousine. That's very nice of you, young lady. What bank did your dad rob?"

I laugh. "He owns Forever Flawless, the chain of walk-in cosmetic surgery clinics."

His whole face changes, and his mouth drops wide open. Oh, *no!* I instantly realize my mistake. He's been in touch with Mom. What if she told him what Jim Monroe does?

He's going to think that's why I'm there. He's going to know who I am.

Slowly his gaze moves to Ms. Kauffman, and they share a look that includes matching shock and awe. She knows about my mom, too?

I brace myself for the what-the-hell-are-you-doing-here attack, but both of them speak at the same time.

"Forever Flawless?" their voices rise in unison.

"Oh, my God, Mel. It's like a sign from above," Ms. Kauffman whispers from behind the hand that's covering her mouth.

"This can't be happening," he adds.

When they both look at me, only one thought registers: *They look too happy to be mad.*

"Are you serious?" Mel asks. "He owns Forever Flawless?"

"He does." My heart is almost back to normal. "Is that . . . a problem for you?"

"A problem?" Ms. Kauffman is kind of hopping up and down in her pink high heels. "No, it's an—"

"An opportunity!" Mel says, that wild look in his eyes that I remember so well. "A golden, amazing, wonderful op-portunity."

"Now, Mel," Ms. Kauffman says, putting a hand on his arm. "This poor girl is going to think we're crazy."

"We are," Lizzie says, stepping into the fray. "Welcome to the Nutter-house, as we like to call it."

That's what we called our family, I think with another twinge of envy. Okay, more than a twinge. I'm pretty twisted up with jealousy, even if that nickname came from another universe, but I manage a smile.

"What's the opportunity?" I ask.

"Let's take the limo," Ms. Kauffman says. "And stop by Mel's house on the way. Ayla can come with us."

Mel brightens, then shakes his head. "You can't be late for your own wedding shower," he says.

"Seriously, Mom. Do we really want to drag Ayla to Dad's house?" Lizzie argues.

She calls him *Dad? Already?* "I'm game for anything," I assure them. "What's the big deal?"

"I don't care about being late," Ms. K. insists. "They can't have a wedding shower without me! I'm the bride. And this . . . this . . ." She gestures toward me. "Is too good to be true."

I'm totally confused and must look it, because Mel gives me a sympathetic pat on the shoulder. "You thought you were taking a little tour of your new town," he says. "And here we are dragging you into our adventure."

"What adventure?" If someone doesn't clue me in, I'll go crazy.

"Ayla," Lizzie says. "We've been trying to get to the top management of Forever Flawless for ages with an idea my about-to-be dad has to sell to their clinics."

An idea? I can't help smiling at him. Some things never change, even across time and space. "What is it?"

"It's a—"

"No." Ms. K. cuts him off. "Let's show it to her. Let her see for herself."

"Come on, Ayla," he says, putting a friendly hand on my back. "Let's go take a look."

"Thank you, Mr.—"

"You can call me Mel. Heck, you can call me anything you want."

I know what I want to call him.

Dad.

I have a sneaking suspicion what this invention might be, but manage to tamp it down and talk to Lizzie in the limo.

Mel lives a few miles away, and we pass South Hills High on the way there. It looks pretty much the same, white brick and jail-like, but Lizzie shows it off as though it's the best high school in the world. Did I love it that much when I was here?

"My mom let me cut today," she tells me with her brown Lizzie eyes dancing as they always do. "Because of the wedding." She makes a little "eek" sound and glances at Mel and her mom, who are cuddled in the corner of the back bench, whispering to each other in between asking me questions about my possible move to Pittsburgh.

I'm just making stuff up when I answer, trying to act really happy, even though my dad is marrying my best friend's mom. Because, inside, I'm not happy. I'm crazy with jealousy, my mind spinning with plans to get Mel to meet my mom in Miami and steal him away from Ms. Kauffman.

But that's *wrong.*

So, I go along for the ride, resisting the urge to ask Mel a million questions like: Why did you let my mother get away?

In a matter of minutes, we're pulling up to a pretty nice

two-story house in the next borough, set on a hill and sur-rounded by trees. Looks like Mel has more cash in this uni-verse, just like his ex/other/former/better wife.

"We'll go through the garage," he tells me, that bounce of excitement in his step that I remember so well.

"Isn't he great?" Lizzie whispers to me as we follow him.

I give her a shaky smile. Yeah, he's great. *He's my dad!*

But, then, I didn't think he was so great all the time when I lived with him, did I? So maybe she deserves him. And I mean that in the nicest possible way. Maybe I just didn't appreciate the old goof when I had him, and this is the universes' (both or all of them) joke on me.

"He seems really nice," I say casually. "I guess you're happy to have a dad."

"Oh, you have no idea." She loops her hand through my arm, a move so natural it kind of takes my breath away. She's affectionate like that, and I welcome the connection. "My mom has been single since I was two. I don't even remember my real father. But this guy . . ." She nods toward Mel as he unlocks the side door into the garage. "He's everything I ever wanted in a dad."

"Everything . . . ," I begin, but then I kind of freeze, staring at the garage.

It's spotless. I mean, it looks like the *Clean House* crew left about five minutes ago. Containers are stacked and labeled, tools are hung on a Peg-Board, the floor is so clean you could lick it.

"It's so neat." I can't keep the dismay and shock out of my voice.

And disappointment. Why couldn't he have been like that with us?

"Mel's a neat freak," Ms. K. says, giving him an affectionate hug. "It's going to be a challenge for us, but I'm changing my sloppy ways."

For some reason, this hurts more than anything. More than the wedding, more than Lizzie being my dad's daughter. What did we do to Mel Nutter to turn him into a hoarder?

I swallow that guilty thought and ask, "So, what did you want to show me?"

"It's in the basement," Mel says. "C'mon down." He opens a door that leads to the cellar, on the same level as the garage, like it is in many houses built on the side of hills. But this is no cellar. It's not even fair to call this a finished basement.

This is a game room, complete with pool table, bar, leather couches, and a massive flat-screen TV.

"I think I could have some great parties down here," Lizzie says.

"So, you're moving in here?"

"Next week, after they're officially married and back from the honeymoon. Who would want to live on Rolling Rock Road when we can move up to this?"

"Now, Lizzie," Ms. Kauffman says quietly. "For one thing, I doubt any of this is very impressive to a girl who arrives in her own limo. For another, money isn't what makes a family happy."

You got that right. I smile at her and follow Mel around the corner to a separate room.

"This is my work area," he says, almost apologetically,

holding up a hand before I enter. "So it's not as pristine as the rest of my house."

Thank God, a glimmer of the man he once was. Maybe I'll find a stray screwdriver that hasn't been filed under S. Hopeful, I follow him in, then stop again.

I knew it. I just *knew* it.

CHAPTER THIRTY-ONE

"Wow," I manage to say, the word sticking in my throat. "That's amazing."

His prototype is way more sophisticated than the first one I saw. This mirror is much better quality than the one Mel made in the other universe, with no hot-wire mess coming out from the back, no red numbers stuck on 143.

"Well, you're already at your ideal weight and completely gorgeous," Lizzie says, stepping next to me. "Look what happens when I stand in front of it."

I'm a little dizzy. A little breathless and wobbly and stupefied as I stand in front of the mirror. Waves of déjà vu roll over me, making me nauseous.

"Isn't there a computer or iPhone to, like, run it?" I ask.

Mel looks surprised and impressed. "Good question,

young lady. I have incorporated the computer into the mirror. Think of it as a network of circuitry that's already in place. Very delicate, of course, but when we manufacture the real thing, we'll make it sturdier."

"Looks pretty sturdy to me," I say, especially compared to the one my mother destroyed with a magazine.

"We call it the Dream Mirror," Mel says. "But that's just a working name. If one of these puppies goes into every Forever Flawless, they can call it anything they want."

"You see why we want your father's wonderful company to look at this," Ms. K. says excitedly, stepping beside Lizzie to see herself in the mirror. "I mean, if you can see what the results will be before you get plastic surgery, it'll just make you want more. I mean, if you can be picture-perfect, then—"

"That's what you should call it," I say. "Picture-Perfect."

They all just stare at me for a minute, then break into a chorus of hoots and hollers.

"Yes!"

"Oh, my God. Brilliant!"

"I love it!"

They're all jumping up and down and excited, especially Mel, who might be *neat* in this universe, but he still isn't *cool*. My heart is just floating and breaking at the same time, and all I want to do is throw my arms around him and call him Daddy.

"Do you think your dad would like to see this?"

"I'm sure he would," I say without thinking. He's already stolen Charlie's mirror for the same reason. He'd positively blow a gasket over one this sophisticated-looking.

"Can he look at it today?" Ms. K. asks. "I mean, we're kind of busy tomorrow."

"I don't know." I consider that as they all stare at me expectantly.

"I know it's a lot to ask," Mel says. "But this is like serendipity, you dropping on our doorstep. Like it's meant to be."

Yes, it is. And maybe if I had access to *this* mirror, I'd have an even better chance of throwing those electrons and photons and gluons into the right place. Or maybe I could just help this man, who, in another life, means the world to me.

"Let me call him and see if I can get him over here."

The three of them explode with shouts and hoots, and you'd think I'd just arranged a meeting with the queen.

"You can do that?" Lizzie squeals, hugging me. It feels so good to hug her again, I think I would promise anything at this moment.

"I'll try," I say, squeezing tight. "If I tell him what it is, I have a feeling that he'll be here very soon."

"Then, call him," Ms. K. says. "And while you do that, I'll phone the girls and tell them I'm going to be late for the shower."

"No, Barb," Mel insists. "I'll stay here with Ayla if her dad can come over. You can't miss your own wedding shower."

"Not a chance I'm leaving until we know if he'll talk to you." She grabs Mel's arm and pulls him close. "This could be the best wedding present ever. This is the most brilliant idea you've ever had, and you've had quite a few doozies."

That's for sure.

Mel stares at her, a little lost, like he used to look at Mom on Sunday mornings when she'd make coffee with her pajama top on inside out. "I love you so much, Barb," he tells her.

My whole body kind of dissolves.

"Ooookay," Lizzie says with an uncomfortable laugh. "Awkward!"

"There's nothing awkward about love," Ms. K. tells her, pulling away just enough to put her arm around Lizzie and face me as part of a threesome. "Nothing awkward about being a happy family. Right, Ayla?"

"Right." I already have my cell out, so I wave it and step away. The power of all this happy love is almost too much to take. "Why don't I call my dad, then?"

I dial in the other part of the basement, perched on the armrest of the cushy leather sofa. No pleather in this universe for Mel. My eyes are drawn to a wall of certificates and awards. A diploma from Penn State College of Engineering.

That's what he always wanted, but never had the time or money for. But without a surprise kid—*me*—he was able to achieve his dreams. He's got everything now.

Lizzie comes out to stand next to me while I'm dialing, giving me that big old Lizzie smile. The one she gave me in second grade when the other kids made fun of the ribbons my mother had put in my hair. The one she saves for me after school when we get on the bus and dive into a day's worth of gossip. The one I love.

"What is it, Ayla?" Jim Monroe's voice breaks into my thoughts.

"Oh, um, Dad, I need to tell you something."

Lizzie steps away to give me privacy, but Jim says, "I'm very busy."

"But this is important. You know that—"

"Oh, for Christ's sake. Whatever it is, just buy it. I'm in a meeting."

"I don't want to buy anything. I need you to meet me some—"

"Ayla, I am too busy to turn this into some kind of vacation trip. You've got what you need. Now let me—"

"It's about the mirror." I turn away and whisper the last word.

Silence. Then, "What about it?"

"I am looking at a much larger, much more refined, much more impressive version."

A longer silence. "How is that possible?"

"Because it is," I say softly, making sure the others can't hear me. "This one not only changes what you see but shows you your ideal weight and body mass index. This one is even better than the one you have." Which, it occurs to me, he will return to me once he sees Mel's mirror.

"Holy shit. Where are you?" Jim asks.

"I can send the limo for you," I tell him.

"All right. I'll come and see it."

I go to the other room and give them a thumbs-up, causing a frenzied cheer.

"What is that noise, Ayla?"

"It's just a family."

A really happy family. I try to ignore my jealousy, but it's not easy.

Mel convinces Ms. K. and Lizzie to go to the wedding shower, sealing the deal by suggesting that the limo driver drop them off on his way to get my dad.

I wait in the kitchen, looking around at the world this man has made of his bachelor home.

It's clean, organized, spare in décor, but what's there is obviously high quality. The house needs a woman's touch, that's for sure, but not to make it any neater. Just to make it less austere.

"So," he says, bounding into the kitchen. "Can I get you a soda, Ayla? Water? Something to eat?"

"No, I'm fine, thanks. Your house is pretty."

"Probably not as pretty as yours."

I shrug. "Ours is fancy."

"Well, I'm a confirmed bachelor, so mine's not so fancy. But now? Guess that will change with two ladies living here." He gives me an easy smile, then opens the fridge and grabs a cold bottle of water, holding it up. "You sure?"

"Okay, I'll take water." Because my throat is dry, closed up with words I want to say but know I shouldn't.

"So, what do you do, Mr. Nutter?" I know the answer, but it seems appropriate to make small talk.

"I'm an engineer," he says, twisting the top off his water and flipping it easily into the trash. "Dull as dirt compared to your dad."

I shake my head. "You're not dull. You invent cool stuff."

"Never really sold anything, though."

"What else have you invented?"

He takes a long pull of water before he answers. "Well, my favorite was this device that—don't laugh now—made sure you got the same amount of toilet paper squares every time."

"The Rip-Off." The words are out before I can stop them.

"Excuse me?"

"That would be a good name for something like that," I say quickly. "The Rip-Off."

He laughs softly. "Except that has some pretty negative connotations, being ripped off."

Exactly what he said in that other universe. "What else?"

"Oh, nothing very special. A beach blanket."

With flip-flops to hold it down. "Not a lot of demand for those in Pittsburgh."

"That's what they told me." Leaning against the counter, he regards me closely, an odd smile on his face. "You know, you remind me of someone, and I can't pinpoint who it is."

My gut tightens. I know who I remind him of—my mother. I know Mom's been in touch with him, at least exchanged one email, but she didn't tell him she's married to Jim Monroe of Forever Flawless. At least, I don't think so. Or wouldn't he have asked her for the introduction?

"Do I remind you of a movie star?" I joke with an awkward laugh.

"No, that's not it." He narrows his eyes, tilting his head, studying me like an artist about to paint a portrait. "But it's someone."

"I get that a lot," I say, taking a sip of the cold water. "I must look like a lot of people."

"Your eyes are green, but you still remind me of . . ." I see the moment it dawns on him.

"Someone special?" I ask.

He searches my face. "Where did you say you live again?"

He's going to put two and two together really soon. He's a smart engineer, and I'm in over my head. "Miami."

A little color drains from his face. "Ayla . . ." His voice trails off. Did she tell him her children's names in the email exchange?

"I'm Emily Zimmerman's daughter," I say flatly. "I think you might remember her."

The rest of the color goes, leaving him pale and a little stricken. "What are you doing here?"

"Nothing," I say at the accusatory tone. "I wanted to meet Lizzie and—"

"Emily sent you here."

"No." I stand quickly, ready to defend my mom. "She didn't. She has no idea I'm here. She'd kill me."

"But you've talked to her about me." I can hear the words strangling him. It's like he's scared of her. Or me. Or the past.

"Not really. I mean, you are her ex and she has mentioned you."

"Jim Monroe." He says the name slowly, and I can practically hear the puzzle pieces snapping into place. "I knew she went to see a guy named Jim . . . then never came back. I didn't know her Jim was *that* Jim."

We both hear a car door slam outside.

That Jim has just arrived.

"I can make him leave," I say, but even as I do, I know it would be next to impossible. Jimbo wants to see that mirror, and now I've got to deal with this.

All Mel does is shoot me a dark, distrustful look as he walks to the door.

"Mr. Nutter, really, this has nothing to do with . . ." *You.* That's not true. It has everything to do with him. "My mom."

He ignores the comment and heads outside.

"Hello there!" I hear Jim's boisterous, upbeat used-car-salesman's voice. "I'm Jim Monroe. And I hear you've got a magic mirror, my friend."

I head out slowly, like I'm moving through water, wishing I could change the last two hours. Two days. Two weeks.

I see them shake hands, Jim like he's pressing the flesh, Mel like he's reluctant to touch the other man.

"It's right in here," he says, directing Jim back to the basement door.

Jim barely says hello to me, and if Mel notices that, he doesn't say anything. I follow them through the game room to the workroom, nothing but agony in my head and heart.

My real dad doesn't believe me. He thinks I have some ulterior motive in coming here.

Well, he's right, isn't he?

"This is what we call the Dream Mirror," Mel says, indicating the mirror with a little less pride than before. He spares me a quick look, his eyes still full of suspicion.

That hurts, so I just stay in the doorway to observe. Maybe if Jim loves the mirror—and how can he not?—then Mel will forget his accusations, or forgive them.

"The concept is pretty simple," Mel says. "But the execution is actually quite an engineering feat. You see, by programming the—"

"You patent this yet?" Jim asks, practically shoving Mel aside as he circles the mirror on a stand.

"Patents for some of the individual components are pending, but I—"

"Anyone else see it?"

"Only some family and friends. I thought I'd—"

"No other plastic surgeons?" Jim stops in front of the mirror.

"No, sir," Mel says, his voice softer. "I was trying to get to Forever Flawless first, since you are—"

"The only franchise of walk-in cosmetic surgery clinics in the world," Jim interrupts, then beams at the mirror, then at Mel. "You're smart."

"I had a heck of a time with your lower-level management. No one wanted to talk to me."

Jim steps away from the mirror, shaking his head. "Well, I don't know, Merv."

"Mel."

"I just don't know." Jim circles again, until he's crouching behind it. "Looks complicated and expensive."

Mel inches around to the back. "Well, a prototype is, of course, but if you mass produce . . . Uh, be careful, Mr. Monroe."

"What's this—"

From where I'm standing, all I can see is the mirror shimmying a little, and shaking. Mel lunges forward just as Jim stands so fast that he loses his balance, grabs the side of the mirror, and it topples, everything moving in slow motion.

Mel's sudden shout is drowned out by the crash and clatter of a thousand pieces of broken glass, wires and tiny semi-conductors poking out of the shards.

"Oh, Lord. What have I done?" Jim says, giving the glass and wires a quick kick.

"Dad!" I scream, coming forward.

"Stay back, Ayla! There's glass everywhere."

Behind the mirror, Mel is on one knee, a hand on a splintered wooden frame, speechless as he stares at the mess.

The expression is eerily, frighteningly familiar.

I stare at Jim as he gingerly steps over glass. "Why did you do that?" I ask.

"I didn't do anything on purpose, Ayla." He brushes his hands over his pants, as if he can wipe the guilt away. Then he bends over and picks up a sizeable chuck of mirror, turning it over like he could find something to blame. "I lost my balance, for Christ's sake. Really sorry about that, Merv."

Mel finally looks up, still unable to form a word.

My heart feels a little like the mirror. Shattered.

"What?" Jim asks, pointing at Mel with the shard. "Look, pal, you're lucky I'm not the litigious type. You got a big fat lawsuit waiting to happen here. And, sorry, I'm not interested in your little fun house mirror. It's not the kind of thing we could trust at Forever Flawless. We're not about visualization tricks. I run a medical practice and we don't need gimmicks, just the finest doctors with excellent skills."

That nausea rises again, and this time, I really think I might throw up.

Mel is still stone silent.

"Come on, Ayla. The driver's waiting." Jim strides by me, but I stay rooted to my spot.

Finally, Mel looks at me. "You should be ashamed of yourself," he whispers. "Trying to wreck my life like this."

I am ashamed. So, so ashamed. But all I do is leave.

CHAPTER THIRTY-TWO

"You know who you remind me of?" Jim points at me with the mirror shard as I climb into the limo.

The person I reminded Mel Nutter of, I suppose. "My mother?"

He chokes softly. "God, no. She doesn't have a corrupt bone in her body."

I'm *corrupt*?

"Ivanka Trump."

"Who?"

He knocks on the privacy panel. "Let's move. I want to get out of here, stat." Then back to me. "The Donald's daughter."

"The guy with the bad comb-over?" I curl my lip. "Gross."

"Not gross. She's going to run his empire." He leans

across the open space and carefully hands me the piece of mirror. "Don't let this cut you. But I want you to keep it. As a symbol of where you're going and just how far you can get when you walk in my footsteps. I'm proud of you, Ayla. So very proud. You came up with this whole mirror business, researched it, found sources. You . . ." He grins. "You are my daughter, through and through."

Oh, God. "Why'd you do it? Why'd you break his mirror?"

He kind of snorts. "Getting me over here to see what the competition is up to under the pretense of buying that mirror? What can I say? Abso-freaking-lutely brilliant. You know"—he plucks at the crisp crease in his trousers—"I've had some misgivings about Trent. He's kind of a weakling. But you? You got a pair, girl." His eyes are merry. It's the most affection I've seen directed toward me since I first met this guy.

It makes me a little sick. Sicker.

"Forget the spy work with your mother; she's a lost cause. But you're going to kill it at the helm of Forever Flawless. Would you like to speak tomorrow at the grand opening? You know, just to get your feet wet?"

"No." I kind of hate him right now, and have to fight the urge to fling the glass shard I'm holding. "And I really did think you'd be interested in the mirror, because you stole the one Charlie made."

"Proving, of course, that there's nothing that special about this mirror thing. We can get our R&D people to make one. But we have to be fast and beat this Nutter character to the patents. How the hell did you meet him anyway?"

"Facebook." I blow out a breath and shift my attention to the mirror shard. "Surely there was another way to handle this."

"Long, involved, legal, and expensive. We try to avoid those ways, if possible. You'll learn." He's got his phone out and is talking to someone before I can answer. "Wait until I tell you what my brilliant daughter did. She sure swims on the right side of her gene pool."

But right at this moment, I am drowning in that particular pool.

At midnight, as I stand on the balcony of a hotel and gaze out at the Monongahela River right where it meets the Allegheny to form Pittsburgh's Golden Triangle, a plan slowly starts to emerge.

I have to see Lizzie and explain this to her. I can't let her go the rest of her life thinking I'm this purely awful, even if she doesn't know me. I just can't.

I don't have a phone number for her so I grab a jacket and my purse, then snag a waiting cab in front of the hotel.

Jim's in his own suite, and I doubt he'll miss me.

If the cabdriver thinks it's weird that I want to go to the South Hills at this hour, he doesn't say, leaving me in a peaceful silence as the car travels across town and through the Liberty Tubes.

Everything feels foreign to me, I realize with a thud of sadness.

I'm more accustomed to the MacArthur Causeway than

the tunnel that cuts through a mountain and takes me from the city to the suburbs where I grew up.

But *I* didn't grow up here. Maybe in another life, another world, another dimension, Annie Nutter grew up here, but in this one, Ayla Monroe doesn't even have a place.

Trying to change that was wrong, I realize, and in the process, I might have hurt Lizzie. And Mel Nutter. And that's what really hurts me.

There's still a few lights on at Lizzie's house, and that gives me a burst of hope. I pay the cabbie and wait until he leaves, then stand outside the house, remembering what it was like to live here.

It was secure. It was happy. It was subpar, below average, and shabby. But it's where I belong. Not in the back of Jim Monroe's limo being handed the keys to a kingdom I don't want—as a reward for being a slimeball.

That's not what I'm made of, not in any universe.

I don't have the nerve to walk up to the door and ring the bell. Instead I circle the house, slowing down when I come to my room. The lights are on, and I can see some posters and bright yellow walls.

Lizzie's favorite color.

The window isn't quite closed all the way, and through the screen, I can hear some voices and laughter. A loud, sharp laugh that is definitely not Lizzie but sounds so familiar.

I hear it again, then Lizzie's much softer giggle and some talking, so I strain to make out the words.

"Oh, my God. Carla Nicholas, you are such a dork!"

The laugh again. Who's Carla Nicholas?

Could it be *Courtney* Nicholas? *Nickel-ass!* I remember that she's in Lizzie's Facebook profile picture—not really looking like the most popular girl in school. Maybe she doesn't have the same cool name, either.

Of course. Realization dawns, and I reel with it because this is another one of the universe's little jokes on me. Courtney/Carla is my replacement in this life. She's Lizzie's bestie, spending the night and sharing inside jokes and probably watching old *SpongeBob* reruns and sucking on watermelon Jolly Ranchers, because life doesn't get any better than that.

Why didn't I realize that when I had it? Why did I want to be popular and pretty and rich and cool?

I step up to the window, empowered by my thoughts. Near the window is one of those giant trash bins that they made everyone in the South Hills switch to, big enough that if I climb onto the kick bar, I might be able to see inside.

I get up and peek in.

There's my old room, in different colors, but the bed and dresser are in the same place. Courtney (or Carla, but she'll always be Courtney to me) and Lizzie are curled on the bed, a laptop open, a TV on without sound. Yep. It's the episode where Squidward moves to another town. But they're not watching. They're talking, heads close, pajamas on, a half-empty candy bag on the bed.

Longing to be part of it, I pull myself up higher, accidentally rolling the trash can. It smashes into the side of the house, and I gasp, dropping off the bar and ducking into the bushes. Dang!

The smell of garbage roils my stomach a little, and I cringe, crouching into the shadows and trying to be small and silent.

"Did you hear that?" The window squeaks as someone pushes it up. "Is someone out there?"

Ohmigod, ohmigod, ohmigod, please don't let me get caught.

"Maybe it's Shane Matthews!"

An explosion of giggles makes my head spin. Lizzie's crushed out on Shane Matthews in this universe, too?

"Hey, Shane! You're cute!" More laughter.

Oh, what I could tell them about Shane Matthews . . . or Ryder Bransford . . . or any of those guys. *Don't waste your time, girls.*

They're still at the window, so I stay completely frozen, holding my breath, closing my eyes, praying for this nightmare to be over.

"Probably an animal," I hear Courtney say. "A squirrel or raccoon. C'mon. Let's finish watching the video."

"I don't know." There's another grunt of wood against wood as the window goes up higher. "I'm still spooked by that creepster girl who used me on Facebook to get to my dad."

Oh, *God.*

"Maybe she's a stalker," Lizzie adds.

"Just forget her, Liz. She's nobody."

I hear Lizzie sigh. "She's not a nobody, but . . ."

"But what?"

"I don't know, Carla. I just had this funny feeling about her. Like I wanted to trust her. Like I *knew* her."

You do! I almost pop up, but fight the urge with everything I have.

"Well, you Facebooked with her, so that's normal."

"It was more than that. It was . . ." Her voice fades out as she closes the window.

A stalker. A nobody.

What should I do? Tell Lizzie the truth? Or just stay hidden and sneak away? I wait a full five, ten seconds trying to decide, just as the clouds break enough for a three-quarter moon to beam down on me like a spotlight.

I stand, holding the trash bin for support, but my handbag gets caught on the handle on the side and gets knocked off my shoulder. The motion almost makes me push the bin over. With a soft cry, I grab the top-heavy container to keep it from tumbling, and my bag slides off completely. It spills everywhere with a clatter that sounds deafening in the quiet of the night.

I bite my lip and cringe, just waiting for someone to come running up to me, accusing me of even more heinous crimes against the Kauffman-soon-to-be-Nutter family.

But no one does. There's just silence, and my shaky breath. I bend to retrieve my stuff, blinking at a flash of light.

The mirror. The broken mirror Jimbo gave me is on the grass, faceup, capturing the moonlight and reflecting it right back into my face. I blink at the sharp beam, blinded for a fraction of a second.

In that split second of time, everything changes. It's like the world shifts under me. My ears buzz and my arms and legs feel heavy and tingly.

"Oh, my God!"

I hear the words, but I'm not sure if I've said them or someone else has. I force my head up, looking away from the light, but I can't see anything but sparkles and flashes, like I just had my picture taken by fifteen different cameras at once.

"She *is* a stalker!"

It's Lizzie and Courtney, and one of them is shining a flashlight into my face and onto the mirror. I open my mouth to say something, but I can't. Everything is just paralyzed, white sparks of light everywhere.

Then I realize what's happening. I'm leaving this universe! The moment I figure it out, I can see again, just for a second, just long enough to catch a glimpse of Lizzie charging toward me. I don't know if she's going to push me or hit me or run past me. I don't know anything, but I'm floating and sparking, and everything is hot and cold and terrifying.

The flashes are blinding, and Lizzie comes in and out of my vision like someone is turning a light switch on and off sixty jillion times, so I can see her, then nothing. In one flash of light I see her drop to her knees.

She's reaching for the mirror. She's going to look at it. She's going to get transported with me. She's going to lose everything and end up somewhere . . .

"No!" I lunge toward her and pull her to the ground. "Don't touch it!"

And then everything goes complete black and I have no idea where I'll wake up or who I'll be when I do.

CHAPTER THIRTY-THREE

"What in the name of Sam Adams are you doing?"

I open my eyes, vaguely aware that grass is tickling my nose. I smell earth and a scent of burned grass. The voice is muffled, coming from above, and something is pressing down on me.

No, not something. Someone.

"Should I call the police or get your mom, Liz?"

"No, wait," the voice says. Lizzie is what's pressing down on me, I realize. "If I get up, are you going to kill me, Ayla?" she asks.

Ayla. I'm still Ayla?

"So, nothing's changed?" I manage to ask into the grass. I don't know whether to be crushed or totally relieved. I go with relief. "We're still here?"

"If by 'here' you mean my backyard at midnight with you hiding in the trash, then, yes, we're here."

"And you're still Lizzie Kauffman whose mom is getting married tomorrow, and I'm still Ayla Monroe with the money and the dad from hell?"

"Uh, yeah."

"Then, no, I'm not going to kill you."

Very slowly Lizzie gets up, releasing me. "You better have a really good explanation."

I lift my head and look around, half-terrified to find out where I am. But it's still the same yard. The same house. The same moonlight. The same Courtney Nicholas (so not hot in this universe) and the same . . . mirror.

The mirror!

Lizzie has picked it up, and Courtney shines the light onto it.

"Don't!" I warn her, pushing the flashlight away. "You could . . . end up somewhere you don't want to be."

Lizzie holds the mirror shard. "Someone could get hurt with this, you know."

"I know." I swallow and swipe some hair from my face. "Lizzie, I have to talk to you."

"Let me get your mom, Lizzie," Courtney says icily. "This girl is totally unstable."

"No." Lizzie and I say it together, exactly like we used to answer questions in unison all the time.

"Please," I say to her. "Give me a chance to explain. I can. It's a long and complicated story."

"Why would we care about your story?" Courtney asks.

I look up at her with a smile. "Because, in it, you're the most popular girl at school."

She lifts a brow that seriously needs a wax.

"And you," I say to Lizzie, "are my best friend."

Lizzie doesn't reply, but searches my face like the answers could be there.

"And in this story," I add slowly, "your new dad is my old dad."

Her eyes widen.

"Give me a chance, Zie," I whisper. At the use of my private nickname, her eyes flicker. Not really recognition but curiosity. And something else. Something that lets me know that telling Lizzie the truth is the only way to go.

"I want to tell you everything."

"And Carla, too," she says, as though she's negotiating. "This is my friend Carla Nicholas."

"Of course," I agree, forcing myself to think of Courtney as Carla.

"Let's go into my room," Lizzie says.

"Actually, it's my room."

I love Lizzie for a lot of reasons, but mostly because she doesn't argue and leads the way.

"Nickel-ass?" Carla clicks a Jolly Rancher indignantly around in her mouth. "You guys called me *Nickel-ass?*"

Lizzie smacks her with a pillow. "That whole story, that whole blasted story with the mirror and the money and the boy taped into a box, and all you care about is being called Nickel-ass? I can't believe I didn't think of that years ago."

Carla laughs sheepishly, showing braces she never needed when I knew her in my old life.

"You deserved it in that universe," I tell her from my corner of the bed, my arms wrapped around one of Lizzie's pillows. "But not in this one," I add. "You seem much nicer than in the real world."

Lizzie shakes her head, studying me. "This *is* the real world, Ayla."

"Annie," I say softly. "And, yeah, I guess it is. I mean, do you believe me?"

They look at each other, and Carla's full of doubt, but Lizzie bites her lip and nods. "Only because I felt something outside. Something weird. It was all numb and warm and sparky for a second, but I thought that was just terror because I was jumping a virtual stranger behind the trash cans in my yard."

"You were almost transported to another universe."

"Where I'm popular," Carla interjects. "So I'm not sure if I buy the story, but I like it."

"Believe me, Carla, being popular is not all it's cracked up to be." I move the pillow and lean forward. "All I want to do is go back to my old life."

"What happens if you leave this world?" Lizzie asks. "Does the old Ayla come back to Miami?"

"Honestly, nobody has any idea. Maybe I'll be the same as I was or as I am or some whole new version of me. We have no way of knowing."

"Yeah, no email between universes," Carla says with a laugh.

"Speaking of email," I say, and reach for my bag. "Let me get your phone numbers right now. No matter what happens, we have to text." I press my iPhone, but nothing happens. "Oh, no. This can't be good. Did we fry it with the mirror?"

Lizzie puts her hand over mine. "Don't worry. We have Facebook. But what if you do go back? Should I try to stay in touch with Ayla? Will she still be you?"

Carla laughs. "I'm confused."

"It's confusing," I acknowledge, throwing my fried phone back into my bag. "I don't even know if I can go back. I mean, I can try, but . . ."

"But what?" Lizzie prompts.

"I told you about Charlie."

"That's your boyfriend?" she asks. "Charlie with the sick sister?"

"I really like him. Like, *really*." I pluck at a candy wrapper as déjà vu vibrates through me. How many times in my life have I sat on a bed with Lizzie and talked about boys? Many. And she always, always knows the right thing to say. I look up at her and she's playing with the mirror.

"Be careful, Zie," I say softly. "You could blast into a million electrons and go flying through time and space."

She sets it down quickly. "I like my life. I don't want to live another."

"Well, somewhere, you probably are living a lot of them. Maybe an infinite amount of them."

She makes a classic Lizzie face of disgust and confusion, crinkling her nose so that a zillion tiny freckles smoosh together. "I don't know about those lives. I only know about this one. And I really like it."

"I know," I say. "Your mom's marrying a good guy and you have a nice BFF and it's good."

"Even if I am a nobody."

"Being an invisible nobody is not the second level of hell. At least not the only one. The price for popularity is high."

Lizzie regards me for a long moment, then leans forward, her voice a whisper. "You know what I think, Ayla? I think you have to figure out why you were sent to this universe. I think there's a reason you're here."

Her words resonate. She's so smart, always right about deep things like this.

"Maybe it's to give those popular girls what for," Carla suggests. "Look what you did in that bathroom. You are, like, the hero of invisibles and nobodies everywhere."

"You think?" I ask.

But Lizzie is shaking her head, carefully touching the rough edges of the mirror as she thinks.

"You can't change those people, Annie," she finally says. "Oh, you might be able to embarrass them or get them momentarily off their high horse or even get them to share their precious bathroom with the band geeks. But they are programmed to be mean girls, and they aren't going to magically change just because one of their own develops a conscience."

I marvel at the overall smartness of that observation. "You're always so right, Zie. In any world."

332

She smiles, but her eyes are very serious. "I think there's a bigger, more important reason you were sent here."

A fine chill tickles my skin as I wait for her to tell me what it is. Even though I kind of already know. "Charlie?" I ask.

"Missy."

For a moment, nobody talks.

"You're here to help Missy."

"How?" I barely breathe the word, because she is right. I know it in my gut, deep in my soul. "How can I help her?"

"Well, for one thing, you have a whole boatload of money."

That's true. Millions that could be used for even more research, and a better place to live, a tutor, music. And no strings attached that say Charlie has to go to Crap Academy. "I could help her. That is if she and her brother and mother haven't gone off to a better universe."

"Do you think they have?" Lizzie asks.

I shake my head. "I don't think that mirror works, except to kill phones. I'm here for good."

"And for a reason," Lizzie says again. "There's a reason you traveled across the universe and got to keep the same good soul. And that's to make sure Missy Zelinsky has the best life possible."

I get a little flutter in my stomach and more goose bumps. "You think?"

She nods.

"Ah, Zie. You're the smartest girl I know. In any universe."

"I am," she agrees in her inimitable Lizzie way. "And if I

don't get to bed, I'm going to be the tiredest-looking maid of honor in wedding history."

"You're the maid of honor?"

"Of course."

A bittersweet pang squeezes my chest. "That's nice. And I'm really sorry about Jim and the mirror. You know I wasn't behind that."

"I'm glad I know that, but, really, don't sweat it."

"How could I not? I mean, that mirror is a cool idea, and Jim just destroyed it."

She waves a hand. "Dad's got two more at his office at Process Engineering, and spent the afternoon filing patents. No one is worried."

More relief floods me. "I'm glad I came, then. Just to find that out. But now I guess I better go."

She stands slowly, and offers a hand. "I'm glad you came, too, Ayla. All the way across time and space."

I smile at her, then impulsively give her a hug, which she gives right back in true Lizzie fashion.

"Hey, don't forget Nickel-ass," Carla says, joining the hug.

When I leave, Lizzie gives me the piece of mirror and a kiss on the cheek for luck. I have a feeling I'm going to need it.

CHAPTER THIRTY-FOUR

The flight home late Saturday afternoon is way worse than the one up. The closer we get to Miami, the more storms there are. All I can do is stay buckled in my seat behind Jim and stare at the flashes of lightning through the rain-spattered window.

I have to talk to Charlie. I have to talk to Charlie so bad, it actually hurts every cell in my body to think about it, and my phone is truly dead. And as spoiled as I am, Jimbo refused to let me take one minute out of the grand opening schedule to get a new one.

So Charlie doesn't even know what happened to me in Pittsburgh. For all he knows, I teleported across the galaxy.

And for all I know, so did he.

I close my eyes as the plane drops through the rain, the runway lights of the executive airport in sight.

Things don't improve when we land, as Jimbo insists on heading straight home. I broach the subject of a side trip to Hialeah and get shot down instantly. In this weather, he's taking the limo out tonight, and I can stay home for a change.

Like that's going to happen.

I have to wait until Dad leaves, and while I do, I email Charlie, but he doesn't write back. No one I know would have his cell phone number. Maybe Facebook.

But he's not on Facebook.

Where is he?

The minute I hear Dad leave, I fly into action. I'm driving to Charlie's house in whatever car I can get my hands on. I have to tell him my plan for Missy, my decision to stay and use all my considerable resources to make her life a happy one. I want to be with him, part of his happy family, and help all of them live the best life they can. Right here and right now.

Burning with the need to share this, I don't even hesitate to grab the keys to the Aston Martin. I already think of it as my car. Yeah, this universe has perks.

As I pull out of the garage, the rain instantly drenches the car, with thunder rolling in the distance. I close my eyes and hear Missy's voice.

It was a car accident, four years ago. Four years ago in less than a week on November seventeenth.

Holy crap! I hit the brakes on the drive and fishtail a

little on a puddle. That's today. This very day. November seventeenth!

We were on our way home from my soccer game, which had gotten called on account of lightning.

Is that where Charlie is going—back to the place where the accident happened? Just like he told me to do with my mirror?

I struggle to remember Missy's exact words.

We were on Old Cutler Road. You know that really winding one down south? We were just turning onto 168th Street, and . . .

I have no idea where that is! With shaky hands, I punch numbers and words into the GPS. I have to get there before he does. Before he leaves.

I bang the steering wheel, waiting for the satellites to tell me how to get to that intersection. To take me there.

To take me to Charlie.

As the woman's voice starts spewing out directions, I follow, gripping the wheel, staring through the slap and smack of the windshield wipers. I can't see a thing, and I have no idea where I'm going. But I won't let that stop me.

Thump-woof. Thump-woof. Thump-woof.

Somehow the GPS lady gets me through Coral Gables to a winding street called Old Cutler Road. Lined with an umbrella of banyan trees, the street is dark like black soup. My lights are barely enough to keep me from driving off the snakelike road.

How will I ever find him?

I tamp down the question and check the street numbers

with the next flash of lightning. I'm at 144th. I do some math to figure out that I'm twenty-four blocks away from the intersection. The street winds, there are no "blocks," and I can't see a damn thing.

But I power on.

As I get closer, a gash of white lightning slices through the sky, almost immediately followed by a roll of thunder. Peering through the swish of the wiper blades, I scan for his Jeep, imagining him parked on the side of the road, holding a curved mirror out the window to catch the light.

But there's no one out tonight. No other cars, no people.

Just as I reach 168th Street, the light turns yellow. I hesitate for a second, knowing I can cross safely because there are no cars anywhere. I've made it halfway through when suddenly a car comes barreling toward me, toward the intersection.

I blink at the headlights of the oncoming car, blurred in the downpour and darkness. They're oddly shaped. High, round, close together.

Jeep Wrangler headlights, and they are making a left turn directly in front of me!

I slam on the brakes, hydroplaning wildly on a puddle, and fishtailing, but I can't stop. I'm going to hit that Jeep. I'm going to hit that Jeep exactly like it was hit before, when Missy was paralyzed.

I pump the breaks and jerk the wheel, doing everything I can scare up from driver's ed, but it's like the world's in slow motion and I am careening right toward that canvas top and plastic windows.

Screaming, I just squeeze the steering wheel as the front

of the Aston crunches into the Jeep, a noisy, horrific bang of metal against metal, followed by the air bag smacking me in the face and stealing the breath I was holding.

Then everything is silent, but for the rain on the roof and the slow hiss of the air out of the bag under my head.

I'm alive. I'm alive! But what about Charlie?

With trembling hands, I fight the air bag and manage to get my belt off. I throw open the door and stare into the pouring rain. The intersection is empty. Where did he go?

Another universe.

"Oh!" Choking on rainwater and emotion, I turn to see how bad the Aston is. Then a flash of lightning bathes the intersection in white and I see the Jeep on the side of the road.

"Charlie!" I tear across the street, trying to process that Charlie and his mother are taking Missy out and putting her in the wheelchair.

"Ayla, no. You can't be here!"

I freeze at the words, at the tableau of the three of them standing in the middle of the storm, about to get hit by lightning. Then I see the mirror Charlie is holding.

"No!" I scream. "You're going to get killed!"

"We have to do this!" Mrs. Z. cries from behind the wheelchair, her hands on Missy's shoulders. "We have to try!"

Missy's eyes are filled with hope. I can see it burning there, firing through her like the bolt of lightning she's waiting for—unadulterated hope that she can get to a better place.

"Charlie." I reach for him, and he wraps his arm around me.

"What are you doing?" I ask. But I already know the answer.

"An experiment," Charlie says, lifting the drenched mirror. "We have to re-create the scene, to the minute, everything about what happened that night."

"And get killed trying?"

"We're not going to get killed," he insists.

"You almost just did," I fire back, gripping him and fighting the desire to shake some sense into him.

"You shouldn't be here, Ayla," he says. "I thought you were already . . . gone."

"I didn't go, Charlie."

"When you didn't call, I figured—"

"I fried my phone. And it didn't work." I point to the mirror. "I don't think it's going to work, Charlie. I have a better idea. A different idea."

"Please, Ayla, let us go," Missy cries. "We all want to live our lives in a different universe, one where this accident never happened."

"But you live in this one," I insist, swiping the water off my face. "And I have the means to help you even more than some company. I can make your life better." I put my hand on the mirror, and it angles toward me, reflecting my face.

But it's not my face. It's . . . Annie's face.

"You see it, don't you?" Charlie asks.

I just nod. "How did you do that?"

"With the picture you emailed me. We all see ourselves the way we want to be. Just ask Missy."

"I'm on a skateboard," she says with a mischievous grin. "You should see me fly."

"I want to see you fly," I say, tears rolling and mixing with rain. "That's why you should stay and let me—"

"Annie." Charlie puts his hand on my cheek. "You can't do that for her. But this can."

I close my eyes and tilt my head into his palm. "I'll miss you so much. I don't want to be here without you."

"Hey, look at me."

I open my eyes and get lost for a minute in his, so dark and comforting. "What?"

"You don't want to be here, either, Annie Nutter." He angles the mirror again and tilts my face to look at it. "You want to go home where you belong. With your family and your friends."

I can't speak, my throat is so tight with tears. He leans forward and kisses me softly. He tastes like rain and . . . home.

"C'mon, you two! You're supposed to be thinking about where we're going, not where you've been," Missy says.

She's right of course, and Charlie and I break apart. As my eyes open, I look to the mirror, to Annie Nutter. Yes, that's where I want my soul to reside. Right there in that—

A huge flash of lightning whitens everything, freezing the instant in stark, blinding light that reflects off the mirror.

Sudden, intense heat slams through my whole body as I blink into the light and see Charlie doing the same thing.

I try to speak, but everything is tingling, sparkling, prickly heat. My arms and legs are heavy. My head feels so light, it's as if I'm floating on air.

I can see Charlie, he's in front of me, his whole being radiant and light. Everything else has disappeared; the world is dark and airless, and all I can see or feel or experience is Charlie.

I cling to his hand, though, electricity zapping through both of us.

He's breaking up, his color fading, his light dimming.

"Charlie! Don't forget me!"

He's disappearing and so am I.

"I won't, Annie. One-four-three! I love—"

The world goes completely dark. All I can hear is a weird noise. A loud, deep rumble right in my ear.

Is that the wind? Is that a motor? Thunder? Or is it . . .

With every ounce of strength I can muster, I open my eyes to come eyeball to eyeball with a boy who is burping in my face.

CHAPTER THIRTY-FIVE

"Theo!" I try to scream, but it comes out almost as a growl.

"Sorry, but Mom told me I had to wake you up, Annie. It's almost seven-thirty and the bus'll be here in half an hour."

Mom. The bus. *Annie*. Is this possible?

"And I gotta tell you." He lowers his voice and gets closer, killing me with his peanut butter breath. "Dad and Mom are barely talking. It's actually worse than yesterday."

"Yesterday?" Oh, this is too good to be true. I did it. *We* did it. Back to the right world, the right time. "What about Charlie?"

Theo backs up and looks at me like I've grown another head. "Who's Charlie?" he asks. "Does Mom have, like, a boyfriend or something?"

"What?"

He almost falls onto my bed. "I heard them talking about some guy, and I heard her say she loved him."

I throw the covers back and sit up, vaguely aware of the SpongeBob sleep pants that I missed while I was in the other universe. And my room. My tiny, crowded, not-very-glamorous room. It looks wonderful. Even my brother looks . . . I almost pull him to me to kiss him, but common sense rules the day. "You misunderstood, I'm sure. I'll go talk to her."

I barely look around, heading right out to the hall toward the kitchen, where I hear water running. "Mom?"

She turns from the sink, her eyes puffy. But it's her. My mom with the little wrinkle between her brow and a few extra pounds and home-colored hair.

"Oh, God, Mom." I can't help it, I just throw my arms around her. "You can't let him do this to you."

"Daddy didn't—"

"Jim Monroe."

She freezes a few seconds, then inches away from me. "This isn't about him."

"Yes, it is. It's about you having second thoughts and wondering about what you did and why you did it." I grip her shoulders, the conviction of what I know practically shaking me. "You would never have been happy with him."

"Annie, I—"

"Listen to me. You wouldn't have. He made you feel inadequate and . . . and imperfect."

She almost shrugs, unable to disagree.

"And Dad makes you feel . . ." I squeeze tighter to make my point. "Flawless. Flawless on the inside, and, Mom, that is what really matters."

"But, Annie, you don't know—"

"I know this, Mom," I insist. "Dad loves you for who you are. And, really, Mom, that is worth a billion dollars."

She blinks, and one last tear falls.

"You're wrong, Annie." At the sound of my dad's voice, I turn to see him in the door that leads to the basement, an empty box in his hand. "It's not worth a billion dollars," he says. "Because you can't put a price on how I feel about your mother. It's priceless."

Behind me, Mom sniffs again.

"And everything else in this house is worthless." He raises the box. "I'm cleaning up today. Everything. No more Nutter Clutter. I'll do anything . . ." His gaze shifts over my shoulder and settles on my mother. "Anything to keep your mother happy. She is the most beautiful, wonderful, exquisite creature in the world, and I don't know how I won her, but I am not about to lose her."

"Oh, Mel." Mom sweeps by me, arms outstretched as she reaches for Dad. He pulls her into a warm hug, dropping the box so he can use both arms.

"One-four-three, honey," he whispers into her hair. "One-four-three."

I can't even swallow the lump in my throat, it's so big. And so is the hole in my heart. Whatever universe Charlie has landed in, I hope someday he finds someone to love like that.

Theo burps from the hall, and Watson comes lumbering in to howl for bacon. The Nutter chaos reigns again. Then Mom jumps out of Dad's arms and hollers, "Oh, my God, Annie. The bus is going to be here in ten minutes."

"I'll drive her to school," Dad says. "Annie hates to ride that stupid bus."

I shake my head. "Lizzie's expecting me," I say, heading down the hall. "I'll be ready in ten minutes."

"When did she get so grown-up?" I hear Mom ask.

I pause to listen to Dad's answer. "It's like it happened overnight."

Well, not exactly.

Lizzie, freckled and grinning from ear to ear, is waiting in our usual seat when I climb up. One glance to the back tells me why she's smiling. Shane Matthews is already on the bus, sitting with some boys, already acting stupid.

"Please, Zie, don't make me smack you. We hate him, remember?" I know, a funny thing to say to your BFF when you've been apart so long, but technically I just saw her last night when she had a sleepover with Nickel-ass in another universe.

"That's not why I'm smiling," she says.

"Oh, you're just happy to see me?" I've already decided I can't tell her the truth. Not with my landing back here the next day; no time has passed for her, yet. She'll think I had a weird dream. If I relegate the past few weeks in a parallel universe to some kind of *Wizard of Oz* dream state, it'll mean I dreamed up Charlie, and I want to believe that somewhere he exists. I have to believe that.

"Didn't your dad tell you?" she asks.

"My dad? Uh, things were a little crazy at my house last night. What's up?"

She gives a little clap of joy. "He and your mom set my mom up on a blind date with his friend from Process Engineering and they went out last night."

"Really?"

"Ohmigod, Annie, he's soooo nice." Lizzie squeals a little. "This could be the one."

"The universe has a way of making things work out," I say, feeling worldly and wise. And really glad that Lizzie might get her engineer dad in this world, too. "Anything else happen while I was . . . Last night?"

Lizzie gives me a sympathetic look. "Obviously you didn't go on Facebook. Nickel-ass had to brag about her stupid dare, and Shane . . ." She shifts her eyes over her shoulder. "He's dead to me for what he did to you, Annie. I don't care if he's the hottest thing that ever walked. He's a tool."

"Totally." I brace myself as the bus turns the corner and heads up a hill to the stop where Courtney and company get on. More tools on the way. But now they can't bother me.

"Maybe she got a ride today," Lizzie says, as though she can read my mind.

I shrug. "Couldn't care less. She doesn't affect me."

"*Riiiight.*" Lizzie drags the word out with plenty of disbelief.

"I mean it. You don't know what goes on behind closed doors. She might be miserable inside because her family's a wreck or she can't trust her friends. You just don't know."

Lizzie draws back, ready to joke. Then her face falls. "Wow, that Shane thing really got to you, didn't it?"

"No. Well, maybe." I'm going to need an excuse for my new philosophies, and if Shane Matthews provides it, then he'll be good for something.

As the bus stops, I don't look out the window, but I can hear Courtney's chatter as the doors open and she flounces up the stairs, pausing right in front of me to turn to one of her handmaidens behind her.

"Oh, my *gawd*, Miranda. Did you see? I must have that. Must. Have. That."

The girl behind her gives a gentle push. "Get in line."

Still laughing, the two of them head to the back, and I duck before any bags hit me.

"Uh, excuse me." A low voice comes from the sidewalk, pulling Geraldine's attention.

"Are you the new kid?" the bus driver demands. "You gotta have your paperwork, son. Signed by the dean, or I can't take you on this bus."

Lizzie leans toward the window to see who's talking, since our view is blocked.

"Wow. Who's that?" she asks.

"I have the paperwork, ma'am, but the problem is—"

"No problems, just solutions." Geraldine extends her meaty hand. "Paperwork."

Slowly, a dark head rises from behind the metal plate, and a male hand wraps around the pole in front of me. I stared at the hand for a second, at the lean but masculine fingers. Fingers that look . . . strong but gentle.

The first little flutter of butterfly wings tickles my tummy.

As he steps up, the whole bus hushes, and with good reason. He lets go of the pole to brush thick hair off his forehead, revealing dark eyes under a thick brow, a strong jaw, and just enough stubble that he has to be a senior.

Broad shoulders clad in a loose orange and teal football

jersey rise and fall in a frustrated sigh that is tempered with a quick smile at Geraldine.

"I have a problem, though."

"I told you I don't want your problems. I want your paperwork."

I can't breathe. Can't move. Can't think a single thought that makes any sense whatsoever. Because he looks so much like . . .

"Ashton Kutcher." Lizzie whispers the words under her breath. "Only, you know, seventeen."

"Can you just wait a minute?" he asks Geraldine. "My sister is coming and . . ." He bites his lip and glances through the bus windows. "It might take her a while."

His sister. I wrap my fingers around the backpack on my lap, clutching something, anything, to keep from reaching out to him.

"Well, where the hell is she?" Geraldine demands, already shifting her big old bus into gear. "First thing you learn on my bus, Mr. Ned the New Guy, is that we run on time. No waiting for late sisters, no excuses."

"But she's on wheels."

"Well, that should make her faster," Geraldine says, flicking her wrist at him. "Get off and get yourself to school."

"Wait!" The word pops out of my mouth as I almost jump out of my seat, and he turns to me, giving me the first full-on look at his face, and oh, heaven help me, I know this boy.

I *love* this boy.

"Charlie."

His smile falters a little. "It's Chase, actually. I'm new here."

349

Not to me. "And your sister?" I ask, having already shoved my backpack half onto Lizzie's lap, ignoring her wide-eyed stare of pure incredulity.

"She's new, too, but she's—"

"I know, I know." I stand up, knowing that if I'm not on the bus, Geraldine won't go. But if he gets off to get his sister, the bus driver will take off and strand him. I know what I have to do for him. "I'll go get her. I can help her."

As I stand, I come face to face with the new boy, because he's still halfway on the lower bus step.

"She'll be okay," he says, his voice so blissfully familiar. Our eyes meet, and it takes everything I've got not to kiss him. He looks different, of course, but not enough to fool me.

I'd recognize Charlie Zelinsky in any universe.

"Geraldine will wait for me," I whisper, nodding toward the bus driver.

"Then so will I," he says.

I almost melt right into his arms. "I'll go . . ." If I can walk. "I'll get Missy."

He laughs softly. "That's funny. I call her that sometimes. Her name's Malina, and honestly, she doesn't need help."

From the aisle, a distinct throaty (and totally fake) laugh trills through the whole bus. Of course, Courtney has zeroed in on Charlie. "Yes, you go find the missing girl," she instructs me, like I'm one of her handmaidens. Then, she plugs in a thousand-watt smile and points directly at Charlie. "Chase, is it? Why don't you come and meet your new friends in the back?"

"Not without paperwork," he says with a teasing smile directed at me.

Without responding, I slip by him to get Missy, aware of the electrical charge that zaps me as my fingers accidentally graze his on the way down the bus steps.

"Thanks," he says softly, like air on my hair as I pass. "I'll handle the driver."

I leap onto the sidewalk, looking left and right, bracing myself for the elfin girl in a wheelchair. Her mother is probably pushing her, which is why Charlie had to run to catch the bus. It all makes sense.

Now I just have to find—

"Cowabunga! Hold that bus!"

I pivot at the sound, and almost choke at the sight of a slender girl with bright red hair spiked from here to Sunday, crouched down on a skateboard, arms wide for stability, careening down the hill toward the bus stop at top speed.

"Missy!" Tears spring to my eyes as I reach out, not caring what anyone thinks, just so damn overjoyed to see her flying, riding, standing, living her dream.

She hops off the board, kicking it easily to a stop right in front of me, bouncing on skater shoes, about sixteen earrings glinting in the morning light.

"Hey, thanks for holding my ride." She tucks the board under her arm and reaches into her bag to pull out a hat—a fedora—which she pops over her gelled hair. "I had to kill that hill, and Chase said he'd kill *me* if I was late. Is he furious?"

"No," I say, laughing and drinking in the glory of whole, healthy, vibrant Missy. "He's charming the bus driver, who won't leave without me."

She gives me an unsure look. "Do I know you?"

351

You did. You will again, I feel certain. "I'm Annie Nutter."

"Malina." She pulls her pack around front, and I instantly see the violin case. More joy pops in my chest.

"You play violin?"

"Badly, but yeah. Think they'll let me in the school orchestra even though it's November?"

"Oh, my God, yes. I'll sponsor you myself."

"Move it, ladies!" Geraldine's growl comes rolling out the door.

Missy makes a face. "Ruh-roh. He sounds mad."

"She. Maybe. Not mad." I can barely make sentences, I'm so happy. How did this happen? How can the universe be so good to me?

I don't even care that they don't remember. The connection is real . . . in any world.

I climb onboard, and my heart sinks when I see Charlie— I'll have to think of him as Chase—all the way in the back, already surrounded by the posse who will always seize someone who looks like that as one of their own.

So, this universe is different. He isn't a nerd, and he isn't the former homeless kid. And he's hot, so Courtney will be all over him.

It doesn't matter. Missy is healthy, and they are right here in my world, so I count this news as a huge win. How can it not be?

I venture another look at him, and instantly know the answer.

It will hurt to see Charlie turn into one of the populars, but in the space of five minutes, I can see it happening.

Already he's laughing with Courtney, high-fiving Shane, and no doubt planning to take a seat at their royal lunch table.

I see Courtney lean into him, letting her silky hair brush his football jersey. "Go ahead. It'll be funny," she says.

And then he looks right at me, right . . . through me.

Am I an invisible to the very boy who taught me not to hate being invisible?

No, Annie, I remind myself. He isn't the same boy in this universe, just like I'm not the same girl. He wasn't looking at Ayla when he saw a plain, boring nice girl who wanted to help him get onto the bus.

He was looking at a nobody.

Courtney says something again, and suddenly the whole world sort of moves into sickening slow motion.

He stands, and I freeze.

Oh, no, Charlie. No. Don't do this to me.

"Oh, good, here comes my brother." Missy, parked right behind Geraldine in the row next to us, half turns to watch him come forward. "I thought he was going all douchetastic on me, sitting back there." She leans forward to talk to Lizzie. "We're twins and just moved here from Miami. What's your name?"

Their conversation fades as the blood thrums in my head and I stare at him. I can see Charlie's face, but he's definitely better-looking in this universe. Confident. Cool. And headed right toward me, his gaze unwavering.

I know I should sit down, but I don't. I need to brace myself and take this blow. Because it's going to hurt if he—

"Hey."

He sounds just like him. Like the boy who kissed me on the grass and took me home to tell me secrets and made me feel *flawless*.

"Thanks for helping us out," he says to me.

I manage a nod. "No biggie."

"C'mere. Sit with me." He indicates the seat behind us, and I feel Lizzie's fingers clutch my leg, not so surreptitiously. I glance down at her, and she gives me a harsh look.

Don't fall for it again, Annie.

I can read the warning in her eyes.

"I want to ask you a question." He gestures toward the seat, and I . . . trust him. I leave my backpack next to Lizzie and step into the aisle, then slide into the seat.

As I do, I catch Courtney's look. That mean look. That I'm-gonna-make-your-life-hell look.

And I stare right back at her, because, sorry, she doesn't have that power anymore. No one does. Not even Charlie, even if he has gone over to the dark side. Not in this universe, not in any.

The knowledge gives me enough confidence to ask, "So, you guys just moved here?"

"Yeah, up from Miami."

"Wow. It's different down there."

"Like another universe."

The glimmer in his eyes steals my breath. "You're going to get cold here," I warn, searching his face. Does he know? Does he remember? Or is that just my imagination?

"I'll find things to keep me warm," he says, smiling a smile that is probably illegal in this universe and any other.

"I'm sure you will." I fold my hands on my lap, anything

to keep from touching him and telling him, *You were my boyfriend in another life.*

God, that would give those beasts in the back something to howl about.

"You praying?" he asks, nodding toward my hands.

"For a miracle," I shoot back.

"Well, I'm praying for one, too."

The tenderness in his voice pulls at me, and the look in his eyes folds me in half. "You are?"

"I just heard that Saturday night is homecoming at this school."

In front of me, Lizzie's shoulders tense, and her face is angled so she can hear every word. Her gaze shifts to the side, like her eyeball might get stuck trying to see me.

Don't worry, Lizzie. He can't hurt me. Even if he tries.

"That's a fact," I tell him. "Saturday night is indeed homecoming, as I'm sure your new friends in the back told you."

"Them? Um, not my type. I got drummed out the minute I mentioned I play the oboe."

I look up at him. "You do?"

He grins. "Nerd alert, huh?"

"Yeah." I barely sigh the word, but then he puts his hand over mine and turns that sigh into a soft gasp.

"So I mentioned homecoming." The heat of his palm sears me. "'Cause maybe you'd want to go with me."

My heart pounds so hard in my chest that surely he sees it or hears it. I try to swallow, but not a drop of saliva moves in my desert-dry mouth. The bus is silent, and every eye— Geraldine's included—is on me.

'Cause maybe you'd want to go with me.

Charlie knows how much that boy hurt me with those words. Charlie does. But this isn't Charlie. This is Chase, a whole new version, and maybe he's just as mean and horrible as Shane Matthews, only a whole lot worse because this invitation feels *real*.

No, Annie. Don't entertain that stupid thought.

He squeezes my hand. There is no tease in those brown eyes, no spite, no cruelty.

"I told you I was asking for a miracle," he says. "I'm sure you've got a date already."

Lizzie whips all the way around. "No, she doesn't."

"Lizzie!"

He laughs a little. "Really? Then you can go."

Is he serious?

The whole bus shakes, and for a second I think it's shaking with laughter, but it's only Geraldine rolling over the speed bump on the way into the school lot, knocking my backpack off the seat where I precariously set it.

"I'll get it." Charlie is up instantly, then on his knees picking up pens and some books and notebooks that fell. "You think about it, okay?"

"Oh, she will," Lizzie answers. Then she mouths "I think he means it" to me.

"We gotta go, Malina. They want us to check in at the office." Charlie/Chase stands and hands me the backpack, the zipper open. "So think about it, and I'll see you around. Maybe lunch? Here's my number." He hands me a slip of paper.

I just stare at him as he leaves the bus.

Malina scoops up her skateboard and leans close to me when she gets into the aisle. "You should say yes, because he's a great guy," she whispers.

And then they disappear off the bus, into the crowds of South Hills High.

"Oh. My. God." Lizzie can hardly contain herself. "He gave you his number, Annie!"

"I don't know. It might have been a joke or something." With shaking hands, I open the folded paper to see . . . the numbers 143 with a heart around them.

"Is he for real?" Lizzie asks.

I smile. "Yeah. He's for real."

acknowledgments

Every book is a group effort, and I am deeply grateful to the crew who helped make this dream a reality for me. In particular, heartfelt thanks go to:

The entire team at Delacorte Press, especially editor Françoise Bui for "adopting" this book and loving it like it was her own.

The brilliant literary agents at Writers House, in particular Robin Rue, a woman who truly doesn't take no for an answer and gets up as early as I do.

Writer-producer-storyteller-lifelong-friend Jeff Franklin, because he fanned the flames for this story right through to the end.

Dr. Michio Kaku, theoretical physicist, bestselling author, and a man with a gift for popularizing science and simplifying concepts bigger and more complex than the universe itself.

My many writer friends, but in particular I send the love to Louisa Edwards and Kristen Painter, my sisters in pounds-and-pages, with me on this journey every day. Also mad props to Kresley Cole for starting and ending every conversation with the same words: *How's the YA coming?* You can stop asking now.

Always and forever, my home team: Rich, who nourishes my muse and makes me laugh every day (and gets all the credit for *Picture Perfect*—he's brilliant!); Dante, the son who taught me what a teenage hero can and should be; and my dear and darling Mia, who deserves cowriting credit for every line of this book and a shopping spree for all the beta reads. (Not really. Okay, maybe.) I could not do this or, frankly, anything at all without my family.

about the author

New York Times bestselling author **ROXANNE ST. CLAIRE** gave up the glamour of working in advertising and public relations to follow her lifelong dream of becoming a published author. Her adult novels have received numerous awards, including the RITA Award, the National Readers' Choice Award, and the Booksellers' Best Award.

DON'T YOU WISH, her debut young adult novel, has been optioned as a feature film and was inspired by real-life events. (Seriously. Some of this actually happened.) Roxanne lives in a small beach town in Florida with her husband, two teenagers, and a frisky Australian terrier that looks like Toto but won't ride in a bike basket. Visit Roxanne at roxannestclaire.com.

East Smithfield Library

3 2895 00126 8700

East Smithfield Public Lil
50 Esmond Street
Esmond, R.I. 02917
401-231-5150

. St.Claire, Roxanne
SAI

Don't you wish